Open Door Marriage

a novel by Naleighna Kai

Macro Publishing Group
Chicago, Illinois

This book is a work of fiction. Names, characters, places and incidents are products of the author's imagination or are used fictitiously. Any resemblance to actual events or locales or persons, living, dead, or somewhere in between, is entirely coincidental

Macro Publishing Group
Open Door Marriage © 2014 by Naleighna Kai

ISBN: 978-1-7326225-9-3
ISBN eBook: 9781732622579

Cover designed by: J. L. Woodson www.woodsoncreativestudio.com
Interior design by: Lissa Woodson www.woodsoncreativestudio.com

Manufactured and Printed in the United States of America

Open Door Marriage

❧ DEDICATION ☙

My mother, Jean Woodson
My grandmother, Mildred E. Williams
My brother, Eric Harold Spears
My niece, LaKecia Janise Woodson,
a rising star who left us much too soon

To Leslie Esdaile Banks (L.A. Banks),
one of the best storytellers the planet had to offer.

To Anthony "Green Eyes" Johnson,
the real life "Dallas" who taught me
what unconditional love was all about

You are missed more than I can say.

ℭ ACKNOWLEDGMENTS ℬ

Wishing you all—peace and love, light and joy.
—Naleighna Kai

"There's no right way to do a wrong thing."
—JANICE PERNELL, AUTHOR

Chapter 1

"You slept with my aunt?"

The words still didn't register, even though this had to be Tori's fifth time saying them. She glared at her fiancé, still desperately trying to come to terms with the information her mother had blasted to everyone at the packed Thanksgiving dinner table.

"Seriously? How is that even humanly possible when you didn't know the woman four hours ago?" Tori shouted.

"Tori, l-let me explain," Dallas stammered.

Twelve pairs of eyes were now focused on the not-quite-blissful couple standing at the bottom of the stairs just off from the dining room.

"But not here. Let's go somewhere and talk. It's not what you think."

"What did you do?" Tori snapped, glaring up at Dallas. "Trip over the sheets, and your penis somehow landed in a woman nearly twice my age?"

The drumstick in Uncle Bill's hand paused in midair on its journey to his wide mouth. Cousin Tiny's fleshy hand flew to her overexposed bosom and came to rest somewhere above her heart. Even Tori's father's frozen expression of alarm would have been Three Stooges comical if the situation weren't so tragic.

Aunt Yoli was the first to recover. "Did they just say what I think they said?"

In unison, everyone nodded.

"Girl, shut the front door and run out the back!"

A few bursts of nervous laughter sprang up around the table, but they were not nearly enough to chase away the unease that had flooded the room when Tori stepped into the house. She'd gone to drop off Aunt Rose's drunk self at home. Tori hadn't even been in the house good when her mother, Bernice, blurted out that she'd caught Alicia and Dallas together. Alone. In bed. In the nude. Tori had picked up from there and summed it up in one sweep. "You slept with my aunt ..."

"Nothing happened, Tori," Dallas said, his voice shaky. "I didn't sleep with her."

"So, my mama is lying?" Tori asked.

Dallas shifted uneasily.

"Hell naw. I know what I saw," Bernice snapped. She had moved from the dining room table to the end of the staircase, right next to her daughter, poised as if she was ready to go to battle. "Both of you were in bed butt-ass naked." She jabbed a finger in her sister-in-law's direction. Alicia hadn't moved from her spot at the top of the staircase. Probably, because she knew what was best for her. "She was butt-naked. And he was nut-naked," Bernice yelled. "Wasn't an inch of space between them." She flickered a gaze at Dallas. "Look at him. You can tell he just got dressed!"

Tori closed her eyes and took deep breaths to calm the emotions that warred within her.

"See, I told you Alicia wasn't worth a damn," Bernice, crowed with savage satisfaction. "And looks like Mr. NBA ain't much better. You thought he was all that and a side order of fries."

Dallas Avery was the NBA's most valuable player, and a man most women would give their right and left ovary to call their own. But Most Eligible Bachelor or not, he had set Tori's bitch meter into overdrive. Even with his chiseled, handsome face, towering muscular frame and million dollar bank accounts, he was now worth next to nothing in her eyes. Too bad her aching heart didn't get that memo.

Tori didn't know if she was more enraged or hurt that her mother had been all too willing to drive this stake through her own daughter's heart in order to publicly disgrace Alicia.

"Tori, we need to talk about this," Dallas repeated before adding, "in private."

Bernice wore a satisfied smirk as she glared openly up at Alicia, who just kept staring stoically at them from the second floor landing. "The angel of the family has fallen," Bernice said.

"Hey, Bernice," Bill taunted with a hearty chuckle. "Bet you won't say that when Alicia comes downstairs. You know she's gonna put a hurting on you."

"You mean put another hurting on her," Aunt Yoli added, doubling over with laughter.

Tori wanted to scream. Her life was unraveling in front of her and her family was cracking jokes.

Instinctively, Bernice inched away from the staircase and back toward the dining room table. Her hands went up to the small scar on her neck, probably remembering that a year ago on this very same holiday, Alicia had ended a vicious blow-for-blow fight with a knife at Bernice's throat. Almost gave the woman a "Sicilian Smile"—an ear-to-ear slice across the throat.

Dallas reached for Tori's hand. "It's not what it seems."

She snatched away, parted her lips to give him what was left of her mind, but Cousin Tiny chimed in first. "Alicia had every right to take Bernice to the floor last year for that foul mess she said! I would've pulled out my own can of whoop ass behind that one."

Tiny's husband, Thomas nodded his watermelon-sized head.

The rest of the family finally sprang to life, also chiming in at once to defend Alicia, the one woman everyone could count on in a time of need, to lend an ear when it was called for and to dry a tear when no one else bothered to care. That she would do something as low as sleep with her niece's soon-to-be husband was unthinkable. So the family sidestepped that issue for as long as they could, finding it more comfortable to speak on the reason no one had expected Alicia home for Thanksgiving—especially since none of them had heard from her for an entire year.

Dallas maneuvered so he was in front of Tori. "Nothing. Happened."

"If Bernice had said that bull to me," Bill responded, still trying to tackle the last of the drumstick, "an ass whipping would've been the least of her problems." He beckoned toward the last slice of sweet potato pie at the other end of the table. "That has my name written all over it."

"Bernice is lying," Martha said. "Alicia's still got looks and all, but that young stud wouldn't pick her over Tori." She shot an appreciative glance toward Dallas, then leaned to her right and whispered loudly in Yoli's direction, "But, girl, he is finer than frog's hair."

Yoli gave him a lusty once-over. "I'd give him some my damn self. He's the type of man who can make a woman put a for sale sign on one thigh and an open for business sign on the other. Yes, Lawd!"

Tori tried her best to tune out her family. She didn't have the stamina to deal with them right now. "How could you do this? You're my fiancé."

"You're Tori's fiancé?" Alicia finally spoke out. She eased down the stairs, looking first to Tori then to Dallas. Her panic-stricken expression gave Tori pause. Could her aunt really have not known?

Alicia turned back to her niece. "Oh, my, God, Tori. I had no idea. I'm so, so sorry." She didn't give Tori time to reply as she brushed past Dallas, slipped into the nearest pair of shoes—her brother's—and ran out of the front door, oblivious to the fact that she barely had on enough clothing to protect her from the chill in the room, let alone the sub-zero temps of a Chicago winter.

The whole crowd gasped in disbelief as Dallas grabbed his leather coat from the foyer closet. "She can't go out there with nothing on," he said as he stepped into his Timberlands. "I'll be right back."

Tori was ready to spit fire. "Are you kidding me?" she screamed as he quickly laced up his shoes, then darted toward the door. "You're going after my aunt? My aunt!" she yelled, following him. "My heart is bleeding all over the carpet and you're going after her!"

The front door slammed and Tori stood frozen, unable to believe what happened in the last ten minutes. Bernice's voice snapped Tori out of her trance. "Girl, I taught you better than that," Bernice yelled, gesturing to the door. "You'd better go get your man!"

Tori snatched up a coat and scarf and braced herself against the frigid gust of wind that slapped her as she left the house. She trekked across the snow and barely reached Dallas before he pulled off. Banging on the glass, she demanded, "Where the hell are you going?"

Dallas lowered the window. "She's out there unprotected. None of this is her fault."

"So now you're speaking up for her, too?" Tori screeched, pummeling him through the opening. "What kind of bullshit is that?"

Dallas flinched at her vicious tone and reached out to keep her hands from doing any more damage. "I'm going to say two things," he replied in that businesslike tone that had landed him several million-dollar endorsement deals. "I'm sorry that your mother lied to you, but nothing happened." His gaze swept the area, probably searching for the woman who was the center of the chaos. "And I'd be less of a man than you already think I am if I let that woman walk around in this weather without a coat."

Tori gave his words a moment's consideration. Causing a scene wouldn't stop him from doing what he felt he had to do, so she made a dash for the passenger side. "I'm coming with you."

They caught up with Alicia at the end of Harper Avenue, where she made a left and was now struggling up the path a block away from the main thoroughfare. She was shaking uncontrollably from the cold and from the sobs that wracked her body.

"Get in, Alicia," Dallas commanded, trailing the distraught woman as she stumbled along the icy sidewalk in shoes that were three sizes too big.

Alicia covered her mouth as though to keep in the words that threatened to spill out. She continued forward, wavering while trying to balance in the oversized loafers on snow that came up to her calves on unshoveled parts of the sidewalk.

"Don't make me get out of the car," Dallas said through his teeth.

Alicia ignored the threat, forcing the car to continue following her until she made it to a glass bus shelter on Stony Island Avenue. She swept the snow away from the steel bench, crawled on it, then tucked her legs up under her as though preparing to spend the night.

Dallas was out of the car and by her side in the time it took to blink. He whipped off his leather coat, placed it about Alicia's shoulders, then held out his hand to her. It took a moment for her to take it, but finally she stood. Together, they took two steps, then, she crumbled down onto the snow.

"Ouch!" she shrieked. "My ankle."

It took Dallas only a moment to lift her into his arms, then navigate carefully over the slick pavement. He placed her gently, almost lovingly, in the back seat of his rented Benz. Using the sleeve of his shirt, he wiped her tears away.

Tori felt like she was having an out-of-body experience. The way Dallas looked at Alicia. The way he held her. It tore at Tori's gut. "Dallas, what is going on?' Tori asked once he was back in the driver's seat. "How the hell have you connected with her in such a way that you feel obligated to ease her pain and not mine?" The anger was still there, but Tori tried to push it aside, because right now, she needed clarity.

Dallas carefully pulled onto the street and aimed the car back in the direction of the place they'd just left. "We'll talk about this when we get back to the house."

"No!" Alicia cried out, gripping the edge of the driver's seat and causing Dallas to punch the brakes. "I can't go back there. Not right now."

Dallas locked gazes with her in the rear view mirror. "Where do you want me to take you?"

"I don't know. Anywhere but there," she whispered, slumping back down in the seat. "Anywhere but home." Alicia's shoulders shook with an effort to hold herself together, and Dallas' expression softened.

The whole scenario made Tori's heart constrict as though someone had put a vise grip on the very thing that kept her alive.

She had only been gone for three hours. What the hell had happened between Dallas and her aunt?

Chapter 2

8:31 P.M.

Tori and the twenty-eight-year old NBA star had been secretly dating for a year after having been friends for twice as long. It surprised everyone when they became publicly engaged three weeks before Thanksgiving and were on track for a wedding when basketball season ended in April.

Bernice had broken Tori down from her "I only want to be friends" stance by constantly preaching that a woman can't be 'just friends' with a man who was at the top of the food chain.

Over and over, Tori had listened to her mother bitterly complain about how she'd married a man who didn't have the brains to keep his life in order, not to mention the unhealthy relationship Bernice claimed her husband James had with his sister, Alicia. It was like those two had some kind of superhero twin bond – and they weren't even twins. Now, James and Bernice were older than homemade sin, and they had embarrassingly landed back in Alicia's home.

"That Dallas of yours has a never ending supply of money. That's the kind of man we want—I mean, you want." Bernice was constantly in

Tori's ear, reminding her how Dallas had come to their rescue, bailing out her dad after "his worthless hide had lost every damn thing at the casino. That man never met a poker or roulette table he didn't sit down and have a conversation with," Bernice had told her daughter.

Bernice had devised a master plan and she eventually convinced Tori to transition that "friend" into an actual "date" and primed him for the ultimate "husband." Among other things, it called for Tori to withhold sex from Dallas. "Don't trade your virginity for a short-term high of good feelings and wet ass," Bernice had said, while waggling a finger at Tori. "Go in for the kill—a permanent relationship. And don't get all touchy-feely with him. Let him crave you. A vagina is standard equipment on every woman. You'll want him to know that yours belongs only to him—for the right price. Marriage."

She'd closed her sermon with, "And defer to him in everything. Let him be in control! Then when you get that ring on your finger, when you finally add his last name to yours, that's when you have control."

Bernice had coached and manipulated Tori along the way, and finally, Tori had suggested to Dallas that they take their friendship into a more practical area—straight down the aisle and into wedded bliss. Tori had no doubts that Dallas cared for her, but she was still nudging him toward the 'in love' part. As quiet as it was kept, she had been trying to graduate to the 'in love' part herself. Tori had told Bernice, "Mama, I'm not ready to get married. I have my own dreams and goals. I want to be a doctor."

Then, Bernice had sobered Tori from that thought with more pearls of wisdom. "I never understood why you wanted to be a pediatrician in the first place. One wrong step and you could lose it all—your practice, your license, and then what? You're already swimming in student loans."

To this Tori bristled as she snapped, "And why is that?"

Bernice waved away her concerns. "I've already apologized. That little money would've never covered everything any old way."

"One hundred thousand would've given me a great start," Tori retorted, shifting on the sofa.

"Okay, so I messed up," Bernice huffed. "But I'm not going to let you mess this up. Now you can afford to do anything we—I mean, you want. You can work because you want to, not because you have to." Bernice grabbed Tori's hands and pulled them to her lap. "Juanita Jordan walked off with $168 million. Tiger Woods' wife—I don't even remember her damn name, but white girl made off with $100 mil. Dallas is smart, invests his money and is worth three times that amount. Do the math girl and—Go. Get. Your. Man!"

Tori understood her mother's motivation, but wasn't quite sure of her own. Regardless, she had the good fortune of helping Dallas through some of the most difficult times of his life. He constantly stated how much he was indebted to her for saving his mother's life. Thanks to Bernice's guidance, Tori had outmaneuvered, outdistanced, and outsmarted all of the women who were angling to get Dallas.

And now I have to fend off my aunt, too? Tori cut her eyes at Dallas Avery, ready to tear him a new asshole.

Dallas pulled over and flipped on the switch to heat the front and rear leather seats. He tapped a few inquiries into the navigation system, and the directions to a hotel in the South Loop came into view. He swerved toward the meridian and spun the car around in the opposite direction, doing Alicia's bidding without even asking if Tori wanted to go with them. Which she did, but that was beside the point. Dallas was only thinking of her aunt. The only thing he'd given Tori was a two-line disclaimer.

She couldn't hold her tongue any longer. "I don't see why you're—"

"Tori, there's a lot on your mind right now," he said in such a clipped tone that it brought her up short. "But I can't spend the next," he glanced at the dashboard, "twenty minutes arguing while driving in these conditions. We'll talk when we're alone."

Tori glared at him, hoping her look conveyed the extent of her feelings. Unfortunately, his attention was on the icy patches of road. His occasional glances at Alicia in the rearview mirror made Tori fume even more.

"But—"

"I'll take Alicia in a cab and you can drive back home," he said. "Your call."

Tori flinched. It took all she had to harness the words that were doing a tango on the tip of her tongue.

❤ ❤ ❤

Twenty minutes later, the Benz pulled into the circular driveway of the Hyatt McCormick Place, a towering glass and white stone building attached to a sprawling multi-level convention center. Dallas slipped out from the driver's seat and helped Alicia up. The shoes slipped from her feet and onto the pavement as he scooped her into his arms.

"I can walk," she mumbled, struggling to get him to put her down.

Dallas angled to retrieve the loafers and said, "Not in these."

He said it so softly that Tori paused for a moment as she exited the car. There was a tenderness about him that she had never seen or heard before. "Keep the motor running," she told the uniform-clad valet, then hurried to catch up with Dallas, whose long strides were practically eating up the pavement.

As he navigated the revolving glass doors of the front entrance, several people focused in their direction, instantly recognizing Dallas. In his signature panther-like gait—even with the weight of a woman in his arms—he effortlessly maneuvered the green and gold marble floors, right past the gawkers milling about the lobby.

The lattice lighting cast a dim shadow across the polished wood that made up the walls and the registration desk. The trio found themselves in front of a portly, dark-haired man whose silver nametag read Victor.

"I'd like to have your best suite for the night," Dallas said, causing Tori to glower in his direction.

"The best suite? Really?" Tori snapped.

Victor's lips set in a thin, disapproving line as he took a sweeping look at the three people in front of him. "Sir, is everything all right?"

"Just helping out a friend," Dallas answered, as though it were normal for a woman swamped in someone else's coat and shoes, with no hat or scarf, to be out in weather that was cold enough to turn corn flakes into frosted flakes. "Now, can you help us?"

"Yes, sir," Victor replied, as a spark of recognition lit in his eyes. He tore his gaze away and focused back on the screen. "The Presidential Suite is available. How many nights will she be staying?"

"Through the weekend."

Tori choked, but with a steely gaze from Dallas, she bit back her response.

"Could you please put me down?" Alicia asked in a voice just above a whisper.

Dallas looked down at her tear-stained face. "Not until you're in your room." Then he shifted so that Tori, of all people, could retrieve his wallet from the back pocket of his slacks. He nodded when she held up a Black American Express card and his license. She slid both to Victor, who swiped the card, looked at the license, then gave them both back.

"You're on the top floor," Victor said, presenting a slip for Tori to sign, along with the keys for the suite.

Dallas asked him, "Can you have a meal sent up?"

"I swear you act like you were lovers long before tonight," Tori said through her teeth.

Alicia and Dallas shared a speaking glance between them.

Tori's heart slammed in her chest as reality clicked a few wheels in her mind. "You were lovers?"

Victor's pale skin flushed bright red, and he quickly returned his eyes to the screen, trying to act as if he hadn't heard a word.

Tori shook her head in disbelief.

Dallas instructed Victor, "Have them send up something with a Thanksgiving feel."

"I'm not hungry," Alicia said softly.

"And send up the basics for everything else," Dallas told Victor, ignoring Alicia's statement.

Tori couldn't help the angry glare she gave Dallas and the woman still bundled in his arms.

"You've get some serious explaining to do," Tori growled.

With a quick glance, Dallas silenced Alicia when she parted her lips to speak. "Since you want to believe your mother," he began, "the only person you need to be angry with is me. I'm the one who's in a relationship with you."

"You know what?" Tori shot back, but stopped to regain what little hold she had on her sanity. She was livid, bristling at how calm and commanding Dallas was in a situation where he should have been groveling and begging for forgiveness. But Dallas was not one for drama, and if she let loose he would shut down completely. She took a calming breath, then turned to Victor. "Me and him," she pointed a finger at herself, then to Dallas. "We need our own damn room."

Victor looked at Dallas, who simply nodded.

"Would you like the one right across from the suite she's in?" Victor ventured, with a sheepish look at Dallas, then Tori as his pudgy fingers hovered above the keyboard.

"Hell no!" Tori slid the card back toward him. "Put us as far away from her as possible!"

Victor flinched at the venom spewing from Tori. She signed another slip before focusing on the clerk's beet red face once again. "Forgive me," she said in a softer tone. "It's been a long day. And can you ask the valet to park our car." She glared at Dallas. "Since it looks like we'll be staying."

Chapter 3

9:02 P.M.

They entered the elegant Presidential Suite, walked across the ivory marble foyer, and past a spacious kitchen, where they were welcomed by a modern blend of chocolate leather seating in the living room, and white leather and ebony wood in the dining area. Marble floors throughout were complemented by ivory walls and black and white artwork, along with a series of cathedral windows that provided a panoramic view of downtown Chicago and Lake Michigan.

"It should only take a few moments to get her settled," Dallas said to Tori. "Then we'll talk."

Tori grimaced as Alicia tried to get Dallas to release his hold on her, with no success. Tori turned from them, moved toward the living room, but quickly changed direction when she realized he was heading for the bedroom with her aunt.

Dallas gently deposited Alicia onto the bed, settling her atop the plush white comforter. When he turned toward the bathroom, Tori snarled,

"You run her some bath water and I'm going to put my foot so far up your behind, you'll need a surgeon to figure out where it ends." She barely recognized her voice, but with the rage bubbling inside her, she was fully prepared to back up her threat.

"She's still cold. And she needs to soak this foot," he said, staring down at Tori. "Are you going to run some water for her?"

"Does it look like I feel like being the fucking maid?"

Dallas paused for a split second, surprised by Tori's use of profanity, but his head whipped to the woman who moved to the edge of the bed as she said, "I don't need her help. Or yours. I can take care of myself."

He flickered a gaze at a shivering Alicia, then pivoted toward the bathroom. "I can't get into any more trouble with you than I'm already in."

The next thing Tori heard was the stream of water hitting the porcelain of the Jacuzzi.

That bastard!

Unable to see past the tears in her eyes, Tori went to the nearest chaise—a curved leather and steel design that cradled her as though the abstract furniture felt sorry for her.

Dallas had always been a gentleman, but this—the care he was giving Alicia—was too much. It was as if Tori didn't exist. And right now, she probably didn't. Their earlier argument was still ringing in her ears.

❤ ❤ ❤

Five hours ago, Tori had hurried from her parent's living room to the foyer to retrieve her cell from the pocket of her new Sable when Dallas' ring tone sounded.

She didn't get to say hello before he said, "We need to talk." The tone was cold, more than distant. He didn't even say, 'Happy Thanksgiving' and that caused a sliver of alarm to course through her.

"About what?" she asked, pressing her back to the closet to close it.

"I don't hold these kind of conversations over the phone, Tori."

She froze in the middle of walking back to the dining room, closing her eyes as she tried to work through the reasons he would come at her this way. "Can you at least give me a hint?"

"Your latest television interview. Your latest magazine spread. The latest invoices that my accountant just called about," he said, and each sentence was like a hammer blow. "Tori, you landed a contract with a reality show by making a promise that I would make guest appearances? Without consulting me?" He released a frustrated sigh. "We need to rethink this whole marriage thing. Because it's not about me and you anymore. It's about you and the world. I don't know who the hell you've become and I'm not feeling it." He was quiet a few moments as though weighing his next words. "Before we make a mistake, I need to rein this in."

Tori silently cursed, now wishing that she hadn't pressed him to talk. Bernice came to stand in front of her, arms akimbo, frowning.

"So you're not coming for Thanksgiving?" Tori asked as a stab of fear entered her heart. She waved her mother away, but Bernice didn't budge.

"I don't think it's a good idea," he answered. "We'll talk when you get back."

"Dallas, don't leave me hanging," she pleaded, causing Bernice to scowl. "Whatever it is, we can talk about it when you get here. It can't be so bad that it can't be fixed."

Bernice nodded as though she was hearing the other side of the conversation.

"Tori, you're tapping into accounts that aren't even yours. Then you go on national television—The View of all places—and tell intimate details of our love life. Well, what there is of our love life—since the only lovin' that's been available to me has been from my five fingers and a palm."

Tori turned away from her mother's distracting movements. She had never heard Dallas so mad. That's when she realized that she had made a grave mistake by listening to her mother, and that included flying through the budget that Dallas had given her for the wedding. He didn't even know about new bills that would hit in a few days. And the truth was, she didn't know what her mother was spending it on.

With Bernice's recent diatribe about the major risks of Tori's chosen profession—the thought of losing Dallas did not appeal to her in any kind of way.

Now, as she reflected on his earlier words, Tori stared out the window at a midnight blue sky without a single star to interrupt the never-ending darkness.

Tori wanted to demand answers from Alicia, but her heart sank when she remembered that her own words had put a wedge between them so deep that they hadn't spoken a single syllable to each other for the past year.

❤ ❤ ❤

THANKSGIVING DINNER. LAST YEAR.

"It's time for you all to make a move," Alicia said to James and her tone caused all of the guests to turn her way. She held a stack of charred pictures, and her hand was trembling with equal parts anger and sadness. "Bernice is making me believe that life in jail wouldn't be such a bad thing."

Bernice smirked and continued walking with a platter of dinner rolls she had carried in from the kitchen.

"Just one more month," he pleaded from his spot at the head of the dining room table. "That's all we need."

"We aren't going to make it another week under the same roof. She destroyed them on purpose," she said, waving the damaged photos at him. "I know she did!" Alicia raked a look over Bernice and took one step toward her, but James scrambled out of his chair to block her way.

"It was a mistake," James said to his sister. "I'll replace everything."

"Those things were irreplaceable!" Alicia shrieked, her green eyes flashing with fire. "You know they were. She just wanted to get rid of any evidence that could expose her lies."

"Evidence," Aunt Yoli asked, her jowls shaking as her head snapped to Alicia, then Bernice. "Did she kill somebody?"

"Well, she does cut up a chicken real well," Uncle Bill added while stuffing his face with dressing. "A human should be no trouble."

Bernice gave him the evil eye, but he wasn't cowed because he added, "They might be PlayBoy photos."

"My votes on those," Nathan chimed in. "She was a real looker back in the day."

Nathan's wife, Diane, elbowed him in the side and he almost spit out a mouthful.

"Just give us one more month," James said, taking Alicia's hand in his and patting it, as though the mild action would be enough to calm her down.

"Oh, yes," Bernice taunted from the threshold of the kitchen. "Just keep begging, James. She always gives in to you."

Bernice circled the dining room and stood on the opposite side of the table, looking at Alicia with a hatred so strong it felt like it had its own zip code. "Just as he's always catered to your uppity ass." She rubbed a hand across her face. "He only married me because I look so much like you!"

"Uh oh. Here we go again," Uncle Bill said, scraping the chair on the hardwood floor as he got up and fled to a safer spot near the front door.

"Why is that, dear sister-in-law?" Bernice asked. Then, her thin lips curled into a sneer. "Only a woman who's been giving a man some nookie has that kind of hold on him."

Diane scrambled from her seat and joined Uncle Bill, as the others who remained at the dining table gave them curious looks.

One eyebrow raised, Bernice finished with, "So, what's really been going on. Aleeeee-sha? You've been letting your brother have his way with you?"

In the moment it took to draw a single breath, Alicia was across the dining room table and inches from Bernice's face. Bernice struck out and landed the first blow, but Alicia blocked it and threw a punch that tumbled her sister-in-law to the carpet with a solid thud. The rest of the dinner guests scrambled from their seats to give the brawlers room.

This had been a long time coming—and no one wanted to get in the middle. Ever since Alicia had told her brother not to marry that "pure gutter trash," Bernice and Alicia had been enemies. At first, James had listened to his sister until Bernice fired back, accusing James of being "too intimately involved" with his sister to make his own decisions; that Alicia was practically holding his balls. The taunt worked. James eloped with Bernice and the relationship between Alicia and Bernice had traveled the fast lane of Satan's highway ever since.

Alicia was on top of Bernice slamming a fist into her face while growling, "You say some stupid shit like that?" Slam!—"In my house." Slam!

"Stop them!" Tori screamed as Uncle Bill held her back.

"While you're eating my food."—Slam!—"Soaking up my heat and my electricity?"—Slam!—"You're not paying one damn bill in this mother—"

The two crashed into the buffet just as Yoli wobbled all four cheeks and a couple of chins in the opposite direction to get out of their way. Bernice struggled to dodge Alicia's blows, stretched out a hand toward the dining room table, grabbed a fork, and stabbed Alicia's left hand.

Alicia shrieked, then went one better and yanked the carving knife out of the half-eaten turkey, lowering it to Bernice's neck, slicing just enough for trickles of blood to make a run for the carpet.

Tori broke free of Uncle Bill's hold, pulled Alicia away from her mother, then slapped her aunt full on. "What the hell are you doing?"

"You heard what she said!" Alicia protested. "After she destroyed my. . ." Then her gaze narrowed at Tori. "Wait a minute, you know your mother was wrong. You're taking her side against me?"

"Of course I am! You're not my mother," Tori snarled. "No matter how much you want to be." Then she glared at Alicia. "If you're going to be mad at anybody, it should be me. I burned them."

Alicia froze as the brutal words ripped into her. "You? You destroyed them?"

"She said you're using them to blackmail her," Tori said, balling her hands into fists. "How could you do something so low?"

Alicia stared at Tori for a few minutes. Finally, she said, "Did you even look to see what you were burning?" Her eyes crumbled, defeated, not by her enemy, but by friendly fire.

Tori turned just in time to see the ugly grin spread across her mother's lips. Only then did Tori realize that maybe, just maybe, she had fallen for her mother's story when she should've been smart enough to look in those boxes for herself.

Alicia slowly rose to her feet and swept past James and the rest of their shocked guests.

"You see what she did to me?" Bernice said to James as she wiped a stream of blood from her neck, which was instantly replaced by a fresh flow. "Call the police!"

When James didn't move to do her bidding, Bernice hurried toward the cordless phone. "Either she leaves or I'm going to press charges!"

"It's my house! My house!" Alicia shrieked from halfway up the staircase.

James turned toward his sister, a pleading expression on his face. "You cut deep. She's going to need stitches. Alicia, this is serious."

Alicia threw up her hands. "I can't deal with you people!" She ran up the rest of the stairs, into her room, snatched a suitcase from her closet, and immediately stuffed clothes inside. By the time she descended the stairs and hurried across the dining and then the living room, the police had arrived.

James wouldn't let them past the door. "Sir, it was a misunderstanding. There's no need for you to do anything."

The burly officer peered around James, nodding toward Bernice. "Doesn't she need medical attention?"

"My husband will take me," Bernice answered, then gestured toward Alicia. "Y'all just get her ass out of here."

Tori moved until she was directly in Alicia's path. "I never want to see you again," she said, brushing off thoughts that her mother may have tricked her. If Alicia was running, it meant one thing—she was guilty.

Alicia's tears welled up and spilled over as she gave Tori one last lingering look. With her bag in tow, she followed the two uniform-clad men out of her home.

❤ ❤ ❤

Tori wished then and now that she could have crammed those words back into her mouth. For an entire year she had left several voicemails asking for Alicia's forgiveness and begging her to come home. When Alicia didn't return a single call to Tori or anyone else, the family hadn't expected her home for the holidays or anytime soon.

Now it seemed some fences were better left unmended.

Tori looked over at the woman curled on the bed and covered in Dallas' custom designer leather coat. Alicia had failed to make any kind of eye contact with her—and that was just as well because Tori didn't know how to phrase the questions she desperately needed answered. What reason could Alicia have had for sleeping with Dallas? Was this payback for Tori's actions last Thanksgiving? But then, Alicia did act surprised to learn Dallas was her fiancé.

"Auntie . . ." Tori found herself saying.

Alicia didn't move from her spot on the bed. "Tori, I'm so sor—"

Dallas' concerned voice interrupted their attempt at a conversation. "Are you going to be all right?"

Tori turned to answer, and snorted bitterly when she realized that he was talking to the other woman.

If you're truly his friend, then you won't keep leaving him at the mercy of all those gold-diggers and whores.

Tori didn't know why her mother's words popped into her head. Bernice had considered herself the absolute authority when it came to men. It never occurred to Tori that her mother could be wrong.

With his grueling schedule, this was Dallas' first visit to get the seal of approval from her family. Not that Tori needed it. Dallas was the ideal man. He was the perfect example of what a strong man should be—compassionate, generous, sexy and charismatic. Not to mention, honest, reliable, loyal, and purpose-driven. So why would he screw up now, when her dream wedding was only five months away?

"I'm all right," Alicia said, sitting up. "I just need to get in the tub. I feel like my foot is swelling."

Dallas held out his hand to assist her aunt into the bathroom. Her delicate hand disappeared within his massive one and once again, Tori couldn't help but note how at ease they seemed together as he guided her into the bathroom.

The sudden flare of heat between them made waves of nausea pass over Tori. She hurried to the bathroom door in time to see Dallas remove his coat from Alicia's shoulders. In the royal blue and white bathroom, Alicia sat on the edge of a porcelain Jacuzzi that had been built for lovers. Tori's knees nearly buckled seeing the intense gaze that Dallas had locked onto her aunt—and the flash of something she couldn't quite name in her aunt's eyes.

They both glanced in Tori's direction, but she refused to let them see her hurt. To hell with pain! She would stick with angry.

With every aspect of her dreams circling the bowl and making a mad dash for the drain, angry was what she had every right to be.

Chapter 4

Minutes later, Dallas followed Tori into the Grand Suite, their steps slow and weighted on the natural wood floors of a foyer, which led into a dining and living room with tan suede seating. The warm, modern décor was drastically different from the chic, elegant suite they'd just left.

The snowstorm, which had delayed his flight earlier today was what had set this chain of events in motion. Tori had thought the delay would have given him time to cool off—but it also meant he would miss going with her and her parents for their traditional Thanksgiving visit to other relatives.

She'd said, "I'll leave the house keys under the mat on the porch for you just in case you get there before we return."

He'd said, "Fine."

Like she'd expected, he made it to their house before they returned. And somehow, for some reason, Alicia was there.

The hotel room door hadn't closed all the way before Tori whipped around to face him. "What the hell happened between you two?"

Dallas shifted, like he wasn't sure how to answer that question. He had managed to bypass all types of women before this, and it wasn't like he didn't have his pick. Yes, he was a baller, but he'd always shown her that he was faithful. Until today.

He made direct eye contact with Tori. "Do you want the truth or the version that will let us remain friends?"

She blinked for several moments as though taking in the many things his statement implied. "Didn't we say that we'd always be about honesty and trust? I want the truth."

He sighed, then began. "I was tired after my flight and just wanted to take a long shower. I went in the top floor guest room, just like you told me. I didn't realize the bathroom was connected to another bedroom and I walked in there. The last thing I expected to find was the love of my life."

❤ ❤ ❤

FOUR HOURS EARLIER …

Dallas froze at the foot of the bed. When he realized he'd walked out on the wrong side of the bathroom, his first instinct was to turn and hightail it out of there. But then, the woman had shifted and kicked the lavender silk comforter away from her like she was hot. And his eyes had immediately been mesmerized by her legs. Perfect calves, hearty thighs, and then, the triangle that met at the center of her thighs. Her voluptuous body was just like he liked it. He couldn't help it. His eyes lingered, and his manhood rose as if taking in the possibilities. She wore a skimpy t-shirt and sexy lace panties and for the first time since he'd accepted Tori's vow of celibacy, Dallas had the overwhelming urge to have sex.

He shook himself out of his trance and was just about to turn and leave, when the woman stirred again. Her eyes fluttered open, and slowly locked on him. If he was speechless before, he was at a complete loss of words now. It couldn't be!

The woman sat up, staring at him like she was trying to focus, make sure she wasn't dreaming. Then her eyes moved from his face, down to his nakedness, then back up to his face. Finally, she whispered, "Dallas? Dallas Avery?"

Alicia still had those mesmerizing green eyes. Their gazes remain locked as she eased out of bed and moved toward him with a hunger he hadn't seen from a woman in a long time—raw femininity, vulnerability, and sensuality.

She stepped in front of him and stroked his broad chest as though testing to see if he was real or part of her imagination. "You must be the most exquisite creature I have ever seen in my life," she said, her touch every shade of warm, wonderful and sensuous.

His erection got harder, which Alicia noticed. No more words were exchanged as her hand lowered, her fingertips gliding over the veins that thrummed with a rush of blood. She stroked him with gentle touches, which became stronger when he moaned with a pleasure he hadn't felt since the last time he'd made love to her.

Dallas was usually a rational man, but only one head was thinking now, and he eased her tank off. "Just like I remember," he whispered, taking in her full breasts. "Why did you leave me?" he moaned as he caressed her nipples.

"I didn't have a choice," she replied, her voice husky as she continued stroking him. "What are you doing here? You can't be here. I must be dreaming."

"This is no dream," he corrected. "This is fate. I've been dreaming of you since the day you walked out on me."

From the time he and Tori had officially become a couple, Dallas had been faithful. Even after her vow of celibacy, he had warded off groupies, cheerleaders and teammates' wives, now only to be felled by this woman with the hands of a goddess. The minute he reached out and brushed his hands across her delta, and a fingertip across her pearl, she arched toward him and her release was so dynamic, so intoxicating—it fueled a desire to do whatever it took to please her again.

It was the same feeling he had the night she won a date with him at a charity auction. She had turned down the dinner and strictly asked for his autograph. He insisted on that dinner, which later turned into much more. He had kept her with him at his condo for three months—pleasuring her, learning her, listening to her, and without warning, he fell deeply in love with her.

He couldn't resist the silken feel and taste of that honey skin, curves that begged for a man's lips and touch, and thighs that should be no other place but wrapped around a man who could pleasure her from dusk to dawn.

Dallas leaned in and pressed his lips to hers; she parted her lips, inviting him to explore her moist mouth. Their tongues intertwined, then Dallas pulled her into his arms, holding her close. "I'm not going to let you go this time."

She snuggled her naked body closer to him. "Oh, my, God. I can't believe you're here."

Those words suddenly brought Dallas back to reality.

"Wait," he said, pulling back from her, "why are you here?"

"This is my house," she said. Reality must've been setting in for her as well because her intense gaze had been replaced with panic. "Why are you here?"

But before either of them could say another word, the door had swung open and Bernice had burst into the room. Dallas quickly reached for the comforter and covered Alicia as best he could.

That brief encounter and now, the look on Tori's face derailed all of Dallas' plans. Even before seeing Alicia, his intention had been to break up with Tori. He'd wanted to make it through Thanksgiving before he actually had that talk with her, wanting her to enjoy the holiday before she'd have to deal with their breakup.

But now, Alicia had miraculously dropped back into his life, and he had no intention of ever letting her get away again. He never wanted to hurt Tori, and he definitely had no clue they were related. But it was what it was.

❤ ❤ ❤

Dallas had to leave Chicago, but outside the window in the Grand Suite, snow was falling, blanketing the Windy City in another coat of soft, white powder that would make getting a flight back home tonight nearly impossible.

"Dallas?"

He focused on Tori for a moment as he settled into one of the suede seats across from her. She had been waiting patiently for him to explain.

"You remember the woman I told you about," Dallas began, "the one I met at my fundraiser a few years ago?"

Tori frowned, then said, "The woman you said you were in love with? The woman who—"

"Yes," he whispered. "That woman. Beautiful. Green eyes. Knew a whole lot about investing and stocks. Taught me all about how to grow my money."

Realization dawned in Tori's eyes. "Nooooo," she crooned, gripping the edge of the seat. "No, it couldn't be!"

Dallas nodded.

"The woman you asked to marry you," she continued. "Then she up and left and you haven't seen her—"

"Until today."

Tori was trembling so hard she couldn't say a single word. "It was my aunt? God, this can't be happening!"

Dallas gave her a watered-down version of the scene that took place earlier. As her tears fell, an ounce of guilt crept in, but he resisted the urge to comfort Tori. Any gesture on his part could send a mixed message. And, it was a gesture of compassion that had brought Tori and Dallas together in the first place.

Two years ago
Plano, Texas

Dallas found a silent corner in the family waiting room in Baylor Regional Medical Center. He laid his head on the brightly painted wall and turned his body inward to block out any outside presence. His heart was breaking in ways that he had never experienced. His mother was dying. All of the reports from the specialists pointed to that fact. None of them held out hope.

Dallas closed his eyes and said a silent prayer. "God, I'm not going to promise that I'll be in church every single Sunday for the rest of my life. I'm not going to put a lie on the table that I'm going to suddenly straighten up and fly right. It's just that … I'm asking the right questions, but I'm not getting the right answers," he said softly. "So, what I need now is strength. What I need now is guidance. These doctors are supposed to be the best in the business, but God, You know this healing business. You know how much she believes in You. Show me what I'm supposed to do. I don't ask for much, but I'm asking you this, right here and right now…"

The feel of a gentle hand rubbing his shoulder and the scent of a woman's perfume caused his eyes to open. He looked into the face of an angel. He had never cried before, but for some reason he couldn't stop the tears that nearly blinded him. The woman pulled him to her and he hesitated only a brief moment before he held onto her as though they had been life-long friends.

"I'm sorry," she said after a while. "I was trying to find a quiet place to study, and couldn't help but overhear your words." She took the seat next to him. "What can I do to help?"

He peered at her, taking in the golden skin, soft brown eyes, honey blonde hair, slim figure—but it was the white lab coat that brought him to attention. "Who are you?"

"I'm Tori. I'm just a medical student right now," she said, smiling at him. "but in a couple of years, I'll be a resident." She looked around the room as if to confirm that they were still alone. "You're really upset; is there any way I can help?"

Dallas wondered what a medical student could do when the doctors were spinning their wheels. "What I'm most concerned about is that they're treating my mother as if she's already dying from cancer. Whatever happened to trying everything possible?" He shook his head. "I'm not feeling it. I haven't felt it since we first came here."

Tori thought that over for a moment. "Have you already gotten a second opinion?"

"They sound worse than these guys," he said sourly.

Tori picked up an iPad that she had placed on an end table nearby and tapped a few letters on the screen. She turned it to face him. "Have you thought about this place?"

He skipped past the name and went straight to the words that instantly put his mind at ease. At our hospitals, leading cancer technologies are combined with natural therapies to help you fight the disease and maintain your quality of life.

"Natural therapies," Dallas whispered. "Quality of life. That's what I'm talking about." He looked over the words again. "Trying for life, not putting a welcome mat out for a funeral."

Tori nodded and placed the iPad in his hands. He continued to study the screen.

"Baylor is definitely one of the best at aggressive treatment." She tapped a finger on the screen. "But it sounds like what you're looking for is a place that looks at the whole well-being of the patient. Not just the cancer itself."

Dallas sat up and took her hand in his. "Thank you. Finally, someone who understands what I've been saying. They're acting like I'm an idiot."

She gave him a small smile. "Well, you have to understand that each physician always thinks they know best."

"How do I get her up out of here?" he asked. "They're not just going to let me wheel her away, right?"

"You have a right to take your mother anywhere you like. Start with a call to Cancer Treatment Centers of America. The closest one will probably be in Tulsa, but it's so worth it. Then, request that her records are transferred to a physician there."

Dallas was out of his seat and hugging the stranger before he could give it a second thought. Within 24 hours, his mother was transferred. Within a week, she was responding to their treatment.

When he came back to the hospital to locate Tori and thank her, he ended up taking her to dinner that night. And the next night. And the night after that. She had traveled to Tulsa with him several times, and had even gone on her own, when a game sent him to the other side of the country. Tori had met his parents and took the time to research anything he, or his parents, needed along the way. They'd been friends ever since.

The treatment for his mother was a long and arduous journey, but even he could tell his mother was now focused on beating the disease, rather than being beaten by it. For that, he was forever grateful to Tori Mitchell.

Their friendship deepened over the months as he excelled in basketball and at the same time, Tori worked on meeting every goal she set for herself in medical school. The next step after friendship was dating, then the next logical step was marriage, though that step had come from Tori.

The two had been dining in a private area of Tate's, Tori's favorite soul food restaurant that Dallas co-owned with his cousin, Lolita. The place was colorfully decked out in a Motown theme—all the way down to plates that were made in the impression of old school vinyl records. It was a night of celebration—Dallas had won another case involving a frivolous lawsuit from yet another woman who was after him strictly for a quick life-time payday.

Their dedicated servers waited just outside the door of their private dining area as Tori and Dallas partook of the restaurant's specialties—fried chicken, collard greens, 4-cheese macaroni & cheese, sweet potatoes, and fried green tomatoes.

"You know," Tori said softly, around a bite of jalapeño cornbread, "a lot of your problems would go away if you got married."

"You're forgetting women these days," he countered. "They don't care if there's a ring or not."

He reminded her about Helen, the church's young secretary, and her gold-digging friends who'd been through so many members of his basketball team that he'd told his boys to stop attending service if they were only on "pussy patrol." He hadn't seen so many desperate women since Moses parted the Red Sea. Females—young and old, single and not-so-single—weren't waiting for "I do." They were just slipping between the sheets and saying, "Ooops, I did."

Tori laughed at his candid explanation, then looked at him for several moments. "You know a reporter asked me if you and I were an item. I didn't tell her anything."

Even though their friendship had blossomed into a relationship, Dallas hated the media in his love life, so they hadn't gone public.

"I don't mind them knowing that you're my girl," he said.

Tori toyed with her food. "It's funny, she said she didn't believe that we could be together because the rumor was I was a virgin and no way would the great Dallas Avery be with someone who wasn't putting out."

Dallas shook his head. "I don't understand why everyone's always in my business."

Tori shrugged. "Well, I did tell her that part was true. Only one special man will have the privilege of knowing me intimately."

Dallas took a bite from one of the homemade wheat rolls. "I'm still amazed that you've kept it on lockdown all this time," he said, chuckling. "There definitely aren't that many twenty-six year old virgins around."

She grinned, placing her napkin back on her lap. "It's not hard to do. No other men have measured up."

Dallas nodded and put his attention back on his plate.

"You measure up."

Dallas' head whipped toward her. "So what're you saying, Tori?"

She toyed with the fork as she shrugged. "I think it'll be a good idea if we get married. Then maybe you'll stop ending up in these lawsuits with women who have your bank account in their crosshairs," she said. "I listened to that woman in court, it was obvious you hadn't slept with her. She thought you'd just pay her to go away."

"I don't give in to blackmail," he said, his mouth stuffed with food. "The DNA would've told the truth."

"But by then your reputation, your brand would be a little damaged. That's what these women want you to pay to protect. Your brand." Tori took another bite of crispy fried chicken. "Getting married means you'll have one place, one woman to come to for everything. Love. Sex. Friendship, and definitely having all those children you swore up and down you wanted." Tori grimaced as she looked over at him. "Although, I think we'll have to cap that number at one. You're not wearing my womb out with eight children."

Dallas put his fork on his plate and stared at her for the longest time. "Tori, at least three children, if that's the case."

"Why're children so important to you?"

"We're educated," he began, swirling a bit of lemonade into the sweet tea in his glass. "And we have morals, and money. Add marriage to that, then we're definitely the type of people who are supposed to have children."

Tori thought about that a hot minute, then raised her glass of wine in a toast. "I'll drink to that." Then she gave him a wide smile. "At least until I get pregnant with the first of our two children."

Dallas chuckled at her attempt of narrowing the number down. "Well, I guess if I'm going to marry a woman," he said touching his glass to hers. "It probably should be to a woman who's always had my best interest at heart. A woman who cares about me, and a woman who I care about, too."

Tori beamed as she asked, "So, Dallas Avery … will you marry me?"

❤ ❤ ❤

Tori had first suggested they elope right away and kept at it until he finally insisted that they wait until after basketball season. He paid for that delay when she began to prepare for a lavish wedding. The amount of money that Tori was spending on their wedding and the extensive amount of interviews that she'd been giving lately had cast shadows of doubt for Dallas on Tori's true motivation of wanting to be with him.

Only in the past few weeks had Dallas realized the crucial mistake he'd made by saying yes to her marriage proposal without giving it the weight he normally gave the heavier decisions that affected his life.

Now they were both paying the price.

Chapter 5

9:31 P.M.

Dallas looked across at Tori as she was still trying to come to terms with the fact that her aunt had more of a claim to his heart than she ever did.

"Did this happen …" Tori said, her voice trembling. "Did you make love to her because I said I wouldn't have sex until we got married?"

Dallas shifted his gaze to the slender, golden-skinned woman, who still looked beautiful even with the effects of pain so clearly etched in her classically pretty features. "I keep telling you, that's not what happened tonight."

"Then fill me in, because my mind's running wild."

He grimaced, once again wondering what it was about Alicia that had caused him to almost have a serious lapse in judgment. Inwardly, he believed fate had landed him and Alicia in the same place tonight. Unfortunately, the timing of their meeting was off.

"Sweetheart," he said, watching as Tori rubbed her temple. "I promise you, we stopped before anything happened."

"See, that's what I get for letting my mother talk me into visiting all those people," Tori said, shaking her head. "I should've been at the house when you got there and this—"

"Tori, you have every right to be upset," Dallas said, interrupting her, "but that wouldn't change anything. Yes, your mother saw us together, but she lied when she said she caught us in bed. You can believe her if you want, but that's the bottom line."

As he had done throughout the last year, Dallas once again quelled his natural inclination to pull her into his arms and give her the comfort she so richly deserved. Tori had never been one for public or private displays of affection—something else that gave him pause about making things more permanent. "A year together and I haven't come close to doing anything like this."

"If waiting was going to be a problem," Tori snapped, "you should have said something before now."

"That's not what I meant," he countered in the most patient tone he could manage. "And let's get something straight—you set the terms for marriage. You didn't ask me, you told me we were going that route. And I went along with it."

She lowered her gaze.

He said, "What I was actually saying was waiting wasn't a problem. I've been celibate for an entire year and never came close to taking another woman up on what they offered—until today."

Tori looked at him with a mixture of weariness and sadness. "You don't have to worry about it anymore. Do whatever the hell you want."

Dallas was never one for knockdown drag-out fights. His parents had years of vicious verbal fights that had left a stain on his soul and he'd vowed never to get into it with anyone that way—whether in his professional or personal life.

Dallas stood, straightened his slacks, swept through the room and went for the door. "Good night, Tori."

"Where're you going?" she asked, moving from the sofa to perch on the edge of the dining table.

"I shouldn't stay here." He held up his hand to ward off her verbal attack. "I have some things to sort out." Taking in the defeated set of her shoulders, he added, "I thought I was doing everything right. Got back in church, got my career going with an NBA contract, was ready to make my best friend my wife. None of my plans included hurting you in any kind of way."

Tori glared at him as she said, "You can't go without telling me. I need to know what really happened. Mama said you were naked. Aunt Alicia was naked. Tell me. What happened?"

He took a breath. "I'd just come out of the shower. I walked into the wrong room. Alicia was already in the bed. I didn't know she was there," he said. He decided to leave out how close they'd really come to making love, not wanting to hurt her even more with all of the intimate details. "Bernice walked in the room and assumed that we'd slept together," Dallas continued. "I. Didn't. Make. Love. To. Alicia. Tonight."

"But you wanted to," Tori challenged, waving her hand in the air.

Dallas stared at the diamond on her left hand that took him hours of working with a designer to create. His answer to her statement was, "Keep the ring, the condo, and the car. I'll have everything paid off and moved into your name." When she didn't respond, he pressed on. "And I'm going to put some money in your account. I don't want you to have to worry about anything while you're starting your residency. I owe you at least that."

Tori blinked twice. Her pink lips opened and then suddenly closed. Several moments later, she finally found her voice. "Are you ending our relationship?"

"Tori, let's be honest," he said slowly. "We're friends. Great friends, but we need to leave it at that." He moved forward to continue his path to the door, but was halted by her voice.

"Wait, but ... I ... You said our friendship is what made our relationship so special," Tori stammered.

"I know, but I was already wavering over this whole thing, and today solidified it. Because I'd turned down every woman that came my way, but Alicia . . . Alicia makes me lose my damn mind." Dallas shook his head. "Now what does that say about me?"

Tori stared at him.

"I have to go, sweetheart," he whispered, unable to spend another moment witnessing the damage he had done. "You can send the things I left at your parent's house to my place."

She caught up with him at the door and placed a hand over his. "Do you …" Tori cleared her throat. Her golden skin flushed considerably. "How can you be in love with her? She's …. She's … old!"

Dallas took in the tears slowly making their way down her face. He resisted the urge to wipe them away. "Age doesn't have anything to do with love," he said, before adding. "And she's not old. She's mature, no games, a lot of wisdom to share. Alicia is every bit of wonderful." He caught himself, sure that was not what Tori wanted to hear.

"So the wedding's off?" Tori asked, frowning.

Dallas released a heavy sigh. "I come to meet your whole family for the first time and this happens? Not exactly a recipe for 'til death do us part'," he countered. Then with the tip of his fingers, he finally wiped away the tears streaming toward her chin. "You won't forget it; neither will they."

Tori placed her back against the door, blocking his exit. "So what I want doesn't factor into it? I haven't even said everything I wanted to say."

He paused, waiting for her to continue. He did owe her at least that.

"You did wrong," Tori whispered, then looked at him and amended, "almost did wrong, and now I'm the one being punished for it."

Dallas placed his hands on her shoulders. "It's not punishment. You deserve a man who can be faithful." He meant that. As much as he adored Tori, there was no way he could be faithful to her now that Alicia was back in his life.

Alicia had stolen his heart, then shattered it by leaving him with more questions than answers. But in just those few moments with her tonight, Dallas experienced a feeling of expectation—of possibilities, of passion, that he never wanted to go away. Chemistry and passion that was missing with Tori.

"Was she that good? I mean, when you were with her before?"

"Tori," Dallas warned. "Don't ask me a question if you can't stand to hear the answer."

Tori fell silent, inching away from him.

"I have to get some sleep," he said as he watched her back up.

He opened the door, but she gripped the edge of his shirt. "We haven't finished."

Dallas placed his hand over hers, giving it a gentle pat. "Get some rest and know that I'm truly sorry."

He kissed her, implanting the memory of her taste and feel in his brain. He was saddened by the fact that he didn't have that same spark of desire for Tori that he had in just those few minutes with Alicia.

"Goodbye, Tori." Dallas walked out of the suite.

Chapter 6

9:31 p.m.

Alicia Mitchell nursed her drink while lounging in one of the comfortable chairs across from a place called The Daily Grind. The bar itself, a maze of glass, mirrors, and high backed seating, hosted only one other patron, who sat talking to the burly bartender in between snatching glimpses of the football game playing on multiple screens. That is, when he wasn't trying to keep an eye on Alicia or checking out the ample assets on the barmaid with fiery red hair.

"Are you good for right now?" the redhead asked Alicia, giving her a smile.

"I'm fine. Thank you."

"Well, let me know if there's anything else that I can get you."

As the woman turned away, Alicia thought: Yes, there was something the woman could get for her. She could help her rewind to the time when Tori unexpectedly dropped into her life.

TWENTY-FOUR YEARS AGO ...

Alicia walked into Michael Reese Hospital, got directions from the security guard, and took the elevator to the maternity ward. She entered a room down the hall from the nurse's station and paused at the entrance. An infant swaddled in white cotton blankets slept quietly in a clear bin.

Bernice was sporting green contact lenses, a wig, and several layers of makeup; the get-up caused Alicia to frown. "Wow, the circus must've needed a whole new clown. You definitely look the part."

Bernice hurriedly slipped on the last of her street clothes and stuffed the hospital gown under the covers. "Glad you finally made it," she said sourly.

"I'm not on your clock. I don't see why you called me in the first place." Alicia noticed that the second bed in the room was unoccupied—highly unusual in a training hospital unless you had major cash. "It's not like we've said two words to each other since you married my brother."

"We had every reason to stay away from you," Bernice snarled. "You told him not to marry me."

"And I had good cause."

"You don't know me, lady," Bernice snapped, shaking a fist at Alicia. "You don't know nothing about me."

Alicia shifted so she was closer to the baby. "But I know women like you, and there was nothing that led me to believe that you had given up your old life."

Bernice's golden face flushed with color. "He told you about that?"

"Of course. My brother tells me everything." She chanced a look at the infant. "Well, he used to tell me everything until you came along. Smart move, making him relocate to Rockford."

Bernice laughed. "It's the only way I could be sure you didn't mess things up for me again. And it worked."

Alicia focused on her sister-in-law. "Then why am I here?"

Bernice marched across the room, grabbed the baby from the bin and shoved it into Alicia's arms.

"Alicia, meet Baby Mitchell. Baby Mitchell, meet your Aunt Alicia."

Alicia quickly secured the baby, smiling down at the little bundle, who was stirring because of Bernice's jerky movements. "So precious," Alicia whispered, stroking a finger across the soft pink cheeks.

"I'm glad you feel that way," Bernice said in a dry tone. "Cause you'll be seeing a lot more of it."

Alicia tore her gaze from the baby. "What are you talking about?" She frowned as it dawned on her. "You want me to take care of your baby?"

"See? He did say you were pretty damn smart," Bernice replied with a grin. "Actually, I signed into this joint as you, babycakes. So the kid's all yours. Free and clear."

Alicia gasped and opened her mouth to speak, but Bernice gave her a cold, hard glare. "You have a choice, dear sister-in-law. Leave it here and let the State take over, or take it home with you and raise it yourself." Bernice scampered over to the unmade bed and thrust the last of her items in a duffle bag. "The way I see it, that old-ass tank you married is shooting blanks. You should be happy to have this bundle of joy to round out your perfect little uppity life. And what makes it even better is that it's your own flesh and blood." She paused, frowning. "Least I think." Bernice quickly shook off that thought, then gestured in front of her. "You get a baby. I get my freedom. Everyone is happy."

"I can't take care of a baby!" Alicia cried, cradling the infant in her arms.

Bernice's eyes narrowed to slits. "You know firsthand what happens to kids in the foster care system, right?" Then she winked as though they were conspirators. "So I know you'll do the right thing."

"Not every foster home is like that!" Alicia shot back. "My grandparents took good care of us."

"But what about the places you lived before you got to them?" Bernice's thin lips lifted at the corners. "James said something about you having to learn to be real handy with a switchblade to live with those people. Almost ended up in juvie at nine years old." Bernice winked again. "My kind of girl. Trust me, we're not so different after all."

Alicia repositioned the baby in her arms, gave a long look at the duffle bag positioned over her sister-in-law's shoulder. "And just where the hell do you think you're going?"

"Someplace other than where I live now."

"Where's my brother?" Alicia asked.

"On another tour of duty," Bernice replied with a shrug. "I'm beginning to think he doesn't care for this whole marriage thing. He stays gone longer than he stays home. That makes this the perfect time to cut my losses." With that, Bernice grabbed her things and dashed out of the room.

Alicia looked down at the child she held, relishing the tiny gurgling sounds. Then a twinge of panic zapped through her. Her husband would not be pleased. He never cared for anything that took her focus from him. And as for herself, motherhood didn't seem like it would ever be an option since her husband was so much older. They'd been having fertility issues, but maybe this ... she glanced down at the baby. Maybe this little girl was the answers to every prayer that she had ever prayed.

"Good afternoon," a blonde nurse said as she entered and came to a halt. "Wow, you look fantastic! Ab-so-lute-ly beautiful." Her gaze swept over Alicia twice before she added, "Couldn't see the real you with all of that makeup you had on. You look totally different from when you got here. Glowing even."

Only then did Alicia understand why Bernice now looked like a hooker on the wrong end of the workday. "Yes, I'm sure I do," she mumbled.

The nurse focused on what was in her arms. "And you're holding the baby. That's a good sign. You had us worried for a moment." She glanced at the chart in her hand. "I know the doctor released you to go home today, but we have to know ... have you made a decision on a name yet?"

Alicia couldn't tell the woman that she wasn't the mother; she was too taken by how the child's little hand had gripped her finger tightly, as if she never wanted to let go. Then there was a gum-filled smile and another sigh that warmed Alicia's heart. Her husband would have to get over himself. "Victoria. Her name is Victoria Denise Mitchell."

"Victoria. What a beautiful name," the nurse said. "Well, let me get all the papers in order and mother and her baby will be able to leave."

The nurse walked out of the room and Alicia said on the edge of the bed. The baby wiggled in her arms and she held her tighter. "Victoria," she whispered. "Tori. My little girl, Tori."

And as she cooed at the baby, Alicia realized that she was already in love.

"Would you like a refill?"

Alicia snapped back to the present and gestured to her half-full tumbler. "Lady, are you trying to get me drunk?"

The redhead's eyes were alight with warmth as she answered, "You just seem so sad. Maybe there's something in that glass that's going to make you feel better."

"Trust me, sweetheart, it'll take more than a drink," Alicia replied.

The redhead gave her a small, sad nod. As she walked away, Alicia wiggled her pedicured toes so the hotel's house shoes would stay put. She pulled the black leather coat around her, inhaling the familiar masculine scent that caused her to drift into memories of the man it belonged to. The hot bath that Dallas had drawn did ease the pain in her ankle, but it did not banish the chill within her soul. She'd come downstairs in search of a little liquid heat to put some fire into her.

Reflecting back, she remembered the night she'd met Dallas, and for the millionth time she wondered how she'd allowed a total stranger to make love to her that way? It was still a wonder to her that the three months that followed had been the most pleasurable mistake of her entire life.

She was startled out of her thoughts when a deep voice said, "Why aren't you in bed?"

Alicia stared up into the handsome face of the man who knew her more intimately than her late husband ever had.

Chapter 7

9:47 P.M.

"I had a lot on my mind," Alicia answered, lowering her gaze to her glass.

Dallas hesitated, then slid into a chair across from her and swept a look across her body that sent the ripple of warmth through her that the drink had failed to provide.

"One question," he said softly.

Her eyes locked on his.

"Why did you leave me that way?" he asked.

Once again, she found an interest in the glass she held. "You wanted more than I could give you."

"What the hell is that supposed to mean?"

"Dallas, it was a fantasy," she said. "You wanted marriage. You wanted children. I can't give you that."

"Can't or won't," he gently said.

"I'm almost twice your age," she shot back, crossing one leg over the other. She quickly wished she hadn't. His leather coat inched open, exposing her thighs. She draped the bottom of the coat over them and sat her hands on her knees to keep it in place. "I knew what you wanted. I know my limitations."

Dallas signaled for the barmaid. "So you just left. Didn't think about talking to me about it or—"

"What purpose would that have served?" she asked, taking a long sip. He adjusted his long legs for comfort and her gaze lingered on his powerful thighs. "It was only supposed to be dinner, Dallas. Then you made it something more. What we had was wonderful, but it couldn't be more than that. Marriage? To me?" She shook her head.

The barmaid stepped into the space between them. Dallas took a quick look at her nametag. "Jane, I'll have whatever she's having." Then he frowned at the dark amber liquid in Alicia's glass. "By the way, what is she having?

Jane gave him a toothy grin. "Three wise men and their bastard cousin."

Dallas slowly shifted his gaze to Alicia, who answered, "Jack, Jim, Johnnie, and José."

He gave a low, throaty chuckle and leaned back in the seat. "You were just waiting for me to come down so I could carry you back to your room."

Alicia ignored Jane's grin and Dallas' comment by lifting her glass in mock salute and taking another sip. Her husband used to make a similar reference to her choice of liquor. Patrick always said that after one glass, he could have his way with her. That was never the case, though. Not that her much older husband hadn't wanted to, he just couldn't. Unfortunate for him. Even more unfortunate for her.

"I'll be back with your drink in a sec," Jane said.

When the leggy woman walked away, Alicia stared out at the courtyard of snow-covered trees and glistening stone walkways that twinkled under the bright outdoor lighting.

He mumbled, "Never thought I'd be spending Thanksgiving in a place like this."

She heard the sadness in his tone, and it certainly matched what she felt at the moment. Facing him, she said, "That makes two of us." She raised her glass and it was almost to her lips when she asked, "Where's Tori?"

"It's over," he said simply. "We ended it tonight."

"Oh, God, no!"

Dallas took the glass from her trembling fingers and placed it on the mirrored table between them.

"You couldn't work it out?" she asked, locking a steely gaze on him as he accepted the glass Jane held out to him. Jane looked at Alicia with one penciled eyebrow raised. Alicia nodded that she was all right and Jane sauntered away, but looked over her shoulder one last time for good measure.

Dallas cupped his hand over hers. "There are too many issues between us. And would you marry a man if his heart belonged to someone else?"

She hesitated. "Who has your heart?" she asked.

His left eyebrow quirked. "One guess."

Alicia inched her hand from under his and retrieved her drink. "You didn't tell her that, right? You wouldn't be that cruel?"

"I wasn't trying to be cruel. I promised to tell her the truth," he answered in a tone that showed his irritation, probably more with himself than with her, since in the three months they were together, he rarely got upset. His eyes swept across her face, then traveled down the smooth lines of her body. "I didn't give her a blow by blow, I just told her that I wanted you. Bottom line. I wasn't trying to hurt Tori," he said, "but seeing you . . . feeling you, proved a point that I was coming here to make anyway."

"And what point was that?"

"That she is not the one." He stared as if he was looking through to her soul.

Alicia closed her eyes, and then opened them, studying his features as though for the first time. She had fallen for tall, dark and handsome when everyone else was into short, suntanned, and sensational. And Dallas was definitely tall, milk chocolate—and a rugged kind of handsome.

And he was built like a stallion, primed and ready to ride.

She pressed her thighs together trying to quell her desire for him, while at the same time she thanked God that they had come to their senses before something actually happened tonight. She couldn't afford to fall for him all over again. Leaving him had been the hardest thing she'd ever had to do and she couldn't imagine going through that again.

"I'm not the one for you," she said, knowing her words were inadequate, but hoping they would be enough to send him back to her niece.

He looked at her as if he couldn't believe what she'd just said. "Really? You must've forgotten how we were together. You must've forgotten our connection."

She spoke before she thought. "I'm not likely to forget the man who gave me my first orgasm."

Dallas nearly choked on his drink and Alicia smiled as she leaned across to give his back a hearty pat. He regained his composure, but his eyes were still filled with shock.

She gave him a small nod, then explained, "My husband, God rest his soul, was a little short in that area. He was a lot older than me. Twenty-five years, to be exact."

"Wow. You didn't tell me that part, you only said you were married for a long time."

"Twenty-three years."

"And you stayed with him all that time? Even though he didn't satisfy you?"

"There's more to marriage than sex," she replied. "He was my grandparents' attorney, and we fell in love. He was a decent provider, and he really cared for me."

Dallas nodded, though his confused expression said he clearly didn't understand.

Alicia shrugged, though she kept the rest of her memories about her husband to herself. There was no need to share the other side of Patrick, a miserable man who wavered between insecurities about his inability to perform in bed and asserting himself as a man. Because of his stubbornness and desire to control every situation, she'd lost any chance of having the child she desired when he told her that he wasn't going to go through with any of the fertility treatments that he'd promised—all because she'd come home with Tori.

When Dallas looked at her over the rim of his tumbler and gave her a smile that was filled with a world of mystery, Alicia forgot about all thoughts of her dead husband. Dallas put the glass to his lips, and in that instant she remembered feeling his lips when he'd given her breasts his expert attention. Fire spread through her body, and she had to close her eyes, trying to bring herself back on point.

"So the first time when we made love ... that was really your first orgasm?"

"Careful, your ego is showing," she teased.

The smile slowly faded from his face. "I thought I missed you before, but seeing you again, what I feel right now is stronger than it was a few years ago." He stood, pulled out his wallet and placed sixty dollars on the table. "I'm going to the front desk; will the weekend be long enough for you?" he asked, his brow creased with worry. "If you need to extend your stay, I'll—"

She waved off his concern with a dismissive hand. "No need. I'll work on finding another place by Monday. Maybe an apartment until I can get another house since I don't have the strength to fight my brother and his psychotic wife."

Dallas removed the drink from her hand and placed it on the table. "You've had enough for tonight," he whispered, holding her gaze for a long moment.

"I needed something that could numb the parts of me that hurt," she answered.

Dallas reached into his wallet and held out his business card. When she grasped it, he placed his hand over hers, sending a jolt right through her.

"I know the timing may be off, but this isn't over. I'm not letting you get away again. I'll let you rest tonight, but here's my new cell. If you need anything before morning," Dallas whispered, tightening his hold on her hand.

Alicia parted her lips to speak, but was interrupted.

"Well, it seems that you two get along real well," Tori said dryly, eyeing their clasped hands. "I guess this is where people come to drown their sorrows or to relive pleasant memories." She scanned the area, then settled on the seat Dallas had vacated across from Alicia. "You don't mind if I join you, right?"

Chapter 8

10:07 P.M.

Alicia stiffened at the sound of Tori's voice, but she was too shocked by Tori's disheveled appearance to say much of anything. Her niece's hair was all over her head, her eyes were bloodshot. Her pain was evident and it hurt Alicia's heart.

Dallas slowly removed his hand from Alicia's. "I was just leaving."

"No, stay," Tori commanded, gesturing to an empty seat next to Alicia. "You owe me at least that."

Tori turned her cell phone to face him. "The next time you want to have a heart to heart with my aunt, make sure your phone is locked."

His number was displayed on her screen, along with a clock timing the call that he'd accidentally placed to her twenty-seven minutes ago.

Dallas frowned, pulled out his own phone and disconnected the call.

"Don't hang up now," she said. "I already heard everything. Enough. Too much."

Dallas settled back into the seat. He and Alicia shared guilty glances.

Tori reached for the half-filled glass sitting on the table and took a long swallow. The liquid came spraying out seconds later as she screeched, "What the hell is this?"

Dallas' lips twitched in an effort to hold back a smile. He removed the glass from her hand and slid it back in front of Alicia, who was trying not to laugh.

For that one moment, Tori took in their humored expressions and actually grinned. The tension between the three of them lightened, but only for a second.

"What are we going to do?" Tori finally asked, looking at both of them.

Alicia searched Tori's face. "What do you mean 'we'?"

"How can the three of us make the best of a bad situation?" she asked pointedly.

Dallas shifted to the edge of his leather seat and peered at Tori. "I thought we decided to go our separate ways."

"You decided that," she shot back. "You didn't let me say much of anything." She looked to Dallas, then Alicia. "So this is what true love looks like? A woman who didn't love you enough to stick around," she taunted. "And a man who falls for a woman who's old enough to be his mother. That's a match made in romantic heaven."

Alicia gave Dallas a knowing glance, then leaned back in her seat as though he should be the one to handle that barb.

"Tori, you're pushing it," he warned. "Throwing shade isn't going to get you good results."

Tori slid her hand forward, resting it on his thigh. "I don't want to lose you," she said in a voice so filled with emotion it caused a slash of pain across Alicia's heart. The fact that her niece couldn't walk away from Dallas spoke to the fact that Bernice had trampled out nearly every ounce of Tori's self-esteem. The fact that Dallas was still in love with "an older woman" must have smothered the rest.

Alicia stood, unable to listen to anymore. "Well, that's my cue."

"Sit down," Tori said in a tone that made Alicia whip toward her. "This concerns you, too."

Alicia looked at Dallas, who gave her a slight, almost imperceptible nod. Only then did she lower into the chair.

Tori wrung her hands in her lap. "Maybe I was wrong to force you into celibacy for a whole year. I know how sexual you are and—"

"I keep telling you—"

"Will you please be quiet!" she snapped.

Three heads looked their way: the lone customer at the bar, the bartender, and the barmaid.

Tori's lips quivered in an effort to contain her emotions. She lowered her tone. "I'm trying to find a way to salvage our relationship." She stole a sideways glance at Dallas, then looked at Alicia before focusing on him again. "Unless it isn't important to you anymore. Unless I'm not important to you."

Dallas went to her and lifted her chin so they were looking each other directly in the eyes. "You're my best friend. You will always be important to me."

The tears that came into Tori's soft brown eyes were enough to make Alicia want to slither away.

"Then why're you trying to end things?"

Dallas released a weighted and weary sigh as he stood erect. "It's not just about what happened with Alicia. It's not just about what happened today. This has been a long time coming, Tori. You hired a damn publicist. And you're conducting a virtual media blitz about our engagement and what doesn't go on in our bedroom." He shook his head. "You know how I am. You don't ever see me talking about my life like that and I'd just had enough, Tori. This isn't our wedding anymore. It's your mother's. It's the media's. I've had it up to here"—he gestured above his head—" with all of it."

Tori grimaced as though hearing his side of things pained her in some way. "I'm sorry about all that."

He shook his head. "I know that you are, but the final straw has nothing to do with you." He paused. "I thought I knew myself," Dallas' gaze went over Tori's shoulder to Alicia. "But I'm realizing that I'm not as strong as I thought I was."

Tori followed his gaze to her aunt. With resignation in her eyes, Tori said, "What if I said I'd get rid of all of that wedding stuff, get rid of the publicist, and," she took a deep breath, "that it was okay for you to keep seeing her for a while." Tori lowered her head, and the defeated movement made Alicia stare openly at her niece. "You know, sort of like getting her out of your system before we get married." She paused, then amended her words. "Before we get married ... or however long it takes."

"What brand of crazy Kool-Aid are they serving your ass in medical school?" Alicia said.

Dallas peered at Tori in a manner that said he totally agreed with Alicia. "You're saying . . . "

Tori nodded slowly, as though hating to confirm his summation out loud.

"Hel-loooo," Alicia crooned, waving a hand in front of both of them.

"Be quiet," Tori snarled at her aunt, who recoiled from the viciousness in those two words. "I'm negotiating the terms of marriage with my future husband. You're just an unfortunate part of the equation."

Dallas tilted his head, frowning before one eyebrow shot up and his lips twisted as though in deep thought. His gaze shifted from Tori, then to Alicia and back to Tori again.

The man was actually considering Tori's offer!

"You're talking about an open relationship? And maybe even an open marriage?" he said, frowning at her.

"It's obvious you have some kind of connection with her," Tori said, as if the admission pained her. "I don't like it, but if you're going to be with another woman, I'd rather it be with her." Tori passed an icy glance at Alicia. "At least she won't go running to the press and damage your brand. And when you get this out of your system, she'll disappear and we can resume our life." Tori spoke with a finality like she'd worked everything out in her head. "And trust me, she knows how to leave. It's what she does best."

Alicia's head snapped to her niece. "Really, Tori?"

"It doesn't matter," Tori replied with a dismissive wave, but the two women's gaze stayed locked for several moments. When neither Dallas nor Alicia said anything, Tori continued. "I was upstairs giving it a lot of thought. We can all benefit from this. Obviously, I underestimated your need for sex, and—"

Dallas interrupted, "I told you this isn't about sex."

Tori ignored his words and turned to her aunt. "I have no intention of changing my celibate stance. So he gets you for a while and I get him for a lifetime."

Dallas and Alicia stared at Tori as if she had grown wings. "Why would you want to do this?"

"Because in the end, this will work for me. You might be all in lust now, but I know you love me, and I also know that you want kids more than anything else. So when that lust shit wears off, you'll long for a family." Tori glared at her aunt again, before turning back to Dallas. "A family that only I can give you."

Tori gave her a quick head-to-toe as though summing her up for the first time, then she placed her hand on her flat stomach. "Women make these kind of compromises all the time. Mostly, it's after they get married but …" She rubbed her stomach to make an unspoken point. "…but it's not a big deal. Because she can't give you what I can."

Dallas and Alicia both stood speechless. The crew cut-sporting busboy swiftly moved about the tables, cleaning the area as the bar prepared to close. The television screens went blank and the solitary patron had left.

But Dallas, Alicia and Tori stayed in their places.

"Why?" Alicia asked. "Why would you even think about such a thing?"

"I just explained it. What part didn't you understand?"

Alicia knew that she should have stomped away as soon as Tori started talking this foolishness. She would never agree to something like this.

Tori stared at her aunt for a few moments. "Did you know he gave Dad the money to come out of bankruptcy, then paid off all the student loans I had to take out because Mom had ripped through my college fund? Did you know Dallas was that kind of man?" Tori looked to Dallas, who tried to keep his expression neutral, before focusing on her aunt again. "He's never laid a hand on me, never raised his voice, never mistreated me. He doesn't do drugs, and—"

Alicia shook her head sadly. Bernice had truly done a number on her daughter. "He's not supposed to do those things, Tori," Alicia said. "That doesn't give you a reason to give him a pass on anything else."

Tori snapped, "Let me tell you something. With everything that he's done for me and my family … he's not the type of man you call a former boyfriend. That's a man a woman calls her husband." She took a deep breath. "And if his only flaw is that he has to be with you sometimes, then that's something I'm willing to deal with."

The silence expanded between them as both Dallas and Alicia stared at Tori.

"Don't say anything right now," Tori said, before she rose from her chair and stretched. "Think about it, figure it out, and I'll see you both in the morning." She took a few steps across the carpet and into the corridor before turning back to Dallas, "You've already paid for two suites; you might as well make use of one of them."

The suggestion hung in the air before Dallas' expression darkened with anger. "Is all this about money? You want my money?"

Tori pressed her lips into a thin line and said nothing.

Dallas continued, "You don't have to marry me for money. I've already given you an 'I fucked up real bad' going away present."

Tori's squinted angrily as she glowered at Dallas. "I told you what this is about," she said before she quickly put distance between them by hurrying toward the elevators.

"Dallas, you were wrong for saying that," Alicia said, insulted for her niece's sake. "Evidently, she loves you, and she's willing to accept a few things that other women wouldn't."

Dallas paused to take those words in, then guided Alicia back down to her chair. He let silence hang between them for a few moments before he asked, "How do you feel about what she put on the table?"

It took her only an instant to respond, "I won't be a part of something like that." She shook her head. Though for the life of her she still wanted him, and Tori's suggestion was swirling through her mind as well. "Earlier, I didn't know you were her fiancé. I won't have that excuse anymore." Alicia took in the conflicted expression on his face and cupped his face in her hands. "You need to go to her!"

"And do what? Beg to be in a marriage that would start on a sour note? That's not fair to her. Or to me."

"This is your chance to make things right. She needs you, Dallas; she cares for you," Alicia whispered. "Do it … for me."

"How can you tell me to do that?" he asked.

"Because I know my niece. We haven't been close over the last year, and really, we were drifting apart before then." Alicia paused, wondering just how much she should share with Dallas. A part of her wanted to tell all: how much she now resented Tori at times, how unfair that was, how hard it was to resist that feeling, though, since she'd given up so much, had made so many sacrifices for her niece. With tears in her eyes, Alicia added, "I'm asking you as a woman who knows what it's like to lose something very valuable—with no way of getting it back." She placed a calming hand over his chest. "So she went a little overboard on the wedding. She said she's willing to give all that up. She has a good heart and you know it."

Alicia wrapped his coat around herself. "I'm going up to my room." She stood on her tiptoes, and Dallas lowered so they could embrace. She pressed a soft kiss to his cheek. "Thank you for taking care of me."

She tried to back up, but he held her in place. With an extra effort, she pushed him away, then made her way to the elevator.

He called out, "What is it about you? Why can't I resist you?"

She paused and faced him, thinking that she had asked herself that same question from the moment the frosty air had blasted her face when she ran from her home this afternoon.

"You take care," was her reply.

To this, he only smiled as he watched her step into the elevator.

Chapter 9

10:28 P.M.

Dallas went into the Grand Suite and trudged past the moonlit dining and living room areas. Tori had planted a seed in his mind, and he needed to figure out why she had even put something like that on the table.

Tori lifted from her lounging position on the bed the moment he paused at the threshold. "You came back to me."

Her soft words sounded more like a question than a statement, but at that moment, the truth was, he was trying to decide his next move. He didn't feel as if he belonged with Tori anymore, but her proposition was swirling in his head. Especially the part about children; his legacy was important. But was it as important as Alicia?

"Thank you for sending up dinner," Tori said, gesturing to the tray of food that had been wheeled in earlier. "Would you like something to eat?" she asked.

A quick glance showed she had barely touched anything. Dallas shook his head and continued his study of her golden features—deep-set eyes, and silky lips. Tori was stunningly beautiful in every way. She was the perfect woman to be his wife—intelligent and driven, and genuine in her friendship with and caring for him.

"So, have you given my proposition any thought?" Tori asked when he didn't respond to her question about dinner.

"I'm still trying to make sense of it," he said, crossing the distance between them in a few strides.

Tori slipped off the bed and met him halfway, wearing only a red lace bra and panties. This was his first glimpse ever of her semi-nude body and he was not moved.

She reached to cup his face in her hands in much the same way Alicia had done minutes ago, which shocked him. He could count the number of times Tori had engaged in any kind of intimacy with him. "It's simple," she said. "You couldn't really love someone like her. It's just sex, Dallas. That's all it is. Just sex. And I know that, and understand that. But, I also understand other things."

"Like children?

"Exactly. My aunt is forty-five; how would she give you eight children? Could she even give you two?"

Her points, her questions were good ones that left him feeling conflicted. Part of Dallas knew that was why Alicia left him in the first place. It was right after they laid in bed and he talked about the children he so desperately wanted to have. The next morning, she was gone.

Tori splayed a manicured hand over his broad chest. "I love you. Enough to let you have us both. At least for a while."

He shook his head. "I can't do that. I've hurt you enough as it is."

"Leaving me will hurt me more. And I know that it won't take long for you to get her out of your system."

She laid her head on his chest, but Dallas withdrew from her. "I don't know how to get you to see it's deeper than that. I just can't do this. She deserves better than that."

Tori glared up at him with an intensity that lasted only for a few moments before a flash of sadness took its place. "She deserves better than that?"

Dallas closed his eyes against the crush of pain he saw on her face. "I already told you that I don't want to hurt you either." Dallas laced his fingers through the streaked blonde tresses that spilled over her shoulders and down her back. "You don't want this."

"Shouldn't I have the right to decide what I want?" she asked in a voice so hoarse with sorrow it made his heart skip a beat. "With everything you've done for me and my family, I'm willing to let you have your cake and the cherry. Why is that so hard to believe?"

Dallas hated hearing the insecurity in her voice. Tori's determination, confidence and compassion had been one of the most beautiful things about her. He would never forgive himself if she lost the best parts of herself.

Tori stroked a hand across his jawbone. "I can't lose you."

Dallas encircled his arms about her and lifted her body so that she was flush against him—a move that sent a tinge of warmth spreading through him, but it wasn't nearly as potent as Alicia's touch. He whispered into her ear, "Do you realize that we've had more physical contact in the past two hours, than we've had all year?"

"You know the reason for that," she said, thinking back to all the times when she'd tried to explain this to him. "I've told you. We weren't like that. I didn't come from a touchy-feely family and I don't know why that's such a big deal."

For at least the thousandth time since he'd found out that Alicia was Tori's aunt, he marveled that the two of them were related. One, so hot! The other, so frigid.

The thing was, as cold as Tori was, Dallas had no doubt that she cared deeply for him. And he felt the same about her. Besides that, Tori was the only person besides his mother that he'd trusted.

He'd been surprised when she'd told him that she'd wanted to abstain from sex until marriage. She'd said that it was the way she'd been raised and when she cited religious reasons, Dallas had gone along with that. He wasn't about to be responsible for messing up Tori's relationship with God.

At first, it had almost been a relief for Dallas. Making the commitment to Tori meant that he wasn't out there, trolling, sleeping with one girl tonight, another one tomorrow, and the whole time, checking condoms to make sure that one of those scandalous females wasn't trying to come up at his expense. But it didn't take long for him to kick himself for agreeing to Tori's stipulation. He'd had no clue that to Tori, no sex, also meant "no nothing else." And for a man who was used to having sex on a pretty regular timetable—having no affection at all was more like he had been dropped into a time warp of ancient times.

"I love you with all my heart," she whispered so softly he thought he had imagined it.

Dallas hesitated, knowing the words she wanted to hear. Finally, he uttered, "I love you, too." That statement was the truth. But was it enough?

As if reading his mind, she said, "Go to her. Do what it takes to make you feel all right."

Tori tried to mask her pain and it tore at his heart. He was at a fork in a rocky road—and neither path was an easy one to take. Stay with Tori and long for what he had with Alicia, eventually hurting Tori in the end? Or go with Alicia, though he wasn't sure that he'd be able to convince her that they belonged together.

Then lastly, there was the ultimate—he could have his cake and his cherry. Have both women. Tori, who had already brought value to his life, who had helped him save his mother and now she held a debt that he could never repay. She was loyal, would be the perfect mother for his children, and he loved her.

And then there was Alicia. Who held his heart. He more than loved her, he was in love with her.

"There's no hiding what you feel for her," Tori said.

Dallas wondered if she knew that her words mirrored his feelings exactly. "Get her out of your system, then come back to me. I promise we'll make everything work."

He thought for another moment, and then, his three choices collided, making him angry. Gripping her upper arms, he growled, "Stop it! If you keep pushing me on that woman, I'm going to take you up on it.

Stop testing me!" he said, shaking her, though he didn't meant to be so forceful.

Tori looked up at him with a calm that was more alarming to him than her anger had been. "Close your eyes for me," she commanded.

"What?"

Tori repeated her request.

Dallas didn't know why, but he did as she said.

Chapter 10

10:46 P.M.

Dallas stood with his eyes tightly shut as Tori pressed her hand on the half-hardened member in his slacks. It didn't twitch or otherwise acknowledge her touch.

Tori leaned in and whispered, "Alicia."

The image of that luscious woman came to mind and his erection sprang to life. Dallas forced himself to take a step back as his eyes flew open. Tori moved with him and stroked that area, punctuating her point with a sly grin.

"You've been semi-hard ever since you walked through that door. And it certainly isn't because you're ready to make love to me." Tori gripped his erection to make her point. "Now tell me that I'm lying about that."

Dallas pushed her away and stormed from the suite. Stumbling through the hall, then into the elevator, he finally made it to the lobby and approached the front desk. First, Alicia pushes him back into Tori's life, then Tori slides him back to Alicia.

His thoughts were awhirl, with no clear direction. Both women filled his mind.

Alicia, with her mesmerizing eyes, the velvety feel of her skin against his, the beauty of her heart-shaped face, her curvaceous body, the sultry sound of her voice, the feel of her hands on him. That was the physical, but they'd connected on other levels. Books, politics, world views, money—he had loved the way she challenged him.

But he knew more about Tori. The things that drove her, her fears, her victories—he knew her in every way except for one.

"Sir? Sir, can I help you with something?" Victor called out from behind the counter.

Dallas looked at him for a moment, then turned away, took five long strides back to the elevator and stepped into the chamber.

The elevator made a slow climb as Tori's words echoed in the far corners of his mind.

You've been semi-hard ever since you walked through that door. And it certainly isn't because you're ready to make love to me.

Dallas stabbed at the elevator's button, which was moving slower than he remembered.

There's no hiding what you feel for her.

He turned his back to the closed doors, resting his head on the clear glass panels.

Get her out of your system, then come back to me.

The elevator opened and Dallas practically ran to the end of the hallway. He knocked on the door softly, as though a part of him didn't want her to hear. Inwardly, he prayed that she did.

Moments later, Alicia peered through the cracked door. "What are you doing h—"

Dallas pushed open the door, reached inside and loosened the belt on her robe. He stood in the doorway, spellbound as his gaze wandered the lush length of her naked body—the full breasts that made his mouth water, the small roundness of her belly, the silky skin of her thighs, which combined caused his erection to thicken to the point it was damn near painful.

He lowered his lips to hers, then kissed a trail to the pulse beating wildly at the base of her throat. When his mouth found her breasts, she whimpered. He could take her this very moment and she'd be perfectly willing to go along for the wicked ride. He captured her mouth with his, giving her a searing kiss that exploded into a world of sensory overload.

Dallas loosened his hold and stepped back, though his eyes stayed on the curves she tried to hide behind the folds of the thick white robe she struggled to secure again.

"Let it go," he commanded.

"We—we—we can't do this," Alicia stammered, backing away from him. "Haven't we done enough damage?"

"Oh, I'm just getting started," he confessed in a husky groan. Dallas gripped her buttocks to hold her in place, then lowered to his knees and spread her open for his tasting pleasure. Her scent was intoxicating; the pure essence of her was one of the most amazing things about her, the most wickedly beautiful thing he had ever witnessed in any woman. And he wanted her to be his completely.

I'm not likely to forget the man who gave me my first orgasm.

Dallas held her steady as a quick move of his fingers opened her, revealing a moist core. He let his tongue go to work, teasing, tasting and giving her a never-ending kiss. She screamed his name, and it caused him to increase the pressure. He nibbled on the outer folds of her core, and she trembled so hard with that first release that her knees gave out and she tumbled into his arms.

Before she could take another solid breath, he stood, swept her from the living room to the bedroom and gently deposited her on the sheets.

"It's all right," he crooned, calming the confusion he saw in her eyes. "Trust me. It's all right, baby."

The splash of winter moonlight filtering in through the windows danced across curves that spread from a small waist and flared into hips that beckoned for a man to do the most pleasurable damage possible.

But it was her breasts that held him captive. Those large nipples called to him, begged for his lips and tongue to have one hell of an intimate conversation with them.

Dallas snatched his shirt over his head, unbuckled his belt, unzipped his slacks and gave a tug, causing belt, slacks and briefs to hit the carpet at once. Nothing else in life mattered except pressing his body to hers, holding her to him, as if her touch alone was a life-giving nectar. He parted her thighs with his knee, then waited for that one sign that this was something she truly wanted.

Alicia reached for him and he centered himself to thrust into her, sheathing himself in that moist heat. There he lost himself, giving in to the direction of her sighs, and the shallow series of breaths that were a melody unto themselves.

He brought about an orgasm that made her pass out, only to come to again in time for another sensual assault where she clasped him to her as though her very life depended on it. The tremors that whipped through her excited him, drove him to keep their intimate connection for as long as earthly possible.

Alicia cried his name over and over, her body following wherever he chose to lead. He gripped her soft, silky strands of hair and pulled her head back to expose the skin along her graceful throat. Dallas buried his face in the smooth curve, trailing his lips upward to tease her until she trembled with the beginnings of another sweet release.

"Dallas, please! I can't take anymore." Her hands came to rest across his buttocks, her thighs tightened around him to still his movements. "I can't take anymore."

Dallas paused only for a moment, but the sound of her breathing coming in small, soft gasps took him over the edge.

"Stay with me, Alicia," he whispered. "Just a little longer."

Alicia gave him a look so open and vulnerable that it moved him. But it was what she did next that sent a wave of pleasure through him.

She parted her thighs, opening to him. He couldn't resist the urge to push deeper, harder, faster into her. The soft whimpers of pleasure guiding him to bring them both to the point where nothing else mattered. The orgasm that slammed through him was so powerful in its delivery, so vicious in its intensity, that every conscious thought took flight, leaving only the essence of her in its wake.

When the sun made its daily ascent into the wintry sky, they were still entwined. The pleasure he derived from being with Alicia was something he couldn't put into words. Every time he held her, he felt a completeness that he never knew was missing. The peace that enveloped him gave him a sense that all was right in the world.

Dallas realized one major thing: "just one more time" with Alicia Mitchell would never be enough.

Chapter 11

Alicia's eyes flew open, and she tried to adjust to the unfamiliar surroundings. She awakened in the comforts of a soft bed with Dallas' arms wrapped around her. His hold was more protective than possessive. She felt safe, wanted and loved—a trio of feelings that had eluded her for most of her life. A trio of feelings that she'd only felt with him.

He'd held her this way the first night they'd spent together. The night when he'd extended their auction dinner into a night of pleasure. He'd held her this way when they'd awakened the next morning and he'd asked her to stay, "just one more day." The one day turned into a week, then a month –until three months later, he said he had fallen in love with her and proposed. The morning after his proposal, she'd had no choice but to leave. Marriage to him was an impossible undertaking.

Alicia snapped to the present and tried to extricate herself from his arms, finding out in the process that she was sore in places she never knew existed. His lovemaking had been so intense that she couldn't remember the exact moment she had slipped into her third and fourth releases.

His arms now slid about her, stilling her movements. She relaxed and settled in, never wanting this feeling of contentment, this feeling of completeness to go away.

"Good morning, baby." His voice rumbled through his body and vibrated through hers.

"Good morning." She traced a path upward toward his chest, following the well-defined contours of muscle.

His hand lowered to cup her buttocks, stroking them as he explored the smooth expanse of skin. The way his hands caressed her body and the gentle kisses along her temple were practically her undoing. She laid her head on his broad chest and closed her eyes.

Dallas drew the sheet up to cover them and took a long, slow breath.

The silence between them was more potent than any conversation. Dallas continued to stroke her body, and the rhythm lulled her back into a comfort zone that caused her eyes to close against her will.

Her last waking thought was, Lord knows, I love this man.

Three hours later, Dallas removed himself from under her and stood at the edge of the bed. "Come shower with me." The words were more of a command, than a request.

"No, I'll wait until you're done."

Alicia glanced at his extended hand, and thought of objecting again. But the intensity of his gaze spoke to the fact that he would have his way, even in this.

She wrapped herself in the sheet and stood several feet away from him.

"It's all right. Let it fall."

Another command. Alicia wasn't sure how she felt about that. She looked at him. He raised an eyebrow and his lips were set in a gentle, encouraging line. She knew from past experience that arguing with him was pointless. She released the sheet, allowing it to slide to the floor.

"Come to me, baby."

She froze. Her feet were unwilling to obey yet another directive.

Morning had brought a whole new reality. What was Dallas really thinking coming to her last night? Whatever this was between them, it couldn't go on. Before, she was too old for him. Now, he was going to marry her niece.

"Alicia?"

She flinched, wanting so much to pull the sheet over her body again. "Oh ... I ..."

He'd seen more of her body in the last sixteen-or-so hours than her husband had in twenty-three years of marriage. But having had the unfortunate experience of attracting the wrong kind of attention as a young girl, it had been impossible for her to develop a true appreciation for her beauty. Remnants of that negative self-image were deeply ingrained.

Even after Dallas had introduced her to what it felt like to have a man truly treasure her body, standing before him completely nude made her feel exposed, vulnerable. She wanted to dive back under the covers more than anything.

"I'm not comfortable with this," she admitted.

Dallas' gaze was unwavering as seconds ticked by. Finally, she found the strength to move toward him and he gathered her into his arms. "You never have to hide yourself from me," he whispered. "Stop fighting me, Alicia. Everything's going to be all right."

She nodded, but her heart rate had increased to the point she had to close her eyes to get her bearings. What was it about him? She was no milquetoast woman, but even though she had the desire to fight him, she couldn't find the strength sometimes. And with everything she had been through growing up, fighting was what she did best. And running. Yes, that, too.

"Dallas, what are you doing to me?"

He placed a gentle kiss on her temple. "Loving you the best way I know how."

The words were enough to bring tears to her eyes, but she refused to let him see that. She should not feel this way—not with him. Anyone but him. Her prayers had been for God to send her someone to love and someone who loved her. God certainly had a wicked sense of humor—sending her a man who not only could never belong to her completely, but who belonged to her niece.

Now she, the woman who had lost everything that mattered to make sure Tori was happy, had hurt Tori in the worst way. She couldn't continue with this, no matter how good Dallas made her feel. No matter how much she loved him.

"Dallas—" she began, but he stopped her protest by placing a finger to her lips.

"Let me show you how good it can be," he said. Dallas guided her into the bathroom. He leaned into the shower, turning the water on and adjusting the knobs that controlled the temperature and spray levels.

The steam rose around him, but her gaze lingered on his handsome face—the beautifully curved lips, the piercing dark brown eyes, the lashes that were too thick for a man as rugged as he was. Then her eyes lowered to the jut of his chin, the broad shoulders and chest, the tight abs, muscled arms, his powerful thighs and legs, all the way to his feet—which made her pause, as she had never seen a pair so well-defined. Her gaze traveled upward to his groin, then went the distance until she reached his most dangerous feature. His body was pure perfection, but his eyes, his eyes were the most intriguing thing about him.

"Dallas, please," she implored him the moment he stepped into the shower and turned his focus on her.

"You're not coming in?"

Alicia shook her head. Finally, some type of strength. "I can't do this, Dallas."

He watched her a moment, then gave her a clever smile as he held out the soap and a face towel. "Just do this for me."

"You want me to bathe you?"

"No, I want you to stand there and look at me for the next hour."

"Don't be a smartass," she snapped, and he laughed. She actually felt the corners of her mouth turn up in response.

Soon his smile disappeared and he was all business again. "Baby, I want to feel your hands on me."

The huskiness of his voice did unspeakable things to her. She inched across the marbled tiles, took the items he held and put the soap in the direct line of the spray. When she placed it against his chest, he flexed. She flinched at the sudden movement, which caused him to grin. As she continued her journey across his skin, he startled her by leaning out to place his lips on hers, his tongue parting her mouth. Her head tilted to give him free reign. And in her moment of surprise, he lifted her from the floor.

She gasped, but Dallas placed a finger to her lips to stop the quarrel that lingered.

"Do you trust me?" he said, holding her to him.

She uttered a breathless, "Yes," before he pulled her into the shower and angled their bodies so the water sprayed over both of them.

He lathered her skin and explored her body with a touch certain of the path it should take. She felt that familiar stirring and closed her eyes, trying to understand what was wrong with her. It was like someone had given her a glass of water to quench her thirst and somehow she couldn't drink it down fast enough. She couldn't drink him in fast enough.

Dallas anchored her. A fingertip teased her pearl, and she gasped at the avalanche of feelings that overwhelmed her.

"Dallas!"

"Yes," he whispered, slipping a finger into her, stimulating her so much that she couldn't keep her hips from moving toward him with a rhythm that matched his.

She gripped him, burying her face into the sharp curve of his neck. "Dallas!"

With that, he centered himself, teasing her first with a series of circular motions on the outer lips of her core. She took in a breath, and that's when he thrust upward.

"Don't ever hide from me," he said against her ear.

Alicia trembled within his arms and couldn't form a response. He thrust in again.

"Do you hear me?"

"Yes!" she cried out.

"I love every inch of you. This," he said as he kissed the smooth hollow of her throat, her shoulder, "and this," he said brushing against her breasts and lowering to her belly.

Dallas picked her up so that her thighs encircled his waist. Each thrust shifted her with the force of its power.

"You're mine now," he said with a note of finality.

Alicia parted her lips to say something—anything—that would stop this sensual possession. What he was demanding made absolutely no sense.

"You're mine!"

He paused, waiting for her acceptance. When she said nothing, he pulled completely out of her body. The absence of him was so profound that she clawed at him, begging him to finish what he had started.

Dallas complied by teasing her core with the tip of his bulbous head. "I'll always take care of you," he said. "Every need. Everything."

She nodded, and he was inside her once more.

"Say it," he demanded on a single thrust that put her over the edge. "Say that you're mine."

The world shifted on its axis. Alicia surrendered to her orgasm, unable to do anything but whisper, "I'm yours, Dallas."

Chapter 12

10:02 A.M.

Dallas slid into the Grand Suite and held the door open for the stocky, dark-haired man who followed behind him rolling a breakfast trolley. He adjusted the shopping bags in his arms so he could sign the bill and pull out a generous tip. The man grinned and handed the money back, presenting a blank sheet of paper and a pen instead. Dallas took a look at the nametag and autographed the sheet before passing it back with the tip.

"Thanks, man!" Hector said, giving him a toothy grin. "You going to take the Mavericks to the top this year?"

Dallas gave the man a grin. "We're going to take them to the top. It's a team, not just me."

"Sure thing." Hector held up the autograph. "Thanks a lot."

Tori stepped into the dining room, toweling off her curls as the door closed behind Dallas. "I thought I heard something."

She surprised him by coming to him and wrapping her arms around his waist. He held onto her for a long while before she pulled away to look up at him.

"I ordered you some breakfast." He pointed to the bags at the other end of the table. "And brought you something to wear."

She blinked twice and suddenly perked up. "New clothes! Nice."

Dallas pulled out a chair for her at the dining room table. Tori took a seat and waited as he put her favorites onto a plate. She lowered her head and said grace, then glanced down at the place where his plate should have been. "You're not eating?"

Dallas had already had Alicia feed him from her plate. It had been another first for Alicia, and he enjoyed getting her to open up to him. "I'll just have some juice for now."

Tori went to the cabinet and returned with a glass. She poured nearly up to the rim, slid it in front of him and then went back to her meal.

"So, did you go to her last night?" she asked matter-of-factly.

Dallas raised a single eyebrow. "Are you sure you want the answer to that?"

She nodded, then shook her head as if the reality of what she'd told him to do, what he'd done was just hitting her. She swiped at her tears with the back of a shaky hand. "I don't know why I'm acting this way. This is all my idea, right?" She groped for a napkin, but her hands were trembling so bad that she couldn't get a handle on a single one of them.

Dallas handed her one of his.

Tori snatched it and dabbed at her face before tossing it on the table. An uncomfortable silence settled around them.

Finally, she looked up and studied him for a few moments. "You seem settled right now," she said. "I don't think I've ever seen you this way."

"A good night's sleep can work wonders for a man."

Tori flickered a gaze over him, then focused on his eyes. She stabbed her fork into a stack of pancakes, as though they had offended her somehow.

"I feel so ... disconnected. So lost." She looked down at her plate and pushed the eggs off to the side to get to the hash browns. "Yesterday I was a woman who was all set to spend the rest of my life with my best friend." She glanced up at him. "Now, I'm doing something I would not have considered three months ago, three weeks ago." She grimaced, and her perfectly arched eyebrows drew in. "Hell, two days ago."

"Tori—"

She waved him off. "You've been the best thing that's ever happened to me. And now it all comes down to this one question: what am I willing to accept so that I can have what I want? And what I want is you."

Dallas slid his glass to the middle of the table and settled back in his seat. "I still don't think this will work. I don't want to hurt you. I don't want to see you crying every time ..."

She glared at him. "It will work. I just have to get used to it being my aunt." She shook her head as if all of this was still unbelievable. "I just never thought I'd be in this kind of situation with my aunt. She's been the one person in my life who I could trust with all of my secrets."

Dallas looked out at the city's snowy skyline, giving her words some thought. "She loves you. Nothing can change that, Tori."

"Whatever," she said, then paused before asking, "How is Alicia taking all of this?"

"She's worried about you."

"But not worried enough to walk away."

"I'm not giving her that choice."

Tori's eyes registered disbelief. "You're really in love with her?"

"I am. But you knew that. I told you about her when we first met," he replied, hoping she didn't press for anything more. He didn't want to talk about how he loved Alicia, how he loved her in a way that he didn't love Tori.

She nodded. "All of this hurts," she said. "But, I'm trying to see the big picture here."

"A woman who's been married to a man for years might have a camera lens that wide, Tori," he said. "But what you're asking us to do, this isn't a 'big picture' kind of thing for a woman who's just getting into a marriage. I'm just not sure that you'll be able to handle this."

"How would you know?" she shot back, waving her fork at him.

"You've never been married. How do you know what I'm capable of handling?"

Dallas shook his head thinking that maybe it wasn't what Tori could handle but what could he handle? He'd had a front row seat to his parents' marriage, all of the conflicts, all of the turmoil. His mother always seemed to be in such pain, never happy. He didn't want to be the man to do that to any woman, but it seemed that he had. Even before he walked down the aisle. At least, though, it had happened now and not after he had taken those vows. What kind of marriage would they have had if he didn't have the kind of love that made a man lose his mind? The kind of love he had for Alicia?

With a softer tone, Tori said, "Believe me, I can handle this. It's better than the alternative, better than losing you." Reaching across the table, she stroked a hand over his arm. "Bring her here and let's see how this is supposed to work."

When Dallas didn't move, she added, "You owe me that much."

Dallas sighed heavily. That was the problem. He did feel as if he owed Tori—in so many ways. He stood, planted a kiss on the crown of her head, then hurried out of the suite.

Chapter 13

10:20 A.M.

Dallas entered the Presidential Suite, rushed toward the bedroom, but stopped at the threshold. He couldn't help but admire the dress embracing Alicia's curves as she turned one way then another to catch her reflection in the full-length mirror. He brushed past her, zipped her up, then took a seat on the leather chaise to get a better view.

"It fits perfectly," she said, giving him a small smile.

"Looks like Victor earned his bonus," Dallas said with a grin, relishing the fact that a genuine smile had graced her sensual lips. "Might have to put him on the payroll."

"Hush money?"

Dallas shrugged. "I don't think our issues are going to end up in the tabloids. At least not by him. I got him covered."

She smoothed the dress along her body. He followed her movements, which ended at the upper part of her thighs. "I can't believe that you got everything right. Even the cosmetics."

He nodded his appreciation. The dress was both sexy and stylish on her voluptuous form. The high-heeled boots made her legs look as if they could go on forever. She had pinned her hair up into a love knot, leaving a few tendrils of hair cascading about a face graced with just a hint of makeup. The woman was well put together—absolutely sexy, with a huge dash of gorgeous thrown in for good measure. And now, after all this time, she was his. All his.

He just needed to make sure she didn't run again.

"How is Tori?" she asked, taking his thoughts away from her.

He motioned for her to come to him; she hesitated. Gently, he patted his thighs and kept his eyes on her until she acquiesced. Still, she moved slowly, until she lowered herself onto his lap and curved her body into his embrace.

When she was settled, he said, "She's getting dressed, but she wants to see you. She wants us all to talk."

Alicia's head tilted as she peered up at him. "Talk about what?"

"Talk about this. About the way this will work out for the three of us. You send me to her. She sends me right back to you. We've got to work this out."

She turned her face away from him, focusing on their reflection. "Dallas, " she began, shaking her head. "I'm not going to do this. I don't want any part of this."

"So, what are you saying? That I should leave Tori?"

"No!"

"Well that's what's going to happen because I'm not going to leave you."

With the tips of her fingers, Alicia massaged her temples. "This is impossible."

"I know, but after all Tori's done for me ... if this is what she wants."

"She doesn't want this."

He nodded. "You're right. An open relationship, and open marriage is not her first choice, but she understands that my relationship with you is—"

"We don't have a relationship!" Alicia shot back. She pushed herself up and moved away so she could stand a few feet from him. "Don't make this out to be more than it really is. It was lust, pure and simple."

"So after today, what?" he snarled, getting to his feet. "We go our separate ways and you'll pretend like nothing happened?"

Alicia met his gaze head on. "I think it's best."

"You're not leaving me again," he said firmly.

Her head snapped to him, green eyes flashing red. "Tori is the one you want to marry. Go make a life with her. Build a home. Have babies ..."

"I don't love her like I love you," he said.

"And I can't give you what she can," Alicia said just as pointedly. She gave him a tired half-smile and moved further away from him. "Besides, there's another variable we keep forgetting. You're young enough to be my son."

Dallas crossed the distance between them, and pulled her body to his. "But old enough to please you in every way."

Alicia blushed and shifted her focus to take in the cityscape images along the wall.

Dallas brushed his lips across her earlobe. "The sound of your voice, the feel of your skin, your taste, your touch. There's a strength about you that's sexy. Class, elegance, warmth—that's just a part of who you are. I want to know more. I need to know more." He splayed a hand across her belly and pressed his growing erection into the swell of her buttocks. "I couldn't let you leave even if I wanted to."

She locked gazes with him in the mirror. Her eyebrows drew together in a stern line.

"This cannot be a good idea," she finally whispered. "Why get married at all if you're going to sleep with other people?"

"Tori said it best. Everyone gets a little of what they want."

"And a lot of what they don't want," Alicia countered.

"It may end up that way, but while I'll never let you go, I don't want to leave Tori if this is what she really wants. She's always been there for me when it counted. My mother's illness, the court battles with all of those women, when I was taking a beating in the press. Every single time she's had my back. And if I marry her, I will be able to have kids and take that issue off the table with us." He paused, turned her around and placed his hands on her shoulders. "But the bottom line remains, it's you that I want. That I need. I owe her. I love you."

"Do you hear how you sound?" Alicia said. "Like some spoiled man who wants it all."

Dallas' chest heaved. "Fine. Then, I choose you."

Alicia shook her head as she fought back her tears. "I can't do that to Tori."

Dallas eased toward her. "Exactly." He lifted her chin. "I don't want to hurt Tori, either. So, I'm going to give her what she wants, the marriage, the fortune, the family. But I want to be happy, too." He stroked her hair, then took her hands. "You make me happy."

Alicia looked down at their hands joined together and shook her head.

"Tell me you don't want me," Dallas said.

He nipped her earlobe, causing her to first melt, then stiffen. She struggled to get out of his grasp and then, she put some distance between them. "Dallas, we're done," she said, holding her hands in front of her to keep him at bay. "I'm not doing this."

Dallas was on her in the time it took to blink. He pinned her to the wall, placing a bruising kiss on her lips. She steeled herself for what was coming at first, but was trembling with the need for him when he was done. Her face darkened with anger as she glared up at him, but her body had told him everything he needed to know. Silenced hummed for a few moments.

"We're done?" He was unable to conceal his satisfied smile. "Are you sure about that?"

Alicia looked away, but his fingers on her chin turned her to face him again.

"Shall I show you how far from over we really are?"

Dallas gripped her waist to hold her in place as he lowered his free hand to her hemline and raised the dress to the top of her thighs. He journeyed upward into the silk panties. Color flushed her cheeks the moment his hand cupped her moistened mound, that telltale sign of her needs betraying her.

He slipped in a single digit, dampening his fingers in her liquid heat. She gasped at the intrusion and barely had time respond to his rhythm. When he removed his finger, he tasted her sweetness, drawing it from his finger while she watched him, her lips parted in wanton expectation.

"I love you," he said again, as if that was the seal on the deal. "So, let's go up and talk to Tori."

She lowered her head and hurried to the bathroom, the set of her shoulders radiating shame and defeat. God help her, but she wanted to do this. But how? How could she do this to her niece?

Five minutes later, he found her at the sink, her hands still gripping the vanity to brace herself.

Dallas turned her toward him, and she struggled to keep back her tears. In her eyes, her saw her vulnerability and the depths of her sensitivities felled him. Sobs tore through her, and she hugged her arms about her body. Dallas knew the reason for her pain—a pain that existed because she was torn about loving him and hurting the woman she considered her daughter.

"What do you want, baby?" he whispered into her ear. "Do you really want me to end this with you?"

When she remained silent, Dallas lifted her chin so that once again, she had to look at him. "Say the word, Alicia. I don't ever want you to be this unhappy."

Still she wouldn't speak, her sullen expression saying that she was working up the courage to tell him to walk out that door and never see her again.

"What about Tori?" she asked.

"What about you? "Twenty-three years in an unhappy marriage," Dallas said. "Where's your reward? Where's your happy ending?"

"Not at the expense of another woman's pain! My niece's pain!"

"Alicia, at least be willing to talk about this. If you still feel the same way after …" His voice trailed off because the thought of being without her made his heart tighten the way it had when she'd disappeared before. He began again. "If you feel this way after the three of us talk, then we'll revisit what we should do. All right?"

He didn't wait for her to answer. Dallas grabbed a towel from the rack and pressed it to her face to stem the flow of her tears.

She lowered her gaze then closed her eyes completely.

"I love you, Alicia," he whispered. "So please, let's go talk about it. And if we can make this work for everyone." He paused. "There'll be no more talk of you leaving me. All right?"

Dallas waited several spells before Alicia moved into his arms. He held her close, relishing the sweet feel of her embrace.

One half of his battle was over.

Chapter 14

10:58 A.M.

Thirty minutes later, a portly driver extended his hand to help Alicia from a black sedan. A sudden squeal of tires made her head snap around. The yellow cab tearing down Harper Avenue came to a screeching halt right behind them. She thought it might be Dallas, who was probably angry that she had given him the slip and left the hotel. "I'll come to Tori's suite in ten minutes," she had told him, knowing she wasn't going to go at all. One of them had to show a little common sense.

But it was Tori who jumped out of the back of the cab, tossed some bills to the driver, then broke into an all-out sprint, aiming toward Alicia. "Wait!"

Alicia stepped around her niece, knocked the snow from the boots Dallas had bought for her, and walked into the house with Tori fast on her heels.

James looked up from the Chicago Sun-Times he was reading and Bernice froze midway across the threshold between the kitchen and dining room. She almost dropped the plate of leftovers she carried.

Alicia made it to the second floor landing, then paused and looked down at her niece, who stood at the bottom of the stairs. Tori wasn't wearing the same dark slacks and silk blouse as she had been wearing the day before. Evidently, Dallas had made sure both women had what they needed.

"Give me a few minutes, Tori. Then we'll talk."

"Oh, this is rich," Bernice mocked, looking from her sister-in-law to her daughter with a scowl that marred her features. "You should have your foot knee deep in her ass, and she wants to talk?"

"Tori," Alicia said, with a pointed look at Bernice, "we should have this conversation somewhere else."

"Fine. Let's go back to the hotel." Tori maneuvered past her mother and moved toward the stairs.

Alicia slid a glance at her brother. An angry vein throbbing at his temple caused her to think twice about having any kind of conversation with him.

Bernice gripped the sleeve of Tori's blouse and shouted, "I want answers!"

"Well, you won't get them from me," Tori retorted, shaking off her mother's hand.

"I have to get my things," Alicia said as she moved down the hall and entered the safety of the guest bedroom. During her absence Bernice and James had taken over her master bedroom.

She rifled through her purse, found her credit card, then took a seat at her computer and navigated to Air India's website. A song trilled out once the intro page came onto the screen.

"Come along, come along with me, and I'll ease your pain," the raspy voice sang.

"If only a plane ride could accomplish that," Alicia whispered. She moved up the departure date on her reservation and quickly printed the necessary documents.

The Mediterranean cruise Alicia was supposed to be on for Thanksgiving had been cancelled due to an outbreak of the Norovirus and it also postponed her trip to India—the last place on her "special things-to-do list." As she'd stood in the airport wondering what she was going to do for the holiday now that her plans had abruptly changed, she'd checked her voicemail and heard the latest of Tori's messages. Her niece had left so many that Alicia wondered if maybe Tori was right. Maybe it was time for her to come home.

So, that's what she did and by the time Alicia arrived at the Harper house after an eighteen-hour sleepless flight, she was soul weary from her year of traveling—first to Sabi Sand Game Reserve in Africa, sleeping in one of their luxury Treehouses for months, reading and meditating before she choose to visit other parts of the motherland, then to Tibet, Switzerland. The call from Tori was perfect timing—a break from trying to repurpose her life.

She'd been grateful when she arrived to find the house empty. She knew everyone was out doing their normal Thanksgiving caravan of visiting friends and family and her plan was to get some sleep before they returned.

Only vaguely did she remember thinking she'd heard the shower; she'd just been too weary, believing that all sounds she'd heard was the carry-over from her travel meds.

So, she'd laid down, closed her eyes, then felt his presence. When she opened her eyes, Dallas was there and . . .

Bernice busted into the room, the same way she'd done yesterday. Her hand was poised on her hip. "How could you do this to her?"

"I would appreciate it if you left my space," Alicia said, hating to be snatched from her memory of Dallas. She moved toward the dresser to collect the few toiletries she'd unpacked.

"I'm not going anywhere!"

Tori entered the room, ushered her sputtering mother out of it and locked the door.

Alicia pointed to her ears, then gestured toward the bathroom. Tori followed her inside. When Alicia perched on the edge of the tub, Tori put the top cover of the throne down and took a seat.

She waited several moments for Tori to say something, and when no words came, she began with, "I'm so sorry I hurt you, Tori. Please believe that—"

Tori's gaze flitted to the marble tiles, then the glass sink and finally landed on Alicia. "So we're in this complicated situation."

"Why did you send him to me last night?"

"Because he longs for you."

Alicia reached out to touch Tori. When she recoiled, the spike of pain through Alicia's heart was almost too much to bear.

"That's no reason to sacrifice your relationship."

Tori folded her hands and placed them on her lap. "Things changed the moment he saw you again." Her golden cheeks flushed with a bright red color as she focused on the seashell designs on the hand towels. "You're a basketball fan! You had to know that he was engaged to me."

Alicia shook her head, folding her arms on her lap. "I detached from my life the minute I left home last year. I didn't care about you, James, basketball, or anything else. So, I didn't know you were a couple," Alicia said. "That's really no excuse, but I'm so, so sorry."

Alicia reached for Tori's hand again. This time, her niece didn't pull away. Instead, she met Alicia's gaze head on.

But then, after a couple of seconds, Tori extracted her hand, finding a sudden interest in adjusting the towels so they hung evenly. "He's in love with you. Did you know that?"

"He couldn't possibly love me. He thinks he does, but he doesn't know that much about me." Alicia hoped her niece could believe that. That was how she explained Dallas. But Alicia had no idea how to explain her own feelings that defied all reasonable understanding. That's why she needed to get as far away from Dallas as humanly possible. India. Yes, India should be just about right. She held a multi-entry Visa that would make it easy to enter the country.

Both women were mute for several moments, and each dodged eye contact.

"I stayed a virgin until I found the man I wanted to marry," Tori whispered. "How did I do all the right things and still lose the man I love?"

Alicia placed her hands over her niece's. "I always encouraged you to respect your body and respect yourself." Then she gave Tori a small bitter smile. "But because of what I went through, I also told you that once a woman found her future husband, she'd better take him for a test drive before signing up for the long program."

Tori's small ears reddened around the edges and she tried to smile, but couldn't. She tilted her head up and looked at the exhaust fan on the ceiling. "I keep thinking all he needs is a little time and we'll be back to normal."

Alicia looked at her niece. "You don't know how much I want that—for you both to get back to where you were."

Tori shook her head. "Now that he's been with you again," she said, "he'll want more. And here's what really scares me: if you're not there, what if he tries to find what you have in another woman? That's something I won't be able to control."

"And you think you're controlling the situation right now?" Alicia asked as she looked at her niece intensely. "This situation's been running the show ever since you dropped that suggestion to Dallas. I don't see why you even went there."

"I'm playing the best hand with the cards I've been dealt," she countered.

"You have so little faith in yourself. You have so little trust in him."

"He's a man," Tori snapped, shifting on the porcelain lid. "Men have that kind of flaw."

"Your father doesn't."

Tori looked down at their joined hands. "Dad has a different type of flaw."

Alicia didn't counter that statement, because she knew Tori was definitely on the money with that one. Between his gambling and his wife; her brother could never think straight when it came to his wife. He had forgiven that woman a multitude of sins.

"I think it's best if Dallas and I continue to live together and he just visits you whenever he can. Until he gets tired of all this." Tori's dismissive wave of her hand showed exactly how she felt about the prospect. "And he will tire of it, right? It's all tied to sex, right?"

Alicia said nothing rather than lie to her niece.

Tori accepted her silence as her agreement. She said, "I have this all figured out. The best thing is for you to stay with us for a little while until we can figure this out. By the time it gets closer to the wedding, things will be back to normal."

"You have lost what's left of your mind!"

Tori gave a bitter laugh, her eyes glassy with unshed tears. "Well if I have, I don't want to lose Dallas, too."

Silence expanded between them as each woman stayed lost in her own thoughts.

"Tori, why not let him go?"

"So you can have him?" she growled, gripping the edge of the sink. "After all the work I've put in on this? I let him go so you can snap him up?"

"That's not what I meant!"

Tori repositioned herself so she was more comfortable atop the toilet seat. "Even last night when he thought I was going to end our relationship, he made sure that the only thing I'd have to do was focus on school. I know he cares about me. It may not be full love, but he was getting there." Tori looked to her aunt as a single tear slid down her face. "I've asked Dallas, but he won't tell me. What really happened yesterday? I really need to know."

Alicia looked at her niece and shook her head.

"Please don't clam up on me now. I need to know how this started yesterday." She paused. "Please tell me what happened."

After too many moments of silence, Alicia began, "It was because of all of your messages begging me to come home. I'd never heard you so excited, and so I thought I'd do it. I only planned to stay one day, so I could see you and James before I hit the road again."

Alicia broke eye contact as the rest of the prior day's events spilled from her mind. "I was only going to shut my eyes for a few moments, then get dressed and surprise you all for dinner." She closed her eyes, remembering how peaceful that moment had felt. Home. Finally. Her own bed. "Then Dallas walked in. I thought I was dreaming.

"It was like I was back in his house all over again." She took Tori's hands in hers. "I don't have any excuse. But I'm going to make things right. I promise."

Tori's brow furrowed with concern.

"I'm leaving for India," Alicia announced.

Tori's soft brown eyes widened in shock. "You're leaving the country? Now?"

She nodded. "I already called the driver I use whenever I'm home and Ray's waiting to take me to the airport. I won't be coming back for a very long time."

For a moment, relief flitted across the younger woman's face; then her lips turned downward. Tori scowled as she shook her head. "If you leave him like that again, with no goodbyes for the second time, he'll never be right. You can't do this to him."

Alicia snatched her hands away from Tori. "So, what do you expect me to do? Stay here and be part of this trio? This open door - whatever you want to call it? It's not right!"

"It's as right as we make it," she countered. "We just have to be discreet. And the only way we can do that is if you move in with us."

"Absolutely not! You're not just playing with fire; you're lighting the dynamite at both ends."

Tori waved off her concern with a flourish of a manicured hand. "When Dallas and I go back home on Monday, you'll come with us. No arguments. But for now we need to get back to the hotel before Mama loses her mind and makes you do something crazy. Like slice her up again."

Alicia cringed at the dark reminder of how close she had come to taking another person's life last Thanksgiving.

Tori asked, "They were pictures right? The things that Mama burned, they were pictures, right?"

"They were precious and priceless," Alicia said on a breathy whisper, hurt filling her all over again.

"If I came home to find someone had burned up all of my prized possessions I might have done the same thing."

Alicia gave Tori a small smile as Tori stood and moved toward the door. "We really should be getting back to the hotel. I'm sure Dallas is losing his mind."

"I'm not going back there. I'm not getting into a relationship with Dallas, and I'm not living under your roof." Alicia held up a hand to silence Tori. "I'm going to India today. And that's final."

Her back was to Alicia, when Tori asked, "Did you enjoy being with him?"

Alicia dropped her chin to her chest, exhaled loudly, but said nothing.

Tori said, "After all that's happened, you owe me at least that much."

Alicia thought about lying, but she did owe Tori this truth. Talking to her niece's back, she said, "If my husband had been even one percent as good as Dallas, I would have wanted to die right along with him."

Tori turned and faced her aunt, blinking a couple of extra times before she said, "Then we—and I'm talking about us as women—" she pointed first to herself, then to Alicia, "have come to an understanding, right? You'll keep his dick happy until the wedding, then you'll leave the country."

It was that moment when Alicia realized how immature and unprepared for marriage Tori was.

"You'll play your position as his other woman," Tori said, her voice wavering with each word. "And everything will work out fine."

When Tori extended her hand, Alicia clasped it and gave her niece a reassuring smile.

There was no need to argue about this anymore. In a few hours, Alicia would be bound for India and there'd be nothing that Tori or Dallas could do.

Chapter 15

11:31 A.M.

The solemn expression on James' face nearly shattered Alicia's heart. Looking down at him, she froze at the second floor landing. Maybe she would speak to James, just not right now.

Tori squeezed around her, scrambling down the stairs with the luggage that Dallas had left there yesterday. She sat it at the front door, then climbed back up the steps, pried Alicia's fingers from the luggage she held, and took it down the stairs.

Shifting her focus from James, who peered up at her from his recliner, Alicia quickened her steps, following Tori to the foyer. She slithered into the supple black leather coat that Dallas had bought for her.

Bernice swept past Tori who was now carrying her own suitcase and placed her hand against the front door, closing it with a slam. "You're not going anywhere."

"Oh, yes I am," Tori snapped. "Listening to you is the reason I'm in this mess. I shouldn't have gone overboard with this wedding spending, and Dallas wouldn't have been rethinking things to begin with."

"Rethinking things?" Bernice bellowed. "Since when?"

Tori ignored her and turned her gaze to James. "Dad, I want you to come to the hotel with me. I need you to know what's going on."

James remained silent for a long while. Only when Alicia finally nodded at him did he say, "I had a poker game this evening, but I'll be there, baby girl."

"Daddy, I thought you weren't going to gamble anymore," Tori said, her voice laced with concern. "I thought you were done with all that."

"It's just a friendly little game," he reassured her, moving toward the foyer. He placed his hand on Alicia's arm. "You're leaving?"

"Actually, I'm—"

"You know I want to put my foot all the way up in your ass," Bernice growled at Alicia. "Why don't you stay gone this time?"

"This is her house," James said to Bernice, moving so he blocked Alicia's view of her sister-in-law. "She can't keep running every time things get a little shaky."

Alicia met his gaze head on. "I've always done what it takes to keep the peace around here. I made that choice when you barged in here … with her." She cut a glance at Bernice, then smiled. "Most people leave their strays at the pound, brother, but you have this uncanny knack for bringing them home, thinking they'll eventually become housebroken."

"Are you calling me a dog?" Bernice shrieked, her bony finger pointing at her Alicia.

"If that's what you want to read into it …" Alicia winked. "James always did say you were smarter than the average bear."

James adjusted his stance so that he was closer to his sister than his wife. "You've never liked her," he exclaimed to Bernice. He took Alicia's hand, no doubt sensing that she was about two seconds away from strangling Bernice. "But you didn't have a problem moving into her house."

"This is your house, too!" Bernice cried out. "Your grandparents left it to both of you. How can she just—"

"She bought me out a few years ago because we needed the money!"

James shouted over Bernice's voice. "She owns this place free and clear. She only let me stay because I'm family; not because I have a claim to this place."

Bernice frowned at James. "What?"

"This is her house," he repeated. "Hers alone. She didn't have to leave last year. She had every right to put us out, but she didn't."

Tori nodded. Bernice frowned and asked, "You knew, too?"

"I found out after you ran through my college fund," Tori said sourly.

Bernice bared her teeth at Tori. "Oh, so now you're all friendly with her, even after what she did to you?"

"Mom, there's going to be some changes around here." Tori's tone made everyone look her way. "I'll be handling the wedding plans from here on out."

"What … what … I …I," Bernice sputtered, rearing back on her six-inch heels. "He slept with her!" she shrieked, looking first to Tori, then to James and back to Tori. "Forget the wedding. He should be paying you not to put his ass on blast."

James stepped forward, but he wasn't given the chance to chime in.

"You know I'm right," Bernice snapped at her husband. "I don't know what happened to all that money he gave you to get your ass out of hock, but we'll make sure he gives us more than enough this time."

"Money?" James shouted at Bernice. "Is that all that's important to you right now?"

Bernice spat, "Why're you barking at me?" Glaring at Alicia, she added, "She's the problem."

"You've always been jealous of her for no good reason," Tori shot back, moving closer to her mother. "Instead of seeing how much I love both of you, you've always made it a competition."

Bernice's thin lips curled into a sneer. "And you don't think she was being competitive when she fucked your man?"

Tori winced as though her mother had physically struck her. She adjusted the scarf around her neck and said in a mild tone, "Mom, that's not what happened here yesterday. I've forgiven him. And I'm done with this conversation."

"So now I'm the bad guy because I call a spade a sp—"

"No, it's because you could've waited to tell me what happened. You didn't have to tell me that Dallas cheated in front of the whole damn family. And it was a lie! I'll never forgive you for that."

Bernice's thin lips curled. "Oh, but you can forgive them?" She made a show of covering her mouth and taking in a deep breath. "No, wait. You said you forgive him. You didn't say nothing about forgiving her ass," she said with a sideways glance at Alicia.

Alicia chanced at look at Tori, who was examining the glass designs on the front door. When she didn't correct that statement, Alicia's heart sank. Of course Tori hadn't forgiven her.

"I'm angrier than you are about all this, and that's just plain crazy," Bernice said, giving a blistering look to her husband as she circled about him. "Wouldn't expect you to be angry, though. You care more about your sister's feelings than mine." Then she favored him with a hard glare. "You're not all up in her face about what she's done. If she can fuck a total stranger, then I don't think a member of the family's all that big of a stretch."

James stiffened, his dark brown eyes flashing with anger, his wide mouth parting.

"I want you out of this house right now," Bernice snarled at Alicia. "And this time, don't come back."

"Hold up, Chief! This be my teepee," Alicia snapped, circling her finger in the air to encompass the area and make her point. "You'd better blow those smoke signals somewhere else." She turned to the foyer closet, yanked down one of the furs inside and slammed it into Bernice's chest. "Someone needs to leave this house, but it certainly won't be me. Not this time! You do not get to continue living in my house after saying that again."

Bernice swallowed hard and quickly put her eyes on her husband as she yelped, "James?"

"I'll help you pack." He was up the stairs and around the corner in the time it took to blink.

"What?" Bernice shrieked. Her hand flew up to cover her slight bosom as she snarled, "You bitch."

Alicia's hands had balled into fists, and she took a step forward.

"Auntie …" Tori whispered, causing Alicia to look her way. That was the only thing that held Alicia in place. That is, before James returned and perched a brown leather overnight case near Bernice's high heels. He positioned himself right in Alicia's punching range.

"I thought you would grow out of this …" his hand made a circular motion that meant both women, "this bitterness. But I see now that it's never going to happen. And I don't have the stomach for it—or you—any longer."

Bernice glared at James. "So what're you saying?" she asked before she looked down at the suitcase that he'd just placed at her feet.

James folded his arms across his sweater-clad chest. "A divorce might be the best thing for us."

Tori grabbed his arm. "Daddy!"

"You're grown now, baby girl," he said. "I think you're ready to handle the hard truth of things. We were on the path to separation long before this. You might want to ask her who Robert is."

A flicker of fear flashed in Bernice's eyes.

"Oh yeah," he said, grinning at her. "You weren't careful this time. My poker buddy called it an even exchange for the cash I owed him." James narrowed his focus on her. "I wasn't going to say nothing. I wanted to see if it would happen again. I lose a lot of money, and you pay up."

"Dear God," Alicia whispered.

Bernice's dark brown eyes narrowed to slits. "Sure, just push me aside now that you're broke and can't pay alimony."

"And what's the reason that I don't have any money, huh? At the rate you're spending money, we'll never be able to move out of this house," James dislodged Tori and moved to stand in front of his wife.

"Oh? And none of it has to do with the fact that you bleed cash at the casino?"

James shrugged. "I've spent our entire marriage trying to make you happy, and I just realized that happy is something you don't know how to be."

Bernice flinched, but then softened her tone. "You can't divorce me. Where will I go?"

James pulled out his wallet, snatched out all of the cash inside and pressed it into her hands. "You'll find someplace, but it can't be here."

She looked at the bills as though they were diseased, then opened her fingers and let them float to the carpet. "This is chump change. How am I supposed to live on this?"

"Maybe you can go back to doing what you were doing before he met you," Alicia offered. "The oldest profession in the world is still going strong."

Bernice glowered at James. "You told her?"

"No," he said with a pained look at Alicia, then to Bernice. "But with the way you act, I guess it wasn't all that hard to figure out."

"This is your fault," Bernice snarled, waggling a finger at Alicia. Then, Bernice turned to James. "She spreads her legs for that young buck, and now I have no home! Where is her punishment? When does she accept the consequences for what she's done?"

"You don't know what she's done," James shot back.

"After I found them—naked, she was looking guilty as all hell. Then he breaks his neck to go after her ass instead of staying with Tori." Bernice folded her arms across her flat chest and leveled her eyes at Alicia. "No, she let him have that old snatch. Turned that young buck out." She grinned at her observation. "I might not know exactly what they did, but I know that they did something that has his nose wide open."

"And Tori's dealing with it," James said in the softest tone that he'd used all evening. "So what business is it of yours?"

"She's my daughter!" Bernice huffed. "She is my business."

Alicia shook her head. "And you put your daughter's business all in the street with absolutely no regard for her feelings."

Bernice didn't have a comeback for that one.

Tears had pooled in Tori's eyes, but she shook off Alicia's attempts to console her. Instead she went to her father and he put his arms around her shoulders.

James said to Bernice. "I don't even have it in me to try with you anymore. I'm too old to keep scraping the bottom or wondering when you're going to come home at night. If I stay married to you, the bottom is where I'll stay."

He extracted his arm from around Tori, picked up the case and held it out to his soon-to-be ex-wife. "Goodbye."

"What about the rest of my stuff?" Bernice asked.

"When you get settled, I'll send it to you."

She held out her hand. "I'll take that money then."

Alicia shot James a look that Bernice didn't miss. He didn't lower to pick the bills up from the carpet.

"Remember, I didn't press charges when I could have," Bernice threatened.

"Remember, I didn't slit your throat when I should have," Alicia replied, giving her a small smile and placing her hand on the knob.

Tori took an American Express charge card from her wallet and stepped forward. "Mama, just check into a hotel until I figure something out."

Only when Alicia gestured outside with a jerky movement of her thumb did Bernice snatch the card and get her skinny legs moving.

"You think this is over?" Bernice snarled as a blast of winter wind came roaring in. "It's just starting. Someone will pay a lot of money for all the secrets this family keeps." Bernice sent a pointed look toward Tori before she grinned at Alicia.

Alicia moved in toe-to-toe with Bernice. "You come against me or my family and your ass is going to need more than a new address; you'll need a whole new continent."

Bernice swept from the house. Alicia slammed the door behind her.

Chapter 16

12:07 P.M.

Dallas stood near the revolving doors, pacing the lobby of the Hyatt, wondering how he'd let Alicia get away. When she hadn't shown up to Tori's spot ten minutes after she promised, he went to the suite and found that she was gone. Tori told him she could find her and hit the ground running. Only a few minutes had passed before Dallas realized that Tori might have been the wrong person to send, that she might actually succeed in making sure Alicia stayed gone.

Gratefully, he was wrong. Tori had called to let him know that she had found Alicia and now, he couldn't stand the wait.

A black sedan pulled into the circular drive, and Dallas practically ran toward it. Tori and James stepped out and retrieved the suitcases from the trunk.

"Where's Alicia?" Dallas asked when James prepared to close the trunk and no one else got out of the car.

Tori nodded toward the back seat. "She's still inside."

Dallas snatched open the passenger door before the trunk closed all the way. Alicia gripped the handle and struggled to pull it back. Dallas wedged his arm in to keep the door open, knowing that she'd never slam the door on him. Silently, he held out his hand to her, begging her, with eyes filled with compassion. Finally, reluctantly, she took his hand and stepped out of the car.

Looking down at her, he asked, "What were you thinking leaving like that?"

"I was thinking that I was doing the right thing for my niece."

She brushed past him and went toward the hotel, and the three followed her. Inside, Tori handed her father the key to her suite. "Dad, can you take my luggage with you? And this, too," she said, pointing to the one that belonged to Dallas.

James nodded and when they reached the floor to her suite, Tori kissed her father's check and gestured to the other end of the hall. "We'll be down in a few minutes. We need to discuss things first."

When Alicia and Tori entered the Presidential Suite, Dallas noticed a calm about both women that he found a little unnerving.

They settled around the seats in living room. He looked first to Alicia, then to Tori, who was giving him a thorough head-to-toe, taking in the team jersey and jeans he now wore. Victor was more than earning an additional bonus by staying around another shift to assist Dallas in whatever way he needed. Maybe if he had pegged Victor as a lookout, Alicia wouldn't have been able to give him the slip.

Dallas peered at Tori a moment, then slid a glance to Alicia before he asked, "Why is James here?"

"My father should know what's going on."

He nodded, then asked both women, "So, you talked?"

Alicia nodded, but quickly averted her gaze the minute he looked toward her.

Tori said, "She's coming home with us."

Dallas caught Alicia's grimace. So, she didn't agree with this decision either.

"That's not a good idea," he told Tori, resting one finger on his temple.

Tori's expression became cold and hard. "This is what will work for me," she replied.

"It's not up for discussion." Dallas crossed the distance between them and took the seat next to Tori. "I can't do this to you."

Alicia stood and walked away from them. She leaned against the wall and turned her focus to the outside world.

"So, what're you saying? That you want to leave me and be with her?" Her eyes darted to Alicia. When she turned back to Dallas, she said, "I thought we already settled this. I thought we'd come up with an agreement. And," she paused, "I thought you wanted children. Because if you do, you can fuck her six ways from Sunday, but you'll never see any real results."

Alicia's drastic intake of breath caused Dallas to leap to his feet. A flash of fire lit in Alicia's eyes, and she held up a hand to keep him from putting his arms around her. "I feel real bad about all this, Tori," Alicia said, her tone low, almost deadly. "But you keep this up and I'm going to slap the cowboy shit out of you."

Tori looked down for a moment. "I have a right to ask questions, a right to know what's really going on. Unless the whole reason you're all right with him leaving me is because you want him all to yourself. Is that what's really going on here?"

Alicia's gaze fixed on her niece for what seemed an eternity as she played Tori's question over in her mind. Then, she lowered her eyes, hoping that her niece couldn't see her guilt. Because that was a good question. Would it be easier for her if Tori were out of the picture?

"The fact remains," Tori went on, taking Alicia's silence as a reason to continue making her case, "I still have some value here. I have the ability to give him the one thing you can't."

Alicia still didn't look up.

Dallas moved to Alicia and he lifted her chin. "Will you marry me?" he whispered soft enough so that Tori wouldn't hear. "Will you consider giving me at least one child, Alicia?"

This wasn't how Dallas had wanted to do this and this wasn't the time. But what Tori wanted to do? For the millionth time he thought about how ridiculous that was, how it would never work. All Alicia had to do was say yes. Then, this would be over and he could begin his life with her.

Alicia weighed his words for a long moment, then shook her head. "Pregnancy can be a pretty traumatic thing for someone my age," she whispered back. "I've resigned myself to never having children." She glanced at Tori, then placed her hand on Dallas' cheek. "But the way she wants to do this? No! This won't work. It's madness. Dallas, let me go. Please."

"Stop fighting me, Alicia." He pulled her against him. "Let me love you." He held onto her until she finally sighed, spent from all the energy she'd used to fight this. "You won't regret it," he said.

Dallas released Alicia and examined her face. She gave him an almost imperceptible nod. He kept his eyes on Alicia as he spoke to Tori. "I'll put Alicia up in a hotel until she picks out a house not too far from us."

"And what?" Tori snapped. She stood and rounded the coffee table. Gripping Dallas' arm, she forced him to face her. "Somebody sees you going in and out of her place, starts talking, and your image will take another hit. With all of those new endorsement deals lined up, you can't afford for that to happen." She glanced over at Alicia. "She moves in with us until—"

"I don't think it's a good thing for you to see us together that way," Alicia said, cutting Tori off. "Seeing us now is probably tough enough on you. How're you going to feel if you walk in and we're . . . together? Do you really want to see that?"

Tori's pink lips curled into a sneer. "The way he tells the story, I might actually learn something."

Dallas moved forward, causing Tori to take a step back. "And you wonder why I'm against this? Your tone, your attitude is going to make things super ugly. None of this is fair ..."

"Fair? You want to talk about fair?" she screamed, slapping her palm on the middle of his chest. "Fair would mean that I would still have my fiancé's undivided attention. Fair would mean that I get at least some of what I want from life. If this is all I can get from you, then doing this is fair to me."

Dallas looked over to Alicia, who just shook her head.

"Look, we're three consenting adults. We can do whatever the hell we want to do." Turning around, Tori swiped the glass on her way to the cabinet. She poured in a heavy-handed portion of VSOP, then stopped and held up the bottle. "You don't mind, do you?"

Dallas shook his head.

She took only a small sip, pursed her lips, then placed the glass down. "Why can't we do things my way?" she asked Dallas. Facing Alicia, she added, "You've practically taken him away from me. Can't you do this for me?"

Alicia ignored Tori and looked up at Dallas. "What is your choice? And be honest."

Dallas raised an eyebrow at Tori, who had folded her arms. "I love you, Tori, for everything you've been to me, but eventually I'll want to marry Alicia. We'll just have to work out the children thing some other way."

Tori stiffened. She ambled to the sofa and sank down into the cushions, a crestfallen look covering her face.

Alicia shook her head. "Now it's my turn to be honest. I've already been married, Dallas. I'm not doing that again. Ever."

The stab in his heart, showed on his face. Alicia added, "And it has nothing to do with you. It has everything to do with the institution of marriage." She trained her gaze on Tori. "She's never been married. And you're a good man. She deserves to take that walk with you."

Dallas shook his head like he had no intention of accepting her words. But he moved from Alicia, and joined Tori on the sofa. He placed his hand on her shoulder. "Before today, I didn't really know there was a difference between love and in love. And now that I know, I'm telling you that you have to believe there's some man out there who will feel the same way about you as I feel about Alicia."

Tori shook off his hand, glaring up at him as she snarled, "So, I guess this means that you're going to adopt children, right!" Her gaze went first to Alicia and back to Dallas. "Because her eggs are old enough to scramble their damn selves!!"

Alicia made tracks toward the door, her hands curled into tight fists. Tori smiled.

Dallas growled, "Apologize right now, Tori. If she walks because of this, you can bet that—"

Alicia whirled to face him. "Don't use me to keep her in line."

"That's not what I'm doing!"

"Bullshit," Alicia snapped.

Dallas winced at the venom in just that one word. "I heard you, Dallas. You're using the threat of being with just me as some sort of tool to control her behavior."

"I apologize," he said, instantly contrite. "I've gone about this all wrong." He paused long enough to sigh, then added, "Everybody's saying what they want, so I'm going to give you my bottom line. I want you and I want to explore these feelings we have for each other," he said to Alicia. Then he shifted his focus to Tori, who was glaring at her aunt. "I need Tori because I do love her. And she'll marry me and give me children. The only one talking about walking is you, and you already know I can't let you go." Dallas pressed a kiss to Alicia's temple and heard Tori's sigh of displeasure. He held his hand out for Tori to come to him, and after a few moments, she did. He kissed her, too, which seemed to pacify her for the moment.

"No marriage? No children?" he asked Alicia, who shook her head and he couldn't help the sense of disappointment that filled him. "Then this is the best scenario. I want marriage, I want children and I want you. So?"

Alicia was thoughtful for a moment. She looked up at him. "We live in separate places."

"I told you why that won't work," Tori countered, taking his other hand. "At least try my suggestion before you rule it out."

A dark shadow shimmered in the depths of Alicia's eyes and Dallas braced himself for what she was about to say.

"Since Tori has to share you," Alicia said, "does she get to take on lovers as well?"

Dallas felt the shock build within him before he could tamper it down.

Tori's eyebrow went up, as though warming to the idea. But that wasn't as disconcerting to Dallas as the smile that spread across Alicia's lips. The question was a set-up for what she really wanted to ask about having lovers as well.

Yes, indeed. Game recognized game.

"I won't like it," he said in the mildest tone he could manage, "but if she insists ..." He let the rest of the answer hang and leveled a stony glare at Alicia.

Dallas couldn't say what he wanted to say. He wouldn't share Alicia with anyone. When they were alone, he would tell her that. He wanted so bad to verbalize that right now. But doing so would just be another dagger in Tori's heart.

"So that means she won't be sneaking off to India any time soon?" Tori asked.

Dallas' eyes widened. "You were going to leave the country?" he asked. "Even after..."

She leveled an icy look at him that spoke to the fact that she wasn't the least bit apologetic for her actions. And it also spoke to the fact that given the chance, Alicia would do it again.

Chapter 17

12:27 P.M.

Dallas peered at Alicia more closely, trying to clear his vision. He gripped her arms and lifted Alicia so they were eye to eye. "I would come for you. No matter where you go, I'm going to find you. You know that, right?"

The small smile on Tori's face vanished the moment Dallas brought Alicia against his chest and held onto her as though even an inch apart was too much.

"Separate houses," Alicia said after a while had passed. "And that's my final answer."

"Fine!" Tori threw up her hands. "That will be the end result, but for now you'll live with us."

Dallas studied Tori for a long while, analyzing the myriad of expressions that she tried to hide. "One last time, Tori. This thing between me and Alicia is not going to end. So, if you want to get out of it now ... ."

"You know what I think?" Tori snarled, a single hand riding up on her hip.

Tori's tone made Alicia walk away, turn back to the window.

"I think your dick's doing a lot of your thinking right now," Tori said. "I think once you've had a few more times with her and the novelty wears off, then you'll realize she isn't so special. She's not going to marry you. She's not going to have your children. So what purpose does she serve other than being someone you can stick your dick into?"

Alicia stiffened, but Tori kept going. "Until we walk down that aisle, she's like the number zero. She's just a placeholder until the real thing comes along."

"Tori," Alicia said, staring at Tori as though seeing her niece for the first time. "You keep attacking me like this and you'll see just how gentle I've been with your mother."

Tori did a little hop and hurried from the suite.

❤ ❤ ❤

Dallas booked a flight to Texas for Alicia and changed the existing reservations for Tori and himself. When he hung up from the call, he turned to Alicia.

She said, "I need to cancel my flight," she whispered, then froze as though realizing that she shouldn't have brought that subject up.

"Yes, about that," he said, taking the opening she had reluctantly provided. "You were running again, and you weren't even going to say goodbye. Just like last time. Why would you do that to me knowing how I feel about you?"

"Because none of this makes any damn sense," she replied, moving back toward the bed. "I feel like I'm all over the place. I want to be the old me again, where everything was predictable. Normal."

"There's no such thing as normal for us anymore." Dallas gathered her into his arms and placed a kiss on her lips. "Are you saying that you wish that we had never shared those moments? Would you have rather lived your life without knowing what real pleasure feels like? What love can feel like?"

Alicia closed her eyes, and he could only hope she was reliving their time together because those moments walked through his mind more often than he could control.

Dallas lowered his hand to her buttocks, pulled her close and buried his head in the soft curve of her shoulder. Then he trailed his lips up to her ear and whispered, "Do you want me to tell you all the reasons I need you?"

Her eyelids fluttered until they closed, and he continued. "Do you want me to bare my soul to get you to understand?" Dallas kissed the vein pulsing at the base of her neck, then the smooth skin along her cheek. "I meant it when I said I love you." He continued until his lips were at hers. "Stay with me. Let me show you how much I care." Then he took the tip of her earlobe between his lips and teased her. "I'll take you to India some other time. I promise."

Slowly, her arms wrapped around him. "Do you know what you're doing, Dallas?"

"What do you mean?"

"You're accusing Tori of biding her time, but you're biding your time, too."

Dallas pulled away. "What makes you say that that?"

"You don't even try to filter your affection for me when you're in front of her. You think that her seeing us together will be the thing that will make her finally give up."

He looked away, and she added, "You're going to hurt her into leaving you. And that's not fair. A clean break—a real clean break, not this wishy-washy bullshit you're doing today—would be better all the way around. You're being selfish, Dallas."

"And I'm not the only one."

Her hands slowly fell by her side.

"I saw the look you gave Tori when she asked you that question."

Dallas watched her expressions, and a slight tint of red flushed her honeyed cheeks. "You do want me all to yourself."

Alicia remained silent for a long time, and she let out a long slow breath. "And I feel so bad about that. What's wrong with me? Why can't I think straight when it comes to you?"

"Because you're falling in love with me." He pushed a few strands of hair away from her face. "I can't say the same for Tori. She's not in love with me and she knows that while I love her, I'm not in love with her."

He kissed her. She tried to resist at first, but soon melted under his touch. "Everything that is wonderful about a woman, I see in you," he whispered into her ear. "I feel comfort, pleasure. I love bringing out your sensuous side. Watching you submit to me is a powerful thing. It's addictive."

Alicia pulled back and glared at him. "I'm not submissive!"

Dallas chuckled and tried to guide her back into his arms.

She pushed him away. "I'm. Not. Weak!"

He peered at her and realized, this was no laughing matter. That word truly upset her, so he conceded, "All right. You're not submissive." Before she protested more, he added, "Come on, let's get out of here. Let's just give this a try and see how it works out. All right?"

After a moment she nodded. "I'll be down in a minute."

"I'm not falling for that a second time," he shot back.

"Dallas, please, give me a moment to be alone and absorb all of this before I step into that madness. Because it's not just Tori who has to compromise. I had my own plans. I had my own life before you penciled yourself in."

Dallas peered at her for a long while, then grabbed her purse and luggage and carted them off, looking at her over his shoulder.

Alicia released a long, slow breath and turned her back to him. His heart skipped a beat when she leaned forward to rest her forehead on the window. He could feel how heavily this weighed on her. But until Alicia changed her mind and decided to marry him, this was the way things would have to be.

Chapter 18

6:16 P.M.
PLANO, TEXAS

Hours later, Alicia stood in the marbled foyer of Dallas and Tori's spacious condo. Once again she was amazed and overwhelmed at the massive open living and dining space with a ceiling that had to be at least eleven feet. The redbrick fireplace was positioned so the flames could easily reflect off the cathedral windows. The place was a perfect blend of rich earth tones and leather furniture. Even now, it felt more like home than anyplace she had been since.

With a sweeping gesture, Tori said to Alicia, "Definitely nothing like Harper Avenue."

Alicia took in the familiar abstract artwork along the living room wall, then gave Tori a patient smile. "Indeed. I should know. I picked out everything I can see from here."

Tori's jaw went slack and her hand fell to her side. But before she could say anything, Dallas took Alicia's hand and moved her further into the space. "I took your suggestions and combined some rooms since you were last here." He gestured toward the back area of the condo. "Now there's three bedrooms, three full bathrooms, a chef's kitchen—though nobody ever uses it," he added on a sour note, then pointed toward a set of spiral stairs. "A loft upstairs and a den with a library right next to it."

Alicia's gaze took it all in. "It's still absolutely beautiful."

"Thank you," he replied.

Alicia could tell he wanted to say more. She was glad he didn't.

"I'll put you in the guest bedroom," Tori said motioning upstairs.

"No, she'll take my bedroom," Dallas corrected, aiming toward the foyer to get the suitcase. "It's much bigger. Women need space."

"You sleep in separate bedrooms?" Alicia asked, unable to keep the shock from her voice as she looked from one to the other.

"It was my idea," Tori said. "Sleeping together would provide way too much temptation." Tori took a seat on the leather chase and crossed one slack-covered leg over the other.

Dallas gave Tori a long look before he turned to Alicia. "I'll move into the guest bedroom," he said, then started to wheel Alicia's suitcase toward the back of the condo. He turned back to the two women staring after him and said, "And I'm starving. Are we eating out or in?"

"In," Alicia answered at the same time Tori said, "Out."

"Looks like I'm the tie-breaker," Dallas said thoughtfully. "I'm all for a home-cooked meal over restaurant food any day." He nodded toward Alicia and said, "I called the housekeeper from the airport and had her stock up. If you're up for it, would you mind—"

Alicia quickly maneuvered around a shocked Tori who remained in the center of the living room long after the other two had left.

An hour later, Alicia put the last of the platters on the kitchen table as Dallas took a seat at the head of the table.

"Shouldn't we eat in the dining room," Tori said, frowning at the spread on the table.

"I thought we could be a little informal this time," Alicia responded softly.

Tori gripped the back of the chair as she said, "So now you're dictating how this house runs?"

"Tori, sit down and eat or don't eat at all," Dallas said. "My stomach is not going to make time for drama."

She plopped into the chair to his left. Alicia settled gracefully in the one on his right.

They bowed their heads as Dallas said grace, ending with, "And bless the hands that prepared it—"

"And the stomachs that have to tolerate it," Tori added dryly.

Both Alicia and Dallas opened their eyes and stared at her.

She shrugged. "I'm just saying."

"And we ask for your patience and guidance in all things," Dallas finished with a pointed look at Tori. "Amen."

"Amen," Alicia added with a wary glance at her niece.

"You both did a great job," Dallas said, grinning as he scanned the spread before him.

"I didn't help with this. I had some studying to do," Tori said, eyeing Alicia with undisguised hatred. "Some of us actually want to work for a living."

Dallas and Alicia ignored that barb as he began to pile up on the Romano crusted chicken, rice pilaf, and steamed green beans and garlic bread.

"Dallas…" Alicia began, eyes widening as she saw her meal disappearing from the platters as though being sucked into a vortex.

"Yep," he said, sliding the salad bowl his way.

"Where are you going to put all of that?"

Tori laughed, lightening up the moment. "Finally, someone agrees that he eats entirely too much."

Dallas wrinkled his nose at her. "I have the metabolism to support it."

"You ain't never lied," Alicia mumbled.

His fork paused midway as he looked at her and smiled. "What?"

Alicia shook her head and he took that moment to slide a little extra food on her plate as she said, "You've lost some weight, so I thought that you had cut back on the amount that you're taking in."

"Nope, I just work out a little more," he admitted. "Balance. Balance works for me."

"And speaking of balance," Tori said, pouring herself a full glass of white wine. "How exactly do we pull this off?"

Dallas took a few bites and glanced at Alicia. When she shrugged, he turned to Tori. "You're the one who suggested it," Dallas said. "How do you see this working?"

Tori froze and for a second it seemed as if she wouldn't answer. "Well, I—I hadn't really thought about it beyond coming here."

Alicia blinked. "Oh, my god. You didn't think this would actually happen."

"No. No, it was nothing like …" Tori withered under Dallas' hard glare, and quickly amended. "Okay, I thought that once you saw our home, what we've built together, you would feel out of place here." She scanned the area and added, "I didn't realize that I'd been living in your shrine."

Dallas' gaze shifted from Tori to Alicia. "Are you still packed?"

She nodded and he stood.

"Wait," Tori said, gripping his wrist to keep him in place. "I don't mean for you to take her somewhere—"

"Tori," Dallas said on a slow breath, "either we're going to do this or not. But we're not going to fight about this every night."

Tori's fork clattered to the plate. Her chest heaved in an effort to rein in her emotions.

"So how is this supposed to work," Alicia asked gently. "We've all walked into this blindly, so let's establish the boundaries, how our days will pan out …"

Dallas pointed to an oversized calendar hanging next to the stainless steel fridge. "Well, until the end of April, I go to training every morning, practice in the afternoons, games most nights. Away games are all put on there and then I'm gone for a few days here and there."

"Okay, that's your schedule," Alicia said. "Let's start with something like cooking," she said to her niece.

But Dallas interjected. "I would love to have home cooked meals for a change. At least some of the time."

Tori opened her mouth to protest, but Dallas said, "This right here," he gestured to his nearly empty plate, "is like solid gold. I'd prefer my meals were prepared by a woman who cares what's being put into me."

Tori smacked her lips. "But we love fine restaurants—"

"We do it because you don't cook—even when you have time. And I can't cook—"

"But you can learn," Alicia jumped in. "Last time I checked, your hands, eyes, and brains all worked just fine."

"If you ever saw me in the kitchen, you'd say something totally different." He gave her a toothy grin. "But I make a mean peanut butter and jelly sandwich," he added with a mischievous lift of her left eyebrow, causing Alicia to laugh.

"Give me a break," Tori muttered and stabbed her baked chicken breast with her fork.

"All right, I can manage to cook breakfast and dinner some of the time," Alicia conceded.

"Sleeping arrangements?" Tori said, softly.

Alicia looked at Dallas, but his focus shifted to Tori. He was silent for a few moments, then said, "We've slept in separate beds for a year, Tori. That's not going to change."

"So you'll sleep in her bed every night," she asked in a tone that sounded like she was trying to keep the tears from her eyes.

He nodded and the tears that she was fighting back sprang to her eyes.

"I'm sorry, Tori." He released a heavy breath as he massaged his temple. "I tried to tell you. This isn't going to be easy for any of us."

Tori took a deep breath and said, "I think that you should—"

The cordless phone rang and Dallas gestured for Alicia to answer since it was closer to her.

She answered with, "Avery residence."

"May I ... speak ... with ... Dallas?" The female on the other end spoke slowly as if she were trying to figure out who'd answered the phone.

Alicia smiled. Katie, Dallas' agent probably recognized her voice, but wasn't sure. After all, it had been a few years.

"Katie?" Alicia asked just to be sure.

"Alicia?"

"Yes. How's it going?"

"When did you … what are you … when did you get back?"

Her gaze shifted to Dallas. "I'm just here for a little visit."

That statement caused Dallas to put his fork down.

"Well, welcome back," Katie crowed. "Is Dallas around?"

"Yes, he's right here." She handed the phone to Dallas who covered the mouthpiece as he looked at her. "A little visit?"

"I didn't know what else to say," she said with a mild shrug.

Dinner was cut short when Dallas trotted up the stairs to the loft to take the call. The two women stayed silent for a long while before Tori pushed her plate toward the center. The chair scraped hard against the natural wood floor as she backed away from the table.

"I have a splitting headache," she said through her teeth and for a moment sadness settled in Alicia's heart.

Tori stood, then looked at the spot where Dallas had sat. "I realize that you might think this—" she circled a finger to mean the kitchen and dining area, "is familiar territory. But please keep in mind that this is my house. I've been here a lot longer than you ever have. I've been in his life a lot longer than you have."

"I'm sure you won't let me forget," Alicia countered before she took a sip of wine and focused on polishing off her meal.

Tori's eyes narrowed to slits. "He's going to get tired of you, you old bitch," Tori snarled causing Alicia's head to whip toward her. "And when he does, he'll realize that you weren't so special. He got over you last time, and he'll do it again. Then, Plan A will be in effect again."

Alicia set her glass down near the half-eaten plate. "Tori, you don't want to go down this road with me," she said in the most patient tone she could manage. "I understand that this is quite … troubling for you. But baiting me is going to get you something you don't want."

Alicia picked up the knife and sliced a small piece of Romano crusted chicken, and placed it in her mouth, savoring it a few seconds before adding, "I try to keep my inner bitch under control. But trust me when I tell you, that you don't want her to start doing all the talking."

Twice, Alicia's "inner bitch" had gotten out of hand. Once with Bernice that almost ended in a funeral. And once before at eight when one of her male relatives ended up with a knife in his genitals because he couldn't tell the difference between his wife and his niece. Alicia landed in the police station that night wearing a blood-spattered nightgown and enough leverage to force DCFS to finally stop shifting her from relative to relative and place her and James with grandparents they wanted to be with all along.

Alicia hated going there with her niece. But they had all agreed to this bad idea. Alicia still found it hard to believe that she was actually doing this. She should've been on the plane to India, but something wouldn't let her leave. Maybe it was because she had deprived herself of true love and sexual satisfaction for most of her life. Dallas was ready, willing and able to finally give it to her. And as much as she loved her niece, in her heart, Alicia longed to put her own feelings first – for once in her life.

Tori leaned against the door jamb and crossed her arms over her bosom. "I made a mistake by not having sex with Dallas. Somehow that made you relevant again." She gave Alicia an ear-to-ear grin. "But I've got plenty of time to rectify that, old woman. Beauty, brains and a damn good body will win out before, barren, soon-to-be wrinkled, and one foot in the grave, every single time."

Tori made it to the threshold but paused the moment Alicia said, "By the way, Victoria Denise Mitchell … I'd like to know one thing."

Tori looked over her shoulder at her aunt.

Alicia smiled over the rim of her glass as she asked, "Who says you were Plan A?"

Chapter 19

7:48 P.M.

Dallas ran back into the kitchen, phone still to his ear as he grabbed his plate. He paused when he saw that Alicia was eating the rest of her meal alone.

He slid his plate back into place, and gestured to the phone.

Alicia nodded, answering his unspoken question that it was all right for him to continue with the conversation at the dinner table. He leaned in to kiss her cheek, reclaimed his seat next to her and made a little more progress on his meal as he entertained Katie's concerns.

A few minutes later, Dallas ended the call with, "Now that's something we can cover tomorrow." He shifted his gaze to Alicia, who was on her dessert. "I'm being a little rude right now, so I've gotta go."

He disconnected the call and set the phone next to his plate. "Where's Tori?"

"I imagine that she's moping in her room."

Dallas sighed his impatience. "I was only gone for ten minutes. What happened?"

"She's got a headache that matches her oversized ego."

Dallas looked at her for a long while, then nodded. "I think in the next week or so, she'll be packing up—of her own accord."

"A week?" Alicia protested. "That long?"

He lifted her hand, brought it to his lips and gave her a small kiss. "I know this is hard, but if I break it off with Tori, number one, she'll be hurt and that's not fair, and number two, I don't know what she'll do if she gets angry. She can be vindictive and there's a lot on my table right now."

Alicia nodded. "And number three, keep her around and you can have your children."

Dallas took a long slow breath, as if he didn't want to have that conversation. "I just said she'll be gone in a week."

"And you're going to use me to accomplish that."

He placed a hand over hers. "I don't have to use anyone, Alicia. And I resent you saying it. She knew about you in the beginning."

"But she didn't know it was me," she protested. "Or that I would be back in the picture."

"Neither did I," Dallas admitted. "And I'm not going to apologize for the fact that I'm grateful that the woman I actually want is back in my life." He locked a gaze with her and added, "You left and I kept on living, but I never really loved again. I couldn't. Because I never understood why you left me ..."

❤ ❤ ❤

CHARITY AUCTION FOR THE PAUL ALEXANDER FOUNDATION
THREE YEARS AGO

"Thank you for your patience!" the strawberry blond host crowed to the expectant crowd who had waited through double overtime for Dallas Avery to arrive. "Folks, our grand prize bachelor is in the house. So let's get this done. " Hearty applause rang out as he reached into the envelope and pulled out a slip of paper. "And the winner for dinner—oh, that rhymed," he said with a laugh and unfolded the sheet. "is ... Alicia Mitchell from Chicago, Illinois.

Dallas, clad in a black tux, left the stage amid a weak smattering of unenthusiastic applause and walked past several crest-fallen women who had also put in a silent bid to have dinner with him.

Alicia was dressed in an elegant strapless emerald gown that hugged her curves as if she were born into it. Poise, strength and sensuality came through as he had watched her progression from the bidding stations all the way to the artwork.

When he made it to her side, she held out a glossy photo of him supplied by the foundation. "All I want is a personal autograph." She presented a pen and tapped it on the edge of the picture. "Dinner isn't necessary."

That right there had set her apart from all of the other hungry fillies who were galloping to him the moment he arrived.

"Don't you want to have dinner with the actual man, rather than curl up with a picture?"

"No thanks," she quipped. "The actual man seems like he's entirely too much work." Then she checked her watch. "Besides, I have a plane to catch. The Red Eye waits for no one."

"I apologize for being late."

"I don't hold that against you," she said giving him a megawatt smile. "The Miami Heat was giving you all a run for the money."

"And we finally spanked that ass," he said proudly. "But I'd like the opportunity to prove you wrong. I'm not really that much work." He grinned.

"You don't have to prove anything to me," she replied, holding out the pen.

"But I want to."

"Turn off the charm, Mr. Avery," she teased. "There are plenty of women you can use it on tonight." She nodded toward the group of sad-looking women who were watching their exchange.

He held his hand over his heart. "How can a Mavericks fan say those things to me?"

Alicia laughed. "Oh, I'm Bulls fan through and through."

"What?" He looked around, then put his arm around her waist guiding her away from the other guests. "Shhhh, don't say that too loud. I don't want you to get hurt."

She glanced over to the few people who were murmuring as they followed their progress.

"I've been a basketball fan since the Michael Jordan era," she admitted. "That's when the Chicago Bulls elevated the game."

Dallas extracted his hold from her. "Hold up, they didn't 'elevate the game,' woman. They played some damn good ball, but that's reaching."

"Watch it, Dallas," she said. "Your fangs are showing."

"Fangs my ass," he countered, pausing long enough to sign an autograph for one of the more zealous women who felt no shame interrupting them. Turning back to the woman, he continued, "Jordan was no saint. Trust me."

"Like you have a halo of your own," she teased, ignoring the woman who gave her a venomous look before stalking off.

"I admit, it's a little bent, but it's still there," he said, pretending to straighten an imaginary halo and causing Alicia to laugh. "So, if you're not feeling the team, then why are you here?"

"I like the cause," she quipped. "You've been on my radar since that interview with Robin Roberts. I've watched so many of those and when they ask that question: 'Why did you get into basketball?' a lot of players answer with the usual stuff: 'to help my family,' 'to get fly cars and mansions,' 'it's all I ever wanted to do.'

"But your response … 'I love basketball, through and through, but right now there is something more important than money. My mother's just been diagnosed with cancer. This contract will give me the funds to get her the best treatment possible … That's my only focus right now. Keeping my mother here on this earth …'"

Dallas stared at her before finally saying, "You memorized what I said?"

She nodded. "I admired that. With all of the egos and grandstanding in the field these days, it was a refreshing change."

Dallas leaned in, pressed a kiss to her cheek, beaming as he said, "So now I have a new mission in life."

Alicia's eyebrow shot up.

"It's my job to make sure you're a Mavericks fan."

"I'll be a Dallas Avery fan," she corrected. "The only time I won't cheer you on is when your team plays against the Bulls. I hope you understand, 'cause loyalty is my strong suit."

Dallas stared into her eyes. "We'll work on that whole Bulls thing."

She laughed and lifted her glass in mock salute. "You can always try."

"So, let's start with that dinner."

And that's what they did. In between snippets of conversation, her knowledge of how to "grow" all the money he had coming in held him captive.

Alicia folded her arms across her breasts. "For me, it was always about being wealthy, not rich. When my husband died, I invested the majority of his insurance money so that I wouldn't have to worry about money for the rest of my life. I work hard to live off the interest. You're younger, so you can take a lot of risks right now and have time to recover. I couldn't do that, so I played it smart and safe."

"So what did you put your money in?" he asked.

"I split my focus," she replied. "Half of it into investments with a guaranteed rate of return. The rest, I basically followed the market. Whatever the top fifteen stocks were that month, I bought them. The next month I sold them and bought the next top ones and kept it going like that for a while."

"The hot hands method."

She nodded. "I've made a mint just on doing that alone." She placed her hand over his. "Don't end up like so many other ones, Dallas. Pay attention to your money. You want your money to still be working for you—even when you're sleeping."

Dallas tilted his head, looking at Alicia as though really seeing her for the first time. "Woman, you're talking my language!"

As the night went on, the conversation ventured from money to politics to their views on relationships.

As each hour passed, Dallas knew that he was attracted to her. Physically, of course, but what had him going was that it was beyond that. He loved her mind. He couldn't think of another woman that he'd ever wanted do much.

He felt like he'd just scored the winning shot when he convinced her to come to his condo. "You were talking about real estate investments, you should check out mine."

She looked at him as if she wasn't sure of his motives, but she agreed.

But they'd decided to stroll to his condo which wasn't far from the hotel, they were caught in a torrential rain and landed in a cab. Dallas loved that Alicia laughed about it rather than being upset over her ruined dress or drenched hair.

When they arrived at the nearly empty condo where Dallas lived, he showed her to the guest bedroom. "You can get out of that wet gown and change into this." He gave her one of his button-down shirts. "I don't think I have any pants that you can wear."

But when she changed and stood in the doorway of his bedroom, he couldn't help himself. His gaze swept across her body and the heat that flamed through him made him unable to look away. He was by her side in the few strides it took to cover the distance. He placed a kiss on the wet curve of her shoulder and trailed upward until he claimed her moist mouth. The kiss deepened the moment her arms curled about his neck.

She arched toward him, and an animal-like lust overtook him. He ripped his shirt from her, kissing her, tasting the warm nectar of her lips, feeling the heat of her body. He wasn't thinking, only feeling, and at the moment, she felt like pure paradise. She trembled under his touch, sighed with each kiss. Every drape of his tongue over any part of her body was enough to bring about a breathy moan that turned him on to the nth degree.

When he scooped her into his arms, and carried her to his bed, she held onto him, returning his kiss measure for measure. He mounted her seconds after he gently placed her on his bed; then paused only for a few moments and looked into her eyes, waiting for some sign that this was something she truly wanted. She parted her thighs, welcoming him into her world, then held onto him, urging him to take her. He complied with a single thrust into those delightfully tight walls, which gripped him so hard that his body was ready for an instant release.

Dallas barely held onto his control as he moved within her, wondering how a woman could be so tight, so hot, so wet, so ... perfect. He thrust into her with every ounce of power he could muster, then slowed his rhythm and made love to her on that second and third pass, relishing every delicious moment as though it would be his last.

When they were sated and he held her in his arms, he asked that fateful question, "Alicia, will you stay for another day?"

"I can't," she replied. "This was ... wonderful, even better than I could have ever hoped for. But I have a life. I have plans to travel and see the world."

"Just one more day, baby," he said, and that was the beginning of a 91-day mantra. Until the ninety-second day when he presented her with a ring, lowered to one knee and said, "Alicia Mitchell, will you marry me and be the mother of my children?"

When she was too stunned to answer, he felt a slight stab of disappointment and stood.

"Dallas..." she whispered and went to him, burying her head in the wall of his chest as tears streamed down her face.

He thought all she needed was some time to get used to the idea. Only later did he realize that he had forgotten one important part of their process … he didn't extract his usual promise from her to stay "just one more day" giving them the time to sort things out.

Alicia was gone the next morning and he hadn't heard a word from or laid eyes on her until fate had landed them in that bedroom on Thanksgiving Day.

Dallas shook his head, bringing himself back to the present. "When you left me, it was never the same," he said to Alicia. "I'm not going to let that happen again. I don't even know why you left me before, but—."

"You asked me to marry you," she said. "To have your kids."

He pulled away to look down at her. "And what the hell was wrong with that?"

"Dallas, you were a wonderful fantasy. An unexpected pleasure. That's all."

"Well, now you know that we're more than that. This time, we're going to work through whatever issues you might have." He stroked a hand across her face. "You feel me?"

Her eyes searched his for a moment before she said, "Yes."

With that one word, and her head laid on his chest, Dallas steeled himself against the onslaught of feelings, which were as powerful as a winning half-court shot in the last second of a championship game.

An hour later, Dallas went up to the loft to give her some time alone. Alicia settled into a bedroom that was the equivalent of three of her master bedrooms put together. The white walls and ceiling, white natural wood floors, and white bedding was a stark contrast to all the bursts of color throughout the rest of the house.

Dallas' room was neat, uncluttered, efficient—just like the man himself. But his closet told the true story. She expected wall-to-wall jeans, jerseys and t-shirts; but not only did she find rows of suits, slacks, Polos and dress shirts, but he chose a more classic style, showing a more mature and conservative taste. She checked out the few simple pieces of jewelry laid out on silver trays atop a white wood dresser right next to three Movado watches. Nothing gaudy or showy. Everything classic and classy. The bedroom and his fashion were Dallas through and through. Simple, conservative and everything in its place.

Later that night, when Dallas came to the bedroom to say good night, she said, "You put me here on purpose. The guest bedroom's right next to Tori's room."

"The walls aren't thin, but you are a screamer, baby," he teased, kissing her shoulder as he pulled her close to him.

"What?"

Dallas chuckled at her shocked expression. "Dallas," he taunted in a high-pitched voice, and put a dramatic hand over her heart. "Oh, Dallas. The world rises and sets with your smile, and—"

The pillow hit him square in the face and he playfully toppled to the bed and spread-eagled.

Alicia settled in the space right beside him and he rolled over to face her.

She stroked a hand across his chest. "Dallas, this is more than just about sex for you, right?"

"It has always been about more than that," he replied, his expression matching his serious tone. "You just didn't give me the benefit of the doubt."

She reached up and touched her hand to his cheek. "I'm sorry for leaving you that way, Dallas. I'm sorry for hurting you."

Dallas nodded, but she could tell from the hard set of his jaw, how much her leaving had hurt.

"You want to put it to the test?" he asked, kissing the back of her hand.

Alicia lifted an eyebrow. "Put what?"

"Whether this is just about sex. Let's test it and take a page from Tori's book. Let's spend time getting to know each other again."

"You mean, we can't make love for a whole damn year?" she shrieked, and he couldn't help but laugh.

"I'm definitely not saying that."

"Well, that's great, because that's what got you in trouble in the first place."

"No, what got me in trouble was trying to turn a friend into a housewife."

Alicia pondered that a few moments before saying, "So now you're trying to turn a one-night-stand into a relationship."

"It wasn't a one-night stand," he protested. "We were together an evening, a night and a day. In total it was ninety-two days, sixteen hours, and twenty-two minutes. I'd call it a Three-peat."

They laughed together, but then, Dallas became serious once again. "Let's take some time and focus on the relationship aspect of this. I want to earn your trust, your respect."

She pressed a kiss to his lips. "You already have my respect. Please believe that."

"Well, I guess one out of two isn't bad."

She cupped his face in her hands. "I don't think we know each other well enough to completely trust each other yet," she said. "But as far as respect, when I left, I kept tabs on you. Well, at least I did up until a year ago," she said. "I loved your interviews, I loved how you've lived up to every single claim that you've made. You've walked your talk and that alone is admirable. You have my respect."

"But your trust."

"Let's give that time," she said.

He nodded and then held her in his arms. As she snuggled into his embrace, Alicia thought about how for the past year, no matter where she went, one thing remained constant—how much she missed him. Everything: the deep timbre of his voice, his smile and laughter. The way he felt when he held her. The way he listened to her. The way he loved her.

Not to mention that toe-curling, panty-ripping fantasies about him always left her wanting more. But then, good sense would kick in and shut things down.

Women like her were not supposed to have those type of experiences. Men like Dallas chose the young and beautiful—women who looked good on the arm. Women who were loved by the camera. Women like Tori.

But though she believed that, sometimes, she allowed herself to dream. She'd close her eyes and imagine that he was in the room with her.

She rolled herself away from him. "Dallas, I can be honest with you about anything, right?"

"Definitely," he said, through half-closed lids.

She took a deep breath. "This relationship right here," she gestured to him, then to her. "I'm scared as hell."

"Why?"

"The age thing ... are you into some mother complex or something like that?"

For a moment his expression darkened. "You'll be everything to me," he replied. "My friend, my lover, my sister, my mother—not because I'm trying to replace my mother's influence in my life—but it's about being everything a woman can be to a man. It's because I want an irreplaceable woman by my side. You are that woman."

Tears welled up in her eyes and spilled over.

Dallas sat up, resting on his elbows as he wiped away her tears. "As long as we talk about things. As long as we're open, we can work through anything." Dallas pulled her back into his arms. "Give it a chance, Alicia. Don't run away before you see how good things can be. It's time for you to have a little slice of happiness." She could swear his voice broke a little when he added, "Don't leave me before we get to the good parts of love."

She nestled her body to his. Dallas was right. She'd damn near lost her husband behind trying to help Tori. She'd made sure everyone was happy—even if it was at her own expense. She was forty-five and it was time that she put herself first. Besides, this had all been Tori's idea.

"I want that, Dallas."

"And I want to give it to you," he said, squeezing her tighter.

Alicia pushed aside the negative thoughts. Hopefully, they could emerge from this arrangement with Tori relatively unscathed, but Alicia's focus was now on her own happiness. And the man lying next to her, who no doubt could provide exactly the type of happiness that could last a lifetime.

Chapter 20

Alicia was at the stove finishing up the last of breakfast when Dallas came up behind her and planted a kiss on her neck.

"Mmmmm, this feels good," he said over her shoulder, while pressing himself against her buttocks, causing her to laugh. "So, what're you going to eat?"

Alicia favored him a startled glance. "Are you serious?"

Dallas slid the platter from her hands and winked. "Yep. This right here … is like appetizers in this camp. Me and good food have always been great friends."

He pulled up to the kitchen table, said a quick grace, then started making headway on the meal. The food on the platter was enough to feed six people, and he planned to put all that away as though it was the last meal he would ever see.

"Dallas, you can't possibly eat all of that!"

"Watch me," he replied around a mouthful of waffles, then moaned when he took another bite. "Did you put vanilla in here? Man, that's good!"

Alicia shook her head and turned back to the stove, aiming to have something ready for Tori before she went off to the hospital.

She yawned and looked at the clock on the stove and realized that a nap was definitely on tap the moment these two were out the door. She barely got any sleep last night, but she still wandered into the kitchen about an hour ago to hopefully get Dallas and Tori's day off to a good start.

"Good morning."

Tori's voice made both Alicia and Dallas turn her way. "Good morning," they replied in unison.

She took a seat across from Dallas and raised an eyebrow at the platter on his side of the table and the empty plate on hers.

Alicia moved forward, snagged a waffle and slid it onto Tori's plate, then lifted the pancake at the top of his stack.

"Hey," he protested, trying to stab a fork in the food to keep it from making an exit stage left.

She managed to slide three whole ones, along with a few pieces of bacon, and a scoop of eggs. "You'll have to wait for part two," Alicia said, nodding toward the items cooking in the skillet. "Tori needs to eat, too."

"Then Tori should've been down at breakfast on time." Dallas gave her a wide smile that caused Tori's frown to deepen.

"Yeah, making out like a short-order cook will be easy to manage since she won't have anything else to do," Tori taunted, as she began to tackle her food.

"Oh, she'll have plenty to do," Dallas said, his fork pausing a few inches from his lips. "Art class, Salsa dancing, cooking class." He finished another bite and said, "Trust me, she won't just be here twiddling her thumbs, waiting for us to come home. She'll have a life, just like we have one."

Alicia turned away from the stove. Leave it to Dallas to make sure her days were occupied. "No wonder you asked all of those questions. You didn't even let me get any sleep last night!"

Dallas finished taking a sip of orange juice and grinned.

"Oh God," Tori said on a sigh. "That's way too much information. I don't ever want to see you all ..." Tori hedged, then shuddered before completing her thought.

"You won't have to," he said, putting his attention back to his breakfast. "We're going to hold off on sex for a hot minute."

Tori frowned. "But I thought that was the whole purpose for this. That you all," she crooked her fingers as quotes, "couldn't do without it."

Dallas' gaze was intense as he told her, "There are some things a man can do without, and there are other things that he shouldn't do without."

"Like what?" she challenged.

"A woman's touch. A woman's feel. A woman's scent. A woman's ... presence."

In just those four sentences Alicia understood more about Dallas than he told her in their nine-hour conversation last night that didn't end until just after dawn. He had everything at his disposal, but the thing he longed for most was a woman who sincerely appreciated him and showed him how much she loved him. And for her, that would be no problem. Dallas made her feel "there," like she mattered. And that was something her husband never managed in all those years. Alicia was more of a conquest to Patrick; something that hid the fact that he was an "underperformer" in several areas of his life. Between Patrick and what she experienced at the hands of some of her male relatives, Alicia had soured on men to the point that she had shut down.

Even the fact that Dallas was already considering her needs—just from things he had gleaned from their conversation last night showed that he understood what it took to please her in something other than the bedroom. Engaging her interests, seeing to her well-being, taking her needs into consideration would make any woman want to see to his needs all the more.

"Wait a minute," Tori said between bites. "If she's going to be doing all that, that means she's going to be out and about. She can't be with you in public." Tori's tone matched her alarmed expression.

"She's not a child, Tori," Dallas replied with an intense look in her direction. "I'm not hiding Alicia away like I'm ashamed of her. An open relationship, and open Marriage means open. The sooner you get used to it, the less likely it's going to be a problem." He gestured to her plate. "Are you going to finish that?"

She shoved her meal in his direction and frowned at him. Then, she glared at Alicia who swiped Tori's half-eaten plate for a fresh batch of food for him.

"Well, at least while she's here she can help with my wedding," Tori said, giving her aunt a smile that didn't quite make it to her soft brown eyes.

Alicia slid the plate on the counter, recognizing Tori's request for the move it was—keep your friends close and foes even closer. This was just another way for Tori to rub it in that Alicia was only temporary. At least, in her mind.

"No, you'll have to fix that mess on your own," Dallas said. "I lowered the limit on your American Express card this morning. Substantially."

Tori gasped and backed away from the table. "You didn't! But my—"

"You want a higher limit?" he said with a grin. "Then you'll need to adjust some things on your end." He lifted his fork as though directing some unseen orchestra. "I see some refunds in your future."

"Dallas, why are you being so damn cheap?" Tori asked, backing up until her buttocks were pressed against the counter.

"Cheap?" He placed the fork on his plate and pushed back from the table. "Tori, let me tell you something—" his gaze flickered toward Alicia who gestured for him to remain calm. "I don't want for much," he continued, lowering back down in the chair. "But I don't just buy up stuff just to say I have it either. Our cars? Gifts from GM. My clothes and shoes? Mostly from endorsement deals. Jewelry? Not too much. Why? Because a smart man doesn't blow it all on something that people can walk off with. He invests it in people, in businesses, and—"

"Experiences," Alicia filled in and he shifted his gaze to her. "And creating a legacy."

"Experiences and things that create a legacy," he agreed, smiling at Alicia who had given him that advice when they first met.

She began to clear away the dishes as she said, "Which means, you have been investing your money so that you'll have passive business income and partnering with people so you have multiple streams of income. Your money is making money while you're sleeping."

Tori sighed her impatience. "Well, thank you E-Trade for the finance lesson, but—"

"And that's my issue, Tori," he snapped, turning his attention her way. "You're spending money without any understanding or consideration for what it takes to make it." His gaze swept the white lab coat hanging on the back of the chair. "If you ask any of the doctors at your hospital, they'll tell you that they have an investment portfolio—the money you'll make at the hospital is limited, but investments are unlimited. You need to know that for your own good."

Tori trained her gaze on her plate, a vein was thrumming at the base of her throat. Dallas reached for her hand, but she stiffened and he pulled back.

"And I want you get something clear in your head," he said, and this time his tone was softer. "Basketball isn't just a sport, it's a business. And I don't know how long I'll be able to play. I'll want to get out while my body's still able to hold up. So, I'll need a wife who'll understand this and will appreciate money, or I'll be just like some of those other players who don't have anything to show for all their hard work."

Tori and Dallas stayed locked in a battle glare so long that Alicia cleared her throat and said, "Soooo, because you all have such crazy busy lives, my contribution to the household is that I'll maintain the house—"

"And my schedule?" Dallas asked, tearing his gaze away from Tori. "I really, really need your help with that. Please?"

"And your schedule," she amended and relished his sigh of relief.

"And mine, too," Tori added, then quickly rattled off an inventory of things related to how she and the maids kept things at their condo.

"She's not going to replace the maid or the housekeeper," Dallas said angrily.

"No worries," Alicia said, giving Tori a knowing smile. "I'm beginning to think you need a wife more than you ever needed a husband."

Tori's eyes shot daggers in her direction.

Dallas chuckled as he polished off the rest of what was on his plate. "You know, my mother said that all the time."

"What?" Alicia asked.

"Every woman needs a wife."

Alicia turned back to the stove, chuckling as she said, "Well, let the church say Amen."

Chapter 21

They fell into a comfortable routine that always left Alicia smiling. Sometimes, Dallas would write poetry and leave it on her pillow so the first thing she would know when she woke up was that he would be thinking of her all day. At night, he would lie on her bed stretched out beside her, reading from a novel until her eyelids fluttered and she fell asleep.

True to his word, he made sure that her days were filled with the things she loved to do, and he enrolled her in an art class to encourage her love for creating beautiful oil paintings. A week after she started, he found a "creative" way to join her, without it being obvious they were a "couple." Dallas hid behind a huge black screen as the bushy-haired art teacher said, "We have a special guest today. You might recognize him, and then again, dressed the way he is right now, you might not."

Dallas stepped out with only a towel covering the Family Jewels and moseyed over to stand next to the art teacher, who gave him an appreciative once-over.

"Class, NBA Star Dallas Avery is our subject for today. Fresh off a win last night from the Mavericks, he's joining us for the ultimate experience."

A sudden hush came over the all-female class. That lasted all of ten seconds. When Dallas turned and walked to the designated spot on the chaise, it set tongues wagging. He heard everything from, "Nice ass," to "Good Lord, I'd like to squeeze that Charmin."

Alicia tried to keep a straight face, but the shock she felt came through, and the women talking about him made her blush.

He winked at her, and she gave him the "evil eye." It had been a pleasant surprise to her when he'd driven her to school that morning. He'd promised to pick her up, so she didn't expect to see him for two more hours.

But after her initial surprise, she focused, working hard on doing justice to the man that she loved.

On their way home from the art studio that day, she was silent for a long while. He opened the car door and extended his hand to her. When she stood in front of him, she placed her hand over his prized package and said, "Next time, drop the towel, sweetheart," and walked into the condo without giving him a backward glance.

Dallas roared with laughter. But then, the next day when she brought the painting of him home, he'd been mesmerized and proud. Alicia had created a piece so life-like and beautiful, he had it framed and hung on her bedroom wall where she would see it the moment she opened her eyes.

They were beginning to build their life together.

❤ ❤ ❤

Dallas had a world class chef come to the condo to give him a private cooking class. The chef tried to teach Dallas how to prepare a few of Alicia's favorite foods. Watching Dallas fumble his way around the kitchen had brought peals of laughter from Alicia, which warmed his heart.

After two hours of torture—where he messed up on simple things like teaspoons and tablespoons; sautéing and simmering, she held her sides, still laughing as she said, "All right Dallas, you've made your point."

Dallas excused the chef, and the moment he cleared the room, Dallas ran over to Alicia and planted a wheat flour laced kiss on her cheek. "I don't have to cook. Thank you. Thank you. Thank you!"

Then he looked at his watch. "Great. We have time for a real meal. Your wine-tasting class starts in a few hours."

"Wine tasting?" she asked. "I didn't mention anything about wanting to be a wine connoisseur."

"I'm hoping it'll help you find an appreciation for something a lot less potent than that swill that's strong enough to put hairs on the glass," he said. "I felt like a punk trying to drink that crap in the bar."

"Oh, so we're not a grown up," she teased, planting a hand on his massive chest.

Dallas caught both of her hands in his. "I'm grown enough, woman, don't play."

She gave him a sultry look and said, "Show, don't tell, honey."

"Woman, don't …"

"Tori's on rotation until tomorrow."

He had her within his arms in the time it took to breathe and carried her off to the bedroom. They made the kind of mad, passionate love that meant she missed wine-tasting class altogether. And dinner. And breakfast. Evidently that "hot minute" of holding off had come to a much-needed end. They didn't even make it through a month.

It truly was all good times for them. Their only arguments came from differing views in politics. While they both agreed that Obama's time in the White House had been marred by the GOP's dogged determination to do the exact opposite of any forum the POTUS put in place to help the average American, they disagreed greatly on how the man went about doing things.

Dallas huffed as they watched another State of the Union address. "He should have went in and gone straight gangster on those fools in the first damn place."

Alicia laid her head on his shoulder. "And have him prove everybody right? That a brother couldn't handle his business without showing his ass?"

"One time and they would've learned that if they didn't play ball, he would take his toys and go home then play his own damn game."

Alicia sighed as they continued to watch their president—each voicing their opinion in such a way that Tori finally came out of her bedroom and banged on the door and said, "Will you two amateur political analysts keep it down! I swear, if you're not fucking like bunny rabbits, you're chattering like squirrels. Give it a rest already!"

The two of them looked at each other and busted up laughing.

They survived the first twenty-one days of Tori's wavering between actually enjoying how smoothly things were shaping up; then remembering that she shouldn't. Every time it seemed as if the two women were mending their relationship, Tori's jealousy would rear its ugly head and they would be back to square one.

Dallas was on the road a lot for his games, but he spent every moment he could at home. Sometimes, he surprised Tori with flowers and jewelry or by leaving a CD of him singing—actually, butchering—one of her favorite songs in her pearl white LaCrosse. Once a week, he had a crew of specialists show up at the medical school and set up shop in the cafeteria to give her, her classmates, and the instructors the royal treatment, which had made her mega-popular at work and toned down some of her anxiety.

And what he did with Alicia was create as many special moments for them together that he could. Many nights, he would take Alicia to a private creek near the woodlands and swim with her under the stars. During one of those times, she had opened to him, telling him of the time when she first learned what fear was all about …

❤ ❤ ❤

ANNAPOLIS, MISSOURI

The wind whipped about and screams rented the air. Six-year-old Alicia and her nine-year-old brother, James huddled in the closet as the roar of what sounded like a thousand engines rattled the house. Alicia's heart slammed against her little chest. Her brother wrapped his arms around her. His shirt was plastered to his brown skin, making it cold to the touch. "We'll be okay," James whispered, rocking her back and forth. "They'll come back for us. You'll see."

Alicia moved closer to James and they sat in the darkness for an eternity. She missed her twin, Lisa, who was at Nana's house learning how to sew. Their parents had left the house when their mother went into labor. That seemed like days ago. Before the rains came. Nana was supposed bring Lisa home and come stay with them while their parents were at the hospital, but the silver-haired woman never made it.

"What if the wind took them, too?" Alicia asked him.

"No, they promised to come back. Mommy and Daddy always keep their promises, don't they?"

Alicia nodded, almost as unsure of his words as she was that the house wouldn't come down around them. The wind had made a shower of branches and limbs slam against the house, breaking the windows and sucking out some of their belongings. That's when they had run from the bedroom to the closet.

James pulled the blanket about her shoulders. He sang to her, just as he always had when the shadows that played about her bedroom wall kept her from falling asleep. James was so brave and smart. He could chase those shadows away with his voice and she would drift into a happy place until the sun touched her face the next morning. But there was no sun this morning. Only dark clouds. An even darker sky. And rain. And the sound of the wind in its angry journey through their city.

As she listened, Alicia noticed there was something different in his voice this time. Something she knew quite well; something that James was beginning to understand. Fear. The feel of his hand trembling as he tried to comfort her; the slight hitch in his breathing was enough to bring on a different thought. If her brother was afraid, then they were definitely in trouble.

She focused on the words of the song. Come by here, Good Lord. Come by here. Yes, they needed God. They needed someone. Against her will, Alicia's eyes began to close and she drifted into an uneasy type of slumber with his arms wrapped around her.

When she awakened, the world was a frightfully different place. They were no longer in the closet. As far as the eye could see, mountains of wood, metal, and glass stood in places that once held houses and families along a tree-lined street. The sky above them was tinged with a murky grey. The wind brushed across them from all sides, bringing with it a biting cold air that made Alicia shiver. Somehow she believed that the wind had carried them faraway, like Dorothy in The Wizard of Oz.

Alicia shook James and he slowly opened his eyes and lifted his head. His eyes widened when he probably became aware of the one thing she had figured out moments ago. She had been wrong. They were still in what was left of the closet, but only the threshold and frame remained. The concrete foundation underneath was now a macabre outline of the once-happy Mitchell family it contained. Their entire house was gone, as well as everything in it.

"My parents didn't keep their promise to return," Alicia finished telling the story to Dallas. "Only later did I learn that it was because they weren't alive to keep it. My nana and twin died that night, too. And ever since then, it feels like I've been drifting … just drifting."

Dallas swam over to her. "Not anymore, baby. Not anymore."

Each time they went to the creek to swim together, Alicia opened a little more to him, telling of her past and the things she had endured before finally arriving on her grandparent's doorstep. Dallas admired her strength and tenacity and was thrilled as she slowly began to lay her heart on the line—for him.

Alicia was beginning to trust him, but he could tell there were things that she held back. Sometimes she would pause, sifting through her memories, filtering out the things she either thought were too painful to share, or too sordid for him to understand.

Dallas tried, on many occasions to reassure her that she was safe with him now. That no matter what life threw at them, he would never leave her.

He understood Alicia, and she understood him in ways that Tori did not—the need for simple things; quiet times, a good meal, peace in his own home. Sometimes they didn't have to say a word—a look, a movement, an unspoken thought connected them, and she responded to him. He adored her.

The most pleasurable moments of his life were seeing Alicia's smile, hearing her laughter, and knowing that he had satisfied her or pleased her in some small way.

And that brought him more satisfaction than he could put into words.

Chapter 22

"You're the one that asked—no, practically, demanded that I come live with you and Dallas," Alicia screamed back at Tori. "Yet you've been giving me hell since I walked through the door." She tilted her head, peering at her niece. "Is there a name for what's really wrong with you?"

"Nothing's wrong with me, dear aunt." Tori's lips lengthened into a sour smile. "I just know that you won't be able to keep his interest for long. Enjoy it while you can." Tori hurried from Alicia's bedroom and was out the door and on her way to the hospital a few minutes later.

Alicia stayed in bed, mulling over yet another argument that always seemed to end this way. And once again, Tori hit on Alicia's sore spot. The older woman had wondered what would happen when things cooled off.

Alicia picked up her cell and noticed there was one missed called from Dallas. He was just leaving practice, and he normally checked on her before he went on any errands. She was glad that she'd missed his call, and she had no intentions of calling him back. She wasn't going to tell him what she was about to do. And she couldn't lie to him—he could always hear it in her voice.

Tori was trying to play hard, but her pain was evident and while Alicia had tried putting her own needs first, Tori had her questioning more and more what was she doing? What would happen with Dallas after the newness wore off? After she fell head over heels, deeply in love with him? That, she wouldn't be able to handle. No. Enough was enough. She needed to get out now. Before she couldn't get out at all.

At dawn, Alicia quietly made an exit from the condo and stole away in a taxi.

The moment the front door closed behind her, Dallas raised up from the sofa and stared at the door. He rushed to Alicia's bedroom, confirmed that her bed was empty, then bolted out the door. He looked up and down the empty street, just in time to see the cab turn the corner.

"Shit!" he yelled. He knew that this was trouble. There was only one reason why Alicia would be up and out of the house as the sun was just starting to rise. He contemplated what to do. By the time he made it back upstairs to get his keys, she'd be long gone. Dallas darted back inside and went straight to the computer. He perused the last searches she had done and quickly found what he was looking for. He threw on some clothes, grabbed his wallet and passport and was hot on her trail.

The auburn-haired ticket agent at DFW International Airport pulled up the cost of the tickets and said, "Sir, are you certain you have to be on this particular flight? It will save you a lot of money if you could catch the next one."

"This one works," Dallas replied, trying to tamp down his impatience.

"But sir, the only ticket we have left is non-refundable. And it's over $10,000."

Dallas didn't respond.

"And do you have a visa?" When he shook his head, she added, "Travel is big business, so they will let you into the airport, but they don't issue visas after you get there, so you'll be stuck in customs."

"I know," he said, trying to keep his voice level. "Thank you for your concern, but I'd like a ticket for this flight. Right now."

"Yes, sir," she said. She took the charge card and passport he offered. When she slid him his boarding pass, she gave him a wan smile. "You have a nice flight."

"Thank you."

With no luggage, Dallas made it through security and hurried to the gate, ignoring the fans trying to get his attention. He scanned the area for Alicia and felt an instant sense of relief when he saw her seated near the window. He leaned on the beam next to the phone charging station at the gate and waited.

Moments later, she frowned and looked up from the novel in her hand, appropriately called, Set This House in Order—something Dallas was having one hell of a time trying to do. Alicia and Tori living together under one roof was the horrible idea that Alicia had warned it would be. Tori went at Alicia whenever she found the opening to whip on the guilt or remind everyone that she would be Dallas' wife.

Alicia's eyes widened with shock, but she quickly refocused on the novel in her hand.

Still he waited.

She tried to ignore him, but occasionally looked up only to find him still watching her.

A woman's thick accented English came over the loud speakers, "Air India, Flight 1267 will now begin the boarding process. First Class passengers, please have your documents ready, as you are boarding now. And thank you for flying with Air India today."

Alicia quickly grabbed her things and hurriedly fell in line behind the passengers who were filing in. She gave the attendant her boarding pass, walked a few feet and turned back to him, her eyes glassy with unshed tears.

Dallas didn't crack a smile as he held up his own boarding pass.

Her shoulders slumped, and she left the line and stood at a spot where there would still be several feet between them and a blanket of white noise that could effectively buffer their conversation. "Dallas, you can't come with me."

He didn't bother to respond.

"You'll miss your game tonight!"

Dallas shrugged, but he never took his eyes from hers.

"You'll get a huge fine, and you'll probably lose your contract."

He leaned against the steel counter and folded his arms across his chest.

"And I know you don't have a visa," she added.

He shook his head, and it caused her to sigh.

"They'll deport you!" she warned. "They'll deport you the minute you get off that plane. And it'll be all over the news."

Dallas raised a single eyebrow and waited. Now he understood why she timed her departure as she did. She thought he wouldn't come for her. From his place at the charging station he simply said, "You get on that plane, and I'm right there with you, Alicia. They may fine me. But I'm not going to lose my contract. And I meant it when I said that loving you is more important than all the money in the world."

Alicia closed her eyes, and a single tear escaped, quickly followed by another and yet another. But he didn't move to comfort her or to keep her from getting on that plane.

They stood in silence for a moment, then finally, she ran to him, and he took her in a deep embrace like he never wanted to let her go. They stayed that way until the wavy-haired attendant came over to ask, "Um, sir, are you and the lady going to board the flight?"

Dallas shook his head and kept his arms around Alicia, ignoring the curious stares and smiles from the people around them.

"Dallas, I can't do this anymore," she whispered as she held onto him. "You're always at practice or a game. And it's just me and her." She looked up at him. "I don't recognize the Tori who lives in your house. And when she finally pushes me beyond my limits, you won't recognize the Alicia who lives in your house either."

Dallas wiped her tears with the back of his hand. He lifted her chin and kissed her lips. "I'll take you house hunting on the way home." With that, he embraced her once again.

They were still entwined long after the plane had left without them.

❤ ❤ ❤

Dallas crossed the threshold of the condo, scooped Alicia in his arms and practically ran with her to the bedroom.

He had skipped training this morning, taking her to see several houses so she could pick out one she'd like. At the last home—all that talk of the kind of bed she wanted, how she couldn't wait to see him walk out of the shower with his dark skin against all that white background, and the wicked things she wanted to try with him—in her new house—made him horny as hell.

The minute they crossed the threshold of the condo, Alicia snatched off her stilettos and took off running toward the bedroom with him hot on her heels. He was out of his shirt and slacks in the time it took him to clear the door.

Alicia tore off her dress and lace underwear, pushed him back onto the bed, and straddled his thighs. She took his hand in hers and held them over his head and said, "Keep them there. You can't touch me."

Dallas grinned, but complied, loving that she had taken control.

She took his erection in her hand, stroking it as though she was reacquainting with a long-lost friend. When she guided him to her moist center, the feel of her tight walls closing around him made him close his eyes.

"No!" she said and his eyes flew open. "I want you to watch me."

And watch he did. She began a rhythm that was slow and teasing, causing his breath to catch and his arms to reach for her.

"Put them down, Dallas. You can't touch me."

"Baby, I've got to …" he hissed with pleasure as she came down on him once again. "Oh shhhhhhh…."

Alicia quickened her movements, and he found it hard not to grip her hips. She gave him an intense look and he forced his hands down by his side. He moved his hips, thrusting in answer to every move, increasing the crescendo into pure bliss.

She teased him, letting her breasts hover just above his lips where he couldn't wrap his lips around her nipples. When he couldn't take anymore, he flipped her over, pulled her to the edge of the bed, spread her thighs with his knee and centered himself within her. Then he thrust into her as she released a low, throaty chuckle. "Ohhh, the big man can give commands," she taunted. "But he certainly can't take them."

His answering thrust caused her to sigh and tighten around him.

Alicia wavered between being submissive and wanton. When she held onto him, thighs securely wrapped around him, hands encircled about his neck, she had cried as he brought her into that third orgasm.

He looked up just in time to see Tori's tear-filled eyes looking in on them. Only he heard the click of her heels as she ran away.

❤ ❤ ❤

Tori ran to the bathroom and braced herself against the cool edge of the porcelain. It was one thing to know that the two of them made love, but seeing it was …

"Tori?"

She looked at his reflection in the mirror.

"Dallas, I can't talk right now." She shook her head. "So y'all are fucking every single day now? Whatever happened to building a friendship first?"

"Done," he said simply. And the sound of finality was like a hammer blow to her heart. He stepped closer to her. "I'm so sorry. We've tried to be careful. I thought you wouldn't be home until later."

She turned and glared at him. "I got off early." She struggled to keep more tears from escaping. If this was her idea, and she knew they would be making love, why did it hurt so much?

"You told me you loved me. When you accepted my proposal, you said you loved me."

He was quiet for a minute, then, "I did. I mean, I do." He pulled his robe tighter around him. "It's just not the way a man should love a woman when they're getting married," he admitted.

"When did it change for you?" she asked softly. "When did I no longer matter."

He sighed heavily. "You always mattered. It's just that . . . well, when you started planning for the wedding, it opened my eyes. With everything with your mother—shit, I felt like I was in a threesome already. I wanted the old Tori. The Tori who knew what her life was all about and didn't need some bitter woman to tell her what to do."

Tori let the tears escape freely. "Dallas, the way you are with Alicia …"

"I'm sorry you had to see that," he whispered. "But the schedule said you weren't supposed to be home until four hours from now."

"I told you, I got off early."

"You do that a lot, you know," he said.

She whirled to face him. "I don't know what you mean."

"You give Alicia one time to put on the schedule, but I've noticed that lately you come in at a totally different time. Almost like you're trying to catch us doing exactly what we were doing."

Tori's lips parted and closed, and a flash of something lit in her eyes. Finally, she looked up at him. "What it is about being with her—I mean, besides sex—that appeals to you so much."

That wasn't a real answer, but Tori was too hurt right now for him to call her on it.

"What could you possibly have in common?" She didn't wait for him to answer. "Sometimes I think that you're just hanging on to her to teach me a lesson."

"That's not it at all. Why can't you just believe that I love her?"

Tori shook her head as if that were impossible.

After a few silent moments, Dallas asked, "Are you sure about this, Tori? You can call it off at any time ..."

"No," she said before he could finish. "We're going to do this. You and I are going to be married. I'm fine," she said as she turned away and stomped out of the bathroom.

Dallas waited a couple of seconds wondering just how much more would Tori be able to take? How much more would any of them be able to take?

Chapter 23

"We need to talk," Dallas announced as he slipped into the space across from Tori at the dining room table in their condo.

James Mitchell's gaze swept over him, and Dallas met the old man's look measure for measure. The man had no right to judge him. He could blame Bernice all he wanted for their financial problems, but James had also committed his own mistakes. The man had a major gambling problem and that was the reason Tori's family was in serious debt. So he wasn't going to take a dressing down from James about something that didn't concern him. Especially from a man who kept inviting himself to this home, flying to Dallas as if it were just down the street from Chicago.

Tori's eyes narrowed in Dallas' direction, but it was Alicia who stretched a hand across the smooth ebony surface of the dining room table and placed it on his arm and asked, "What's wrong?"

He removed her hand from his arm and clasped it within his hand.

"Bernice called my agent," he answered with a pointed look at Tori. "She wants a million or she'll sell a story about us to the press."

Tori jumped up from the table nearly knocking over the vase of flowers. "What?"

James grimaced as he let loose with a string of curses.

Tori rested her fingertips against her temple. Her perfect white teeth held her bottom lip prisoner. "But I gave her—"

Dallas' head whipped to her, his left eyebrow raised. Tori quickly clamped down on the rest.

James sighed with impatience. "I guess we shouldn't be surprised. She's losing a husband. She's been cut off from spending Dallas' money …"

Dallas smirked at Tori, who quickly averted her gaze.

"And she doesn't have a place to live anymore." James shrugged as though the issue was of no serious consequence.

"What are you going to do?" Alicia asked.

"I'm filing a police report," Dallas replied. "Blackmail is a felony."

James helped himself to an apple from the fruit bowl that Alicia made sure stayed on the dining room table. "Do what you gotta do. She brought it on herself."

"Please, don't," Tori said, reaching for Dallas' other hand. "Let me talk to her first."

"She never listened to you before," Dallas replied evenly. "What would make her change this time?"

"Why can't you just give her the money so she'll go away?" Tori asked.

Dallas looked at her for a long while, pissed that Tori would be so cavalier with his money. "If I give her a million, next time she'll want more. You know how these things go."

"But what about me?" Tori snapped, looking at each person sitting around the table. "Suppose she does talk? Do you know what's going to happen when people start talking about the fact that you chose an older woman over me?"

"Seriously?" Dallas said, frowning down at her. "That's all you're worried about?"

"Well, I meant, chose my own aunt over me."

Dallas leaned back in the chair. "Let's say I do pay. There's no guarantee that Bernice still won't run her mouth after she gets the cash."

"Don't turn her in." Her soft brown eyes pleaded with him. "Just give her a little something, and she'll be all right."

"What do you think?" he asked Alicia, whose wry twist of the lips showed exactly how she felt about this turn of events.

"Don't ask me a question about saving her," Alicia answered. "If she was on fire, I'd toss in some lighter fluid to keep it going."

Dallas let out a low whistle.

James cleared his throat, clearly holding back harsh words, but keeping his focus on Alicia.

"But she's my mother," Tori shrieked when no one said anything for a while. "You can't send her to jail!"

"And she's trying to hurt you—for money!" Alicia shot back, staring Tori down. "The way her old trifling ass ran through James' money, even a million more wouldn't last. Dallas has sense enough to realize that. And she doesn't care about that cash you're slipping her under the table," she said. "She's already hurt you in front of your family and now, she's ready to do it in front of the world."

"And you've done a hell of a lot worse," Tori countered. "But you don't see us putting your 'old trifling ass' out to pasture. Now do you?"

Seconds ticked by. The silence between the two women was unsettling. Then there was a sudden movement. Dallas was out of the chair and intercepting Alicia before she made it to the door. "Alicia, you're not going anywhere."

Alicia snatched away. "I'm not doing this shit, Dallas!"

"Baby, don't," he whispered so only she could hear. "You can't keep running."

"So, I need to stay here and endure this?"

"It won't be much longer. I'm sure we're going to find a house that you like soon. And who knows, maybe she'll wash her hands of this before then."

Looking over her shoulder, Dallas didn't miss the flash of envy in

Tori's eyes, but what concerned him was that he also saw a spark of something cold in James' eyes.

Dallas escorted Alicia back to her seat at the table and said, "So we're in agreement?" He looked first to a stone-faced Tori, then to Alicia. "Bernice doesn't get paid."

Alicia nodded.

"I didn't agree to that," Tori replied with a haughty lift of her chin.

"Two out of three is the majority."

"But I—"

"Might want to get used to it, Tori," Dallas said, causing her to pout. "Majority rules in an open relationship. Bernice doesn't see one dime of that money."

Tori sulked as she slid down in the seat.

James glared at all of them but lingered on Alicia as he said, "I think I need a drink."

Tori made a beeline for the cabinet and pulled out a bottle of Jack Daniels and two glasses as Dallas grumbled, "Man, don't get them started."

Chapter 24

"Dallas!" Tori shrieked and it tore him from his spot in the loft and he hurried down the spiral staircase and into the living room.

Tori and Alicia were both standing in the center of the living room, staring at the wide-screen television. The real estate listings of Alicia's final house selections slipped from her fingers and landed on the floor.

Dallas followed their line of vision.

Bernice Mitchell primped a little while the cameras panned first to the host, and then a wider shot of the studio and Los Angeles cityscape background itself.

Dallas was riveted to the screen when the words, *NBA Star's Secret Life* flashed across.

The host crossed one leg over the other, causing her already short skirt to expose even more of her thighs. "So you're the mother-in-law to be and the sister-in-law to the aunt?"

"Yes, I am," Bernice replied. "I'm here to tell it all. The man is having a threesome with relatives."

The shocked gasp of the tow-headed host was more fake than the weave slapped on her head.

"Dallas Avery is known for his charity work, and funding start-up businesses," the host said, looking directly into the camera. "We've only heard a few details of his love life until Tori Mitchell came on the scene. You know, those unfortunate court cases were just a mess." The host looked back at her guest. "We'd love to hear everything. A Threesome. An aunt and a niece." She gave Bernice's thigh a reassuring pat. "Give us all the dirt, honey."

Bernice leaned in as though she and the woman were old friends. "Well, it was Thanksgiving …"

"Uh huh."

"And he was coming to meet the rest of Tori's family."

The host looked at the audience and said, "Looks like one family member checked him out more than everyone else."

"Oh, yes," Bernice gushed. "She sure did. I caught him in bed with my brother's sister right before Thanksgiving dinner."

"Well, that could be a major problem. Doesn't your daughter have this big wedding coming up?"

"Sure does, and I was planning the whole thing." Bernice nodded, looking more like a puppet. "But you know what he did?"

The host leaned in. "What?"

"They moved that man-stealing cougar in with them."

Tori gasped, and inched away from the two standing next to her, mumbling, "She said she wouldn't say anything."

Dallas did a 180. "You've been talking to her?" he demanded, then caught up with her before she could make it out of the room. He whirled her around to face him. "You've still been telling her what's going on in my house?"

She tried to shake off his hands. "It may have slipped out that Alicia was living here."

"Slipped out!" he roared. "Tori, I swear to God you can be dense sometimes. You're the one who said you didn't want people to know and you told your mother?"

"Don't snap at me," Tori shot back, trying to free herself from his grasp. "We wouldn't be in this situation if you hadn't let your dick do all the talking."

Dallas put an instant three feet between. "Yes, all my fault. Got it. Again. You're still here—because somehow I twisted your arm. Got it. Again. And let's not forget one major issue that started it all was you telling too many people my business in the first place. What part of that did you not get? Again."

"Dallas—"

"I don't even want to hear it," he said, waving her off. He scooped up his cell from the coffee table and dialed up his publicist, who finally answered on the third ring. "Y'all watching this?"

"Yep," Liz answered. "The entire staff is in the boardroom taking it all in."

"And y'all didn't have a handle on this?" he demanded.

"Hell, we didn't know this was coming," she protested. "They contacted us about doing an interview with Backstage Pass, but we know you don't do rag mags or gossip shows."

"And you didn't think to mention it when we talked the other day?"

"They didn't say anything about this Bernice person, who is making up these kind of stories," she protested, then paused. "She *is* making all of this up?"

"A little truth thrown in with a whole lot of lies," he replied.

"And that's all it takes," Liz said dryly. "I'll get our legal team on this."

Dallas tossed his cell onto the sofa and went back to stand between the two women. Finalizing house choices was going to take a backseat to getting a handle on this today.

"You should've listened to me," Tori said, folding her arms over her bosom. "We should've paid her the money."

"We? You've been paying her enough!" Dallas yelled. "By the way, where's your American Express Card, Tori?"

She quickly looked away.

"See, that's what I mean. You gave her access to more than enough money, and it still wasn't enough," Dallas growled. "You feed a starving hound, they'll keep coming back to the same bowl. Again and again. This right here," he said, gesturing to the screen, "was bound to happen. Giving her that million or not."

"You don't know that," Tori snapped.

"Oh, but I do. Didn't you say that she ripped into your college fund?"

"Well, the family needed it," Tori protested.

Alicia laughed and it caused both of them to look her way. "James didn't need a damn thing until your mother lost her mind. What did she need twelve damn furs for? It's never that cold in Chicago. Three cars? Really?" Alicia said. "The woman has two-hundred pairs of shoes."

"So she's stylish," Tori protested weakly, then shook her head as if she knew how dumb that sounded.

"Be honest, Tori," Alicia said. "She's always been stupid when it comes to doing what it takes to keep an address and some food in her belly, but she certainly knows her way around the bedroom."

"Well, she isn't the only one," Tori taunted, smirking. "I mean, knowing their way around a bedroom."

"That might be true," Alicia shot back. "but I don't need my husband— or in your case, fiancé—to keep rescuing my ass from financial messes I made." Tori froze, but Alicia kept going. "How long did you think he'd keep doing that? He had to get tired sooner or later."

Alicia was more right than she knew. Dallas had grown tired of relatives and family friends who were continually hitting him up for cash that they thought fell from some orchard of money trees growing in his backyard.

Some of them kept their hands outstretched in spite of the fact that Dallas had given them each a one-time cash distribution when he came into his good fortune. The smarter ones—mostly the women—used it to partner up with Dallas and open up businesses that ranged from bakeries to boutiques and foundations to social agencies. Dallas had received more than a return on his initial investment from them, even expanding some of the businesses for a greater return.

The fellas, on the other hand, thought he was kidding about that one-time rule. They squandered theirs away, then put themselves in line for another hand-out.

So now there were two dinners during the holidays—the early one where Dallas could enjoy his time with his parents and sister, and a second one that Dallas rarely attended because he didn't want to insult everyone by leaving when someone pissed him off, which they frequently did.

And since Dallas kept his business to himself, there were no tabloid stories for his family to sell.

Somehow, Tori's mother didn't get that memo. She was all in for serving up anything that could turn a quick buck. The woman should have been a hooker instead of a wife—she would've made a mint with the way she liked to screw people over.

"Say what you want about what I did," Alicia said after a few moments. "You can't say anything about that fact that I bailed your parents out of a tight spot. And that didn't have anything to do with Dallas, that came from having basic common sense in knowing that a woman has to have four things to survive: An address, food, clothing, and a way to keep bringing in income.

"Your mama thinks it's a man, fancy clothes, and material things—and not exactly in that order. And I'm beginning to think you're a hell of a lot more like her than you think."

When the interview ended, Dallas clicked off the television and said, "Well, she might have done us a favor."

"Are you kidding me?" Tori shrieked, pointing to the screen. "How can this be good?"

"She's put our business all out there in the street," he said, looking over at Alicia. "So, now we don't have to hide in plain sight anymore."

"You're not going to—"

"Damn straight," he snapped. "You let her know that Alicia was living with us. She's on national television making up shit I haven't even thought of doing. Threesomes? Me taking turns with both of you every night." He slapped his palm against his forehead. "Woooooow, that's something I didn't even think to put on the table. I'll tell you one thing, she's got a wicked imagination, which is more than I can say for her daughter."

"Dallas …" Alicia chided in a softer tone, but he silenced her with a look.

"The days of Alicia having to be kept a secret are over," he said. "Thanks to you and your greedy mother, everything you didn't want people to know …"

Tori stormed from the room before he could finish.

Alicia parted her mouth to speak but Dallas held up his hand. "Not one word. Not a single word!"

She held up her hands in surrender as he brushed past her on the way to his loft.

Chapter 25

Dallas pulled his Buick Enclave into his parent's garage and maneuvered it between two other Buicks—a Regal and his mom's LaCrosse. All three were part of an endorsement deal his agent had brokered with General Motors a few years prior. Pops' Regal had never left its original place. A year ago, that was cause for concern. Now, Dallas tried not to give it too much thought.

He sat in his car for a moment, thinking about the grueling two weeks that had passed since Bernice took his private life public. Finally, he entered the house through the den, walked past a heavily decorated Christmas tree, a mountain of presents, the fireplace and an area filled with his high school trophies.

"Hey, Pops."

The nut brown man with graying hair and a stocky build snatched his focus from the football game and gave Dallas a sidelong glance. Pops didn't have a love for any sport, even though he watched a football game from time to time. Never basketball, though. Never basketball.

John Avery never set foot inside of a single court to watch Dallas play—not in grammar school, not in high school and not when he went pro. Pops had done his best to discourage Dallas from participating in sports altogether. And those were some of the biggest arguments in the Avery household. The more vicious ones between his parents were when his mother claimed that John was letting jealousy cloud his judgment.

With not so much as a hello, his father launched into, "Son, you know I'm real proud of you."

Something in John Avery's tone put Dallas on guard. He responded, "Thank you, sir."

John took a swig from his can of beer and shifted on the sofa. "And I'm proud that you put all that money into the church. We really needed those new buildings."

Dallas took a seat on the recliner across from his father. "Yes, sir."

"I'm really looking forward to that wedding with Tori," he ventured.

He realized his father was leading to a place he didn't want to visit. Dallas was hoping a trip to his parents' house would be a nice getaway from all the grief he had been getting inside and outside his own home ever since Bernice's interview.

"She's one fine young lady, that one," John said, nodding at his own observations. "All the times you brought her over here, that's what I thought. Smart. Beautiful. Will make a good wife. Give you babies. Lots of 'em. Give you a family. A real family," he said with a cautious glance at Dallas. "You understand what I'm saying?"

"Yes, sir."

John refocused on the television and Dallas did the same. They were just in time to see the Bears wide receiver miss a perfectly good pass and a clear shot to a touchdown.

"But, son ..."

Dallas braced himself for more of what he'd been hearing for the past two weeks. The public was carrying on so badly that Alicia couldn't leave his condo most of the time. Women's magazines were taking Tori to task over openly accepting Dallas' relationship with Alicia. As far as they were concerned, both women exemplified everything that was wrong with women today.

"Son, what you doing with that other woman?" John's lips twisted in a frown. "You bringing a whole lot of shame on this family. We're a good Christian family." John inched forward until he was on the edge of the sofa. "You carry the Avery name, boy. My family name—a name my grandfather gave himself, not some slave master's name. You hear me, son?"

Dallas put his anger in check and weighed his words carefully so he could be respectful.

"Pops," Dallas began the moment the game switched into half-time and he knew he would have his father's complete attention. "I ask your advice on a lot of things, but my intimate relationships are my business." John's expression went red hot, but Dallas held up his finger to keep him from interrupting. "Now, I never had nothing to stay about things that I saw around here that weren't quite right, so I expect the same courtesy."

John slid back and shifted his focus to the screen, a vein in his temple throbbing at a furious pace. "I've done some wrong things in my time, son, but my dirt wasn't all out there for the world to see." He took another hefty swig from the can. "I don't want you messing up your life the way I did."

Dallas nodded, but then said, "I'm just wondering why everybody's so concerned with what's going on in my bedroom."

"The women are family, son. Family!" he spat, his body shaking so vigorously that Dallas thought he would drop the beer. "That makes it even more wrong."

"So it's fine as long as the women aren't related?" Dallas said, his gaze locked on his father. "It's fine as long as the women don't know each other?"

"Even the Bible says having relations with two women from the same family is a sin."

Dallas didn't miss a beat. "It doesn't say that! The Bible does say that adultery is a sin. But that certainly doesn't stop people." He slid a sideways glance at his father, who grimaced at the not-so-subtle hint.

"Are you sure the older one's worth all this?" John asked, ignoring Dallas' plea to stay out of his business. "The young one is all you need to have a family."

Dallas stood and stretched before making it to the threshold. "I'm going in the kitchen to see Mama and get a plate before Quan eats it all."

John looked up at Dallas and mumbled, "I just want what's best for you."

Dallas walked back into the den and leaned down to give his father a hug. "I know, Pops."

He went into the dining room, where his sister, Carrie, was putting out the last of five plates for the people who would be seated at the table for the next hour. The immediate family ate together before guests came.

Dallas shot a frustrated glance at Quan, his redbone, wavy-haired, freckled faced brother-in-law. Quan tended to think that the fact that all the other family members weren't around gave him easy access to Dallas' wallet.

Carrie shot a mean look Dallas' way.

"What's kicking, chicken?" he asked, hoping the familiar childhood greeting would break the ice. His sister was a beautiful woman, with light brown skin, deep set eyes and a wide, generous mouth. She was smart, educated and could have her pick of men. Unfortunately, she scraped hers from the bottom of the barrel.

Carrie didn't bother to answer. Instead, she stormed from the dining room and went into the kitchen. Dallas looked down to the other end of the table, where Quan gave him a nod along with a shit-eating-grin that made Dallas bristle. "What's up?"

"I'm keeping it light, my brother." Quan extended his fist for a pound. Dallas totally ignored it. "Yes, Lawd, keeping it light," Quan repeated, putting his hands flat on the table. "But not like you, my man."

Dallas peered at him a moment, then decided he was better off not responding.

Quan crossed the distance and caught Dallas before he reached the kitchen. "Heard you've been tappin' a little extra ass man—and some old ass at that. I thought you ballers could have any kinda woman, and you go in for the AARP club."

Dallas ignored him and went straight into the kitchen toward the petite, brown-skinned woman who would break out into a smile on a moment's notice.

"Heeeeey, Mama," he crooned. "My stomach said it's not waiting for the dressing to get done. Let's get to the good stuff!"

She chuckled as he wrapped his arms around her and practically lifted her from the floor to plant a kiss on her cheek.

"Mmmm," she said, giving his back a hearty pat. "You always give the best hugs."

Dallas raised an eyebrow as he lowered her to the natural wood floor. "Sounds like you're trying to butter me up."

"Would I do that?" She nudged him with an elbow as she gave him a wide smile.

"Yep. Sounds like I'll be cleaning gutters before the weekend's over."

"I made your favorite."

He scanned the area until his eyes landed on a lattice crust dessert cooling on the blue granite counter.

"Peach cobbler!" He rubbed his hands together. "Yes, indeed. All right, I'll get to the gutters, clean the garage, attic, and—"

Anna Avery released a hearty belly laugh.

Carrie snatched up the platter of homemade dinner rolls, scampered out of the kitchen and back into the dining room. Dallas watched his sister from behind, wondering what he'd done that would make her give him the silent treatment. She couldn't be that mad over his personal life. Maybe Quan had screwed up again and she was just mad at the world.

Anna placed a hand on his face. "Son, are you all right? That's all I want to know."

"Yes, ma'am," he said, leaning down to give her another peck on the cheek. "I'll be fine. I promise."

She stroked a hand across his jaw line. "Does she—that other woman—does she make you happy?"

"Yes, ma'am. She truly does." He took in the concerned glint in her dark brown eyes. She'd probably been hearing all kinds of things about him and Alicia on the news and from gossiping family members.

Anna withdrew her hand, then switched off the stove. "So, you're not going to marry Tori?"

"Actually, it looks that way."

His mother froze for a moment, then focused on taking the pan of dressing from the oven. "And you're still going to keep seeing that woman?"

She looked over her shoulder at him. Dallas lowered his gaze. Anna nearly dropped the pan as she jerked upward. "Oh, Dallas!" she said in a pained tone. "How could you do that to Tori?"

Dallas leaned against the edge of the counter. "Mama, it's complicated." When his mother remained silent, he added, "Come on, Mama. Don't give me that look. This was the best solution we could come up with."

Anna pulled off the oven mitts and tossed them on the counter as she pondered his words. "So why doesn't that other woman—" She looked up at him. "Her aunt, right?"

Dallas nodded.

"Why doesn't she step away and just let you get on with your lives?"

Dallas looked his mother square in the eye. "I would rather lose Tori than Alicia."

By this point, Dallas really did think Tori would've thrown in the towel. But she was determined. And he wasn't making any progress with swaying Alicia on the marriage issue. His plan to get her to see that she was better suited for marrying him than Tori ever was—had failed. Big time.

Anna didn't move. "How on earth could something like this happen, Dallas?" she whispered.

He could hear the disappointment in her voice, and it saddened him.

"I went to meet Tori's family in Chicago and …" He swallowed hard, realizing he had to filter quite a few thoughts. "Things took on a life of their own. I connected with Alicia in a way that I never have with Tori." Seeing Anna's sour look, he continued. "And it's not like this was my idea. Tori was the one who suggested this whole open marriage thing. I wanted one woman—Alicia. But there are some benefits to having Tori around."

After several moments had passed, Anna nodded, but he could tell from the weary set of her shoulders that she still couldn't understand.

"Alicia," he began, pausing the moment she grimaced at hearing the name. He steadied her, trying to find the words to convey what he felt. "Mama, you know I'm no saint. I've been with plenty of women. But with her, it's something beautiful. I don't know how to describe it, but the thought of not having it, not having her, makes life seem ... dull."

Anna moved out of his reach and placed a top on the sweet potatoes. An expression crossed her features. She suddenly looked as if she understood. "She brings out your passion."

Dallas gave her a smile. "Sort of how I feel about basketball. How understanding it, knowing my position, and how I was supposed to play within the team, made us win most of the time." Her lips lifted in a small smile as he said, "I want to win in my personal life, too. Alicia makes me feel like I've already won five championship rings. Tori makes me feel like I'm still learning to play the game."

His mother turned back to him, her eyes the size of saucers. "You really love that woman!"

"Yes, ma'am."

"But you just met her!" Anna shook her head. There was a world of hurt in that small movement. "Why do I have children who can't have normal one-on-one relationships?"

"Hey! Don't lump me in with Carrie and Quan," he warned. "And the gossip rags are only giving half the story. I knew Alicia before Thanksgiving. I loved Alicia long before I ever met Tori."

Seconds ticked by, the scent of all that good food wafting in from both rooms made his stomach growl.

"Mama, sometimes I don't know what I'm doing. I love Alicia in one way. I love Tori in another. Both are important to me for totally different reasons," he said, hoping his mother would get the message that he was tired of justifying his personal life.

His mother was silent for so long, he thought she wasn't going to say anything else.

"Come here," she finally said, wrapping her arms around his midriff. "I might not agree with—no, let me be honest." Anna looked up at him. "I don't agree with it. But I love you, and I'll support you all the way down the line. You hear me?"

"Yes, ma'am." He kissed the short cap of dark silky curls that graced her angular face. "I love you, Mama."

"I know, number one son. And I love you more."

She went back to the stove, and he peered at her. Somehow he expected his mother, of all people, would want to put Dallas over her knee and whip his ass. He decided to ask her something he'd been wondering for years.

"Those years," he said, trying another approach to a delicate subject, "when Dad wasn't the best husband in the world ..."

She tried to make eye contact but failed. And Anna Avery was never one to shy away from the truth. If you had the balls to ask the question, she had the presence of mind to give the answer. "Your father wasn't doing dirt by himself. I'm just more discreet than your father ever was," she said without looking up from the pot of collard greens she was stirring.

Dallas blinked to clear his vision. When he could focus again, he watched his mother. Her hands were trembling; her chest was heaving in an effort to brace herself for whatever Dallas might rain down on her.

The question that had always lingered in the back of his mind now took center stage. Everyone in his family was his mother's and father's size—petite to average. Dallas towered over them by the time he was in high school. Many who knew the family whispered, "How could those two have spawned a virtual giant like him?" And there were no grandparents on either side who could explain his abnormal stature.

Dallas looked at his mother, waited for her to stop fidgeting with the parts of dinner that were already done. "Am I my father's son?" he asked point-blank.

"You are your mother's son," she countered smoothly, as though she had been expecting the question for a lifetime. "That's all that matters."

"John Avery is not my father," he said in a matter-of-fact tone that belied the pain settling in his heart. If he had known that kernel of truth growing up, it would have made things a lot easier.

After several moments had passed, Anna shook her head. "Do you love him any less?"

Dallas thought about all the lectures over the years about the Avery name and the integrity that was supposedly attached. John had given him his name, but now it made sense why there had been a disconnect between him and the man he affectionately called Pops.

"He'll always be my dad no matter what."

Dallas was poised to ask who his real father was when his mother placed a shaky hand on his arm and asked in a pained whisper, "Do you love me any less?"

He leaned in and pressed a kiss to her forehead, causing her to smile up at him. "Mama, you know the answer to that."

She didn't bother to hide her relief. This was not the time to call his mother into account for not only keeping a part of his life hidden, but coming clean about the fact that she wasn't the innocent, victimized wife he had always believed her to be. No wonder John Avery was always so bitter.

"Now, you get on to the table so I can put some meat on your bones," she said, shooing him away. "Both of those city women don't know how to feed you. You've got to be up to speed when your team meets up with that Kobe fella."

Dallas gave her another hug.

She nodded slowly, while keeping her eyes fixed on his, answering his unspoken question that they would have to talk about his real father at another time.

Chapter 26

3:03 P.M.

Dallas walked into the dining room, and Carrie glared at him. Seconds later, she was out of her seat, straightening the already perfectly positioned napkins. Things were pretty damn serious if Carrie was giving him her back to ponder.

"My man!" Quan bellowed on the heels of Carrie's second disappearance into the kitchen. "Been telling your sis she needs to loosen up a little. Roll like her big bro."

"So, that's why she's giving me the evil eye."

Quan shrugged, put his grubby hands on one of the dinner rolls and crammed it into his wide mouth. "I figure, hey, if you can do it, then I sure as hell can."

"Difference is, I can afford it," Dallas snapped, glaring at the redbone man. Quan glared back with beady eyes and a cat-that-ate-the-canary smile.

Dallas had never liked his brother-in-law but figured he had to have some redeeming qualities since Carrie had snuck off to Vegas to marry him. A few weeks later, she miscarried the baby that no one had been aware of. Now, she was stuck with a man who could barely hold on to a job since, as he put it, the white man was keeping him down. A crock of well-oiled bullshit if Dallas had his say, but since Carrie wouldn't hear of leaving Quan, Dallas held his tongue. He had bought her a house and nestled the money for it into a trust for her and whatever children she would eventually have. Quan wouldn't see a penny if they parted ways. Then, somehow Quan talked Carrie into going behind Dallas' back and trying to put his name on the deed anyway. To this day, Carrie didn't know that Dallas knew. He had attached a "forgivable loan" to the deed—one that would not need to be paid back as long as the house stayed in his sister's hands. So any activity on the house—taxes not being paid, insurance lapse, notices were sent to his accountant, who notified him.

"You can't afford the wife you already have, stud," Dallas said to Quan.

"Well, there's some truth in that," Carrie chimed in, glowering at her husband as she continued her journey toward the den.

Dallas was right after her. "I'll go get Pops."

"Naw, stay here. Make yourself comfortable or somethin'," Quan said. "I'll go get him. Need to see if the Bears are still getting their asses kicked on the field. I've got money on this game!"

Dallas slipped down in a seat, glowering at Quan's retreating back. Hell, where did he get off saying "make yourself comfortable" to the person who paid for the house and everything in it? That was a lot of damn nerve.

Carrie walked back in the dining room, saw that she and her brother were alone, and did a back step that would make any street dancer proud.

Dallas jumped out of his chair and gripped her arm. "So, you're going to keep acting this way all evening?"

"How could you do it?" she growled, snatching away as though his touch was leprous. "It's wrong!"

"When does what's going on in my private life have anything to do with you?"

There was ice in her eyes as she stared at him.

"I take care of everyone," he said, "and that includes Tori and Alicia, Mom and Pop, plus you and that shiftless ass husband." He clenched his jaw as he worked to regain his composure. "No one's complaining, including Tori and Alicia." Well, that wasn't exactly the whole truth, but Carrie didn't need to know that sad fact.

"Now my husband wants to try that nonsense you're doing, talking about some Divine Law that says men should have more than one wife." Carrie flat out punched him in the center of his chest.

Dallas looked her square in the eye. "Your husband's on some religious trip, but the Ausar Auset Society was never about doing things the way Quan's doing it—using women to make sure that he doesn't have to work an honest job. It's supposed to be a collective relationship—not a harem to take care of lazy bums," he snapped.

When she drew back to hit him again, Dallas grabbed her wrist and kept his focus on her dark brown eyes. "You need to admit it; your husband was an asshole from jump. Correction—he wasn't an asshole, he was a whole ass." He held up a hand to stave off her protest. "Now he's only using this religion thing to justify something that he's wanted to do all along—to have some extra in-house nookie. But that's definitely not what I'm doing."

"How is your situation different?" Carrie snarled, waggling a finger in his direction. "What makes you so special?"

"Because both of the women chose me," he answered smoothly. "This idea came from Tori, and Alicia agreed. I'm not hiding behind a belief system. But the real issue here is that I take damn good care of both of my women." Dallas raised an eyebrow. "Can your husband say the same?"

Anna and John froze at the doorway, their heads snapping to Quan, who stood directly behind them. Apparently they'd all heard the tail end of the conversation. John looked over his shoulder and gave Quan a forbidding look that the younger man chose to ignore.

"I can barely stand to look at you." Carrie hit Dallas again, harder this time. "I'm so pissed at you it's not even funny."

Dallas clasped a hand over her fist and leaned in to whisper. "Good! Stay mad for a real long time. Maybe now you and freckles won't tune your lips to ask me for anything else." Dallas pulled back and winked at her. "Take care, little sister."

He looked to his mother, who placed the bowl of potato salad on the table. "Mama, do you think I can get four plates to go?"

"You're not staying?" she asked, her panic-stricken expression tugging at his heart.

Dallas swept a gaze over his ticked-off sister, angry father, and the resident asshole. "I don't think it's a good idea right about now."

"Stay for me," she whispered, maneuvering around the table to stand in front of him. "I don't get to see you nearly enough."

"I know, Mama," he replied, embracing her. "Next time it'll be lunch, just me, you and some … banana pudding?"

She held onto him a moment longer before saying, "I'll get those plates."

"And I need to have a conversation with the whole peach cobbler," he suggested, giving her a smile that caused the corners of her lips to lift. "I'll do all the talking."

Quan spurred into action and blocked Dallas' path to the kitchen. "You're leaving? For real?"

"Most definitely," he replied, sidestepping him.

"But, you know," Quan flickered a gaze at Carrie before whispering to Dallas, "I need to holla at you for a minute, my man."

Dallas gave him a grin. "Ask your wife. She already has my answer."

Quan scowled in Carrie's direction, and she flipped Dallas the bird.

"Don't get mad at me," Dallas said, leaning in so only Quan and Carrie could hear. "I can't help that your husband has the toilet touch. Every scheme, every con always turns to shit." Then he said to Carrie, "But the best con he's got going is you, my sister."

"Pastor called," John said from his seat at the head of the table. "Wants to speak with you in his office sometime next week, son."

More like Pops had put a call into Pastor Braxton and asked him to have a heart-to-heart talk with Dallas. Well, that would be a very interesting conversation indeed.

Dallas was glad he'd followed his first mind and not brought Alicia along. It was safe for her to be home, since Tori had flown to Chicago to be with her parents, hoping that she'd be able to help them mend their relationship.

Dallas did a quick step into the kitchen and focused on making off with the goods and bringing in Christmas with Alicia.

Chapter 27

Alicia paced the length of her bedroom, fuming after a call from Tori. The girl had sunk to a whole new level of low. And Alicia should have seen it coming.

For the last few days, she'd thought that the three of them had hit a mellow stride that was almost symbiotic. Alicia took care of everything related to the house—preparing and cooking meals, maintaining the budget, their schedules, making sure everything was organized and trying like hell to keep Tori within Dallas' wedding budget. While all Tori had to do was focus on her studies. Dallas kept his concentration on his career—and the few hours a week he spent on managing his money. He started bringing her in on that, teaching her what he knew about the stock game. She was a fast learner. Soon she was giving him advice on things.

She also learned that preparing for a game took sometimes seven hours a day—practicing, lifting weights, doing sprints, watching team tapes, all to be ready for a mere forty-eight minutes of play. Alicia focused on nutrition and foods that would help boost his energy and performance, without filling him up with empty calories as he had been doing all along. He still had a healthy appetite, but he wasn't eating as much and as often.

Things had smoothed out to the point that even Alicia had thought an open marriage could actually work. Well, Tori had just poured salt and vinegar in the tank.

Alicia plopped down on the sofa, trying to put her focus on the Bears Game. She didn't fume as long as she thought she would because fifteen minutes later that familiar "click" of the door made her whirl around toward the entrance.

"Why didn't you tell me, Dallas?"

He froze, frowning at her thunderous expression. "Tell you what?"

"James. Bernice. They're together again. In my house. She pulled him out of a gambler's addiction treatment center to put him in marriage counseling."

Dallas sighed, and the sound sucked more of the good vibrations out of the room. "I didn't tell you, because I didn't want to ruin our holiday."

She stopped pacing long enough to glower at him. "The woman accused him of incest—not once, not twice—but every time she wants to piss him off. Then waltzes back into his life as if no damage was done. Unthinkable!"

"Let's not worry about what's going on with them," he said, lifting the plates in one hand and the pie in the other. "I brought dinner."

She frowned and turned her back to him. "I'm not hungry."

Dallas slid everything onto the dining room table and hurried over to her, curling her into his arms. "Baby, don't let them destroy our evening. It's Christmas."

"You should've told me instead of letting Tori do it," she said. "Trust me, she has an ulterior motive."

Dallas threw up his hands and walked away. "Come on, baby. Stop it with the conspiracy theories," he warned. "She just wants her parents to get back together. That's natural."

"I was the one who encouraged James to go to rehab and I paid good money for that," she said. "And anytime Tori spends time with her mother, it's not because she's been lovey dovey. She's trying to come up with a better game plan to get what she wants. Trust me."

Dallas didn't look at her for several spells. A roar went up on the television as the Bears pulled an upset at the last minute.

"It's about time," they said in unison. Then they looked at each other and smiled.

Alicia picked up the remote, switched off the set, crossed the distance between them and led him to the sofa. "Let me tell you who you're dealing with." When they were seated next to each other, she took his hands in hers. "Tori was a little on the plump side when she was in grammar school, and these girls wouldn't let her on the cheerleading team. She worked out, changed her diet, lost the weight and got a member of the squad to help her learn the routines."

"Nothing so sinister about that," Dallas said with a shrug. "That's determination."

Alicia pressed her hand to his chest. "No, listen. She used all of her allowance to hire a well-known professional cheerleader and made sure that the team saw the woman working with her. When they approached the lady, she said she wouldn't help them unless Tori was on the team."

Dallas shook his head. "That's being resourceful. Hell, I would've done something like that."

Alicia nodded and gave him a smile that unsettled him. "Tori made sure the woman studied the captains to find their physical weaknesses, then added parts to the routine that they couldn't perform. The rest of the girls put Tori on as co-captain. One by one, Tori picked off everyone at the top and had them kicked off the team, because now they were the ones who couldn't keep up."

She squeezed the bridge of her nose then looked deeply into Dallas' eyes. "It took a year for her to have her revenge, but she got it in spades. Tori became the only captain, and the other girls never made it on the cheerleading team again. And that's just one instance. That girl can be cold, calculating."

Alicia wrapped her arms about his neck. "Having me here had nothing to do with what the press might do. She was tallying up my strengths and weaknesses, so she could disqualify me when the time came. Smart move on her part, and I played right into her hands."

Dallas looked down at her, as his shoulders slumped.

"At some point, Dallas," she said, stroking a hand over his chest. "You're going to have to stop straddling the fence and actually pick a lawn. Any lawn. Whether it's green or has a few weeds in it."

He was silent for a long while.

"Dallas, you asked me what I wanted for Christmas," she said softly, her gaze focusing on him. "All I want is you. Just you." Alicia lowered her arms about his waist and laid her head against his chest. "You're seeing my refusal to marry you as some sort of slight. You shouldn't." She looked up at him. "I want to be with a man who's in my life because he wants to be, not because has to be."

Dallas took a breath, but she held up her hand to stop him.

"But this thing with Tori, and us ... it's not going to work. I understand all the reasons why you want it to work, but there's one thing you need to know. You don't have to have everything to be happy." She let the statement swirl around for a moment. "I don't have a family—not really. I stayed in a loveless marriage out of misguided loyalty and fear." She cupped his face in her hands, gently stroking a thumb across his cheek. "But right now, I'm the happiest I've ever been in my life; not because I've traveled to every place that I've ever wanted to, well except India," she added dryly, then smiled. "It's because I have you. A man who loves me, with all of my flaws, with all of my imperfections." She closed her eyes for a moment and when she opened them she said, "Loving you, has only taught me that I should love myself more. And that's been the hard part all these years—loving me. And, it's because I've learned to love myself that I know I can't do this anymore."

He pulled her against him. "I hear you, baby. I hear you." When they separated he said, "Can we make a deal?"

She gave him a long side-eye glance. "What?"

"Can you just give me 'til May?"

"May? I can't wait that long."

"I know it's a long time, baby, but here's the thing. I really think Tori will get over this by then, and if she doesn't then, I'll break it off. But by then, she'll be through her last semester, and she'll really be able to start a new life."

Alicia shook her head. "I can't live here with her ..."

"And you won't have to. I'm still working on that house."

The way he grinned made Alicia suspicious. "Have you found something?"

He shook his head. "But let's just say that I know you'll be smiling soon. So, is it a deal? 'Til May?"

"And I won't have to live here?"

"Not that much longer." He shook his head.

Alicia nodded. "All right. But right after ..."

Dallas released a visible breath of relief.

"Four plates," she said, wanting to change the subject. She smiled at the four plates stacked one on top of the other. "Two for me and two for you."

"No, no, no." He pulled himself away from her. "You've got it all wrong, baby. Three for me, and one for you."

She put her hands on her hips. "What?"

"You don't even eat that much!" he protested.

Alicia went to the table and lifted the foil and inhaled the sweet scent of peach cobbler. "Well, at least you brought enough dessert."

"I have to share?" he said in a playful whine.

Alicia gave him a startled look that made him laugh.

Chapter 28

MONDAY, DECEMBER 31—8:09 A.M.
FORT WORTH, TEXAS

Dallas pulled into the freshly paved lot of a set of red brick structures that stretched about a half mile down Christ Lane.

He crossed the grounds and went in through the side doors, passing the donors' wall and glass-encased trophies along the way.

A platinum blonde, breast-baring secretary sat behind the huge desk that served as a gateway to the pastor's domain. If she thought wearing that type of body-hugging dress was going to land her an even better position—like First Lady, for example—then she was in for a rude awakening. Reverend Braxton had been with his high school sweetheart for over forty years. The likelihood of him slipping off with a woman barely out of diapers was about the same as someone winning the lottery without purchasing a ticket.

"Hello, Helen," Dallas said.

She looked up from the set of manila folders in her hand and smiled.

"Oh, it's you," she said softly, blinking her eyes in a fashion she probably believed made her appear innocent. But he knew better. This woman had been on the manhunt trail with both guns blazing.

"You can go right in," Helen said, gesturing to the oak door behind her. "Reverend Braxton's expecting you."

Dallas tossed the water bottle in the trash and could feel her eyes on him as he walked past. When he turned and saw her checking out his rear end, her eyes widened. She dropped the folders, jerked her attention to the computer and stabbed at the keys.

"You wanted to see me?" Dallas asked, poking his head inside the door. He scanned the area to see if they were alone, and then fixed his gaze on an ebony man with kind eyes, a broad nose and a mouth framed by laugh lines created by age and a wonderful sense of humor. Reverend Braxton had lost a few pounds and was sporting a new haircut, trimmed up mustache and goatee, along with a savvy two-piece suit. Very GQ. Someone had stepped up their game.

"Thank you for coming, Dallas." Reverend Braxton gestured to one of the leather wing-backed chairs that flanked his desk. "Have a seat."

Dallas settled in and took a good look around. The office was decked out with a cedar wood desk, the scent of which permeated the entire office, plush maroon carpet, and cherry wood walls and shelving, which was home to a vast spiritual library. It was a drastic departure from that cracker box of an office at the previous place.

Reverend Braxton pointed the remote and switched off the flat screen television. "So, how're things?"

"Pretty good. How about you and Sister Braxton?"

"Fine," he answered softly.

The reverend's grimace made Dallas hone in on the man. Never was there a time when the mention of his wife failed to bring a smile to his face.

"And your mother?" Reverend Braxton continued.

"She's doing all right." Dallas narrowed his gaze on the man. Dots of perspiration were on his forehead. The only time that happened was when the man was full blown into the heat of a sermon, sliding across the pulpit, channeling his inner James Brown.

"And your father?"

Yes, his father. A very good question indeed. He almost wanted to answer, "Which one?" Dallas had lunch with his mother prior to setting foot in church today. She had told him about Paul Alexander and had even taken things one step further, slipping him a sheet with a phone number and address as she said, "Paul wants to meet you. Any time you're ready."

Dallas made the call from the church parking lot. Now he was all set to have his first visit with his biological father right after this meeting. He looked his pastor in the eye, "Reverend..." Dallas crossed one leg over the other, "no disrespect. I like small talk as much as the next guy, but why am I here?"

The pastor nodded, sighing as he did so. "I always liked you, Dallas. You're a straight shooter. Even on free throws," he said, grinning at his own pun.

Dallas gave him a patient half-smile.

Reverend Braxton moved from behind the desk and perched on the edge nearest Dallas. "The recent ..." he cleared his throat. "The recent exploits pertaining to your relationships are not becoming of a good Christian man, a man of faith, a man of honor. Fornication is a sin." Then, he nodded as though agreeing that he had made his point. "You need to bring Tori here to my office so I can marry you in a civil ceremony right away; then y'all can have that big fancy wedding later."

Dallas centered his thoughts and stayed silent, formulating his response.

Reverend Braxton cleared his throat again. "And that second woman, Dallas? You're going to have to stop having relations with her."

Dallas paused before answering, deciding on how ticked off he should be with Pops for calling the pastor about all of this. Funny how Pops could never find time to see the pastor when he was doing his own dirt.

"Are you going to poll every single member and ask them about their sex life?" Dallas asked.

The pastor's weathered brow furrowed as though he wasn't expecting

Dallas to lay down any type of defense. "No, but you're one of our most visible members, an ambassador for our church. A role model for our teens."

Dallas cocked his head. "And whose idea was that? You know, for me to be 'the most visible and a role model.'" He jutted his thumb toward his chest. "I never wanted to be anyone's role model. I play ball and invest in people, progress and pleasure—exactly in that order."

The reverend's lips twisted in a frown, and his eyes narrowed to slits.

"Pastor, I come to this church because I love the choir," Dallas began. Realizing that was probably insulting, he quickly added, "and your sermons—I come for those, too. But I didn't come with the intention of being the face of this church. I wanted to be like any other regular church member."

He scanned to the photos of the pastor shaking hands with various celebrities, accepting checks to benefit one of the many much-needed programs of the church. "I remember you giving me a half-hour-long 'to whom much is given, much is required' speech. So I shelled out the money for a whole new set of structures when we were in a building that could barely hold a hundred people."

"Well, money isn't the only thing I meant when I said 'much is required'."

Dallas fingered the crease of his black slacks. "You were the one who insisted on putting me out front, saying the publicity would be good for the church. And from what my father tells me, it helped you to land some additional grants for the after-school program, the etiquette classes, woodshop and the computer lab."

Dallas glanced out of the only window in the office, which overlooked the solarium terrace, where several senior citizens were seated at café rounds enjoying an afternoon game of Bid Whist.

"When I come through these doors, it's to give respect to the Man Upstairs. And I pay my tithes just like everyone else. So I'll give you my bottom line." Dallas looked back to the pastor, who had pulled out a well-worn Bible, gearing up for an unwanted round two. "If what I'm doing is hurting the church so much, I don't mind giving up all the rest of the responsibilities you've placed on me. Being a regular member has always been fine with me."

Reverend Braxton rubbed his hand over the leather cover of the gold leaf edition Bible. "You know what the Good Book says about fornication. It says that sex before marriage is a sin. That's why I counseled Tori that you both should wait for marriage before entering into a sexual union."

Dallas mulled over those words. "Well, if we're going to be honest, I think a good majority of your congregation is doing more listening than believing in that part of your sermons."

"We're not talking about everyone else," Reverend Braxton shot back.

"Here's the deal." Dallas uncrossed his legs and inched to the edge of his seat, "if you're going to call one of us on it, then call everyone in and let's do a group session. I'd be down for that."

Reverend Braxton's eyes flashed with frustration. "Dallas, your situation is a little different than people just having sex. You're getting into a polygamous relationship! If you're going to continue in that kind of relationship, Dallas, then I'll have to insist that you not come back to service until you're ready to follow the dictates of the Bible."

Dallas settled back in the chair and gave his pastor a long hard look.

"I realize you're upset—"

"Oh, I'm not upset," Dallas said, giving him a wicked smile that caused the older man to stiffen. "I'm about to call it the way I see it. I understand the position my lifestyle puts the church in, so I'll just catch you on television from here on out."

"I'm not saying you should leave the church altogether," Reverend Braxton said, getting to his feet. "I'm just saying—"

Dallas' smiled widened, and it caused the pastor to fall silent. "I'm not leaving the church, Reverend Braxton, I'm just leaving this church. I have a personal relationship with God, whether I set foot in a building or not. I've always known that."

Reverend Braxton put a hand on Dallas' shoulder. "Is she—I mean, that other woman—worth losing your soul's salvation?"

"I don't think you understand, Pastor. I thank God every day for sending her my way, for showing me what it's like to feel truly loved and wanted by a woman who wants me for me. For making me feel … alive."

Understanding dawned in the pastor's eyes, and he averted his gaze to the other hand still resting on the old Bible.

"Everyone—my family, the press, her family—is ripping into me for this. Right now I couldn't care less whether anyone approves."

"As your spiritual advisor," Reverend Braxton said after a long while, "I had to be certain that you know that fornication is a sin, adultery is a sin."

Dallas pictured the buxom secretary outside the office "A married man lusting after a woman other than his wife is a sin too, right?"

Reverend Braxton winced.

Dallas gave him a mild shrug. "What did the Bible say about casting the first stone? Or was it people in glasses houses?" His index finger circled the outside of his ear. "It tends to get all jumbled in my head sometimes." Dallas extended his hand. "Thank you for everything, pastor."

"You're taking this the wrong way," Pastor Braxton said, grasping Dallas' hand, which practically eclipsed his own.

"No, I'm not. Leave her or don't come back here."

The pastor's thick lips pulled into a straight line.

"I'm not giving her up anytime soon, so that leaves me outside of these doors."

Reverend Braxton put a tighter grip on Dallas' hand. "And your commitments?"

"Commitments?"

"To the church."

"Ah, money," Dallas said, nodding as realization dawned. "That's what it all comes down to. So, my presence is unwanted, but my presents are still welcome?"

"Don't misrepresent what I'm saying here," Reverend Braxton replied in a solemn tone. "There's a lot we can do with what you've been sending. We—"

"Unfortunately, my money goes where I go," he replied from the half-opened door. "You know I have several foundations and I'm sure God will add that to my account." Dallas gave him a slow, easy smile. "And since it's God who's actually keeping score, I'm sure He'll say that I'm giving back, even if I'm not giving it here."

Dallas walked from the office and felt the Reverend right behind him. When Dallas made it a few feet past the secretary's desk, he turned in time to see that the pastor's line of vision was right where he figured it would be—on the sexy assistant.

Chapter 29

Dallas parked outside his biological father's house and sat in the car for what seemed an eternity. He was more anxious than he should have been.

Suppose his father was yet another person who would be disappointed with the way he was living his life? A blog that went viral with scathing accounts of the exploits of black men who had hit sports stardom ranked Dallas somewhere among Tiger Woods, Kobe Bryant and Michael Vick. And that was one hell of a place to be.

From the driver's seat, where he sat contemplating his next move, Dallas witnessed something intensely beautiful. Two little brown-skinned girls were playing in their front yard, holding hands. No matter where they traveled on the well-manicured lawn, they continued holding on to one another. One went over to a spigot and turned on the water. She allowed the other girl to take a drink first, and then had her own drink. All the while, their hands remained clasped, as though separating for even a moment was not an option. Why couldn't relationships remain that innocent, that loving, that pure?

Alicia and Tori had been that close once, but because of him they were as far apart as Quan was from getting a real job.

A knock on the driver side window made Dallas jerk forward. When he looked to his left, a man towered over the car, blocking out the sun's rays. Dallas examined the face—a spitting image of his. He had always thought he favored his mother, but seeing Paul Alexander in the flesh, he wondered if his mother's genes had factored into the equation at all.

Dallas pulled the key from the ignition, exited the vehicle and leaned against the driver side door to shut it. A simple gold chain hung about Paul's neck, and a diamond glittered in his right earlobe. A gold bracelet and Movado watch encircled his wrist. His casual shirt and slacks covered a muscular athletic build that mirrored Dallas' completely.

Dallas inhaled the fresh air—well, what passed for fresh air in this part of the country. Paul's tri-level sky cottage had an unobstructed view of the water, and the marine smell was something that took getting used to.

Paul extended his hand, saying, "I thought you'd been sitting out here in your car long enough."

Dallas clasped it and held on for a few moments before letting his hands fall by his side. "I was deciding if I really wanted to meet you at all."

"Now you don't have to make that decision."

Dallas gave his father another once-over and said, "You look just like me."

"I think you've got it all wrong, young blood," Paul said with a toothy grin and a conspirator's wink. "You look like me."

"I guess that's about right," Dallas admitted with a laugh. Then, they were silent as an awkward 'what's next?' moment came between them. "I'm not one to mince words, so I'm going to ask straight up …why?"

Paul moved to take the space next to Dallas, keeping only a few inches between them as he followed Dallas' gaze to the two girls. "She made the choice to marry John while she was pregnant. I didn't want to complicate her life."

"But you knew you had a son?"

"Yes."

Dallas looked out to the river, trying to ignore the pain that stabbed his heart. "And you didn't think that I needed you?" He looked back toward the two girls, who had been joined by another. They were fighting now, each pulling at a single doll that hadn't been there a few minutes ago.

"You already had a father and a mother," Paul countered smoothly.

Dallas could feel the man's eyes on him, but he couldn't look his way.

"I had a dad," Dallas snapped, "but that didn't mean I didn't need you."

Paul gave him a bittersweet smile. "In hindsight, maybe … I should have … but I was young and probably angry that she choose stability over love."

Dallas took a minute to wrap his mind around that admission. "If you loved her, why didn't you come for her?"

"Son…" He paused, grimacing when Dallas' right eyebrow shot up. "Dallas," he amended. "She wanted something different than what I had to offer. I loved her enough to let her go."

Loved her enough to let her go. Dallas stared out at the brownish-grey water.

"I was about to go pro," Paul added. "But I injured my leg and failed to make the draft."

"Who'd you want to play for?"

"The Mavs. What other team is there?" He smiled, but it quickly faded. "It would have put me closer to home. And it didn't hurt that they were talking the right kind of deal."

Dallas looked toward Paul. "So what did you do?"

"After rehab, I finished college, got a degree, then started my own construction company. My father was a carpenter and bricklayer by trade. Now I specialize in building structures like this one." He gestured to the place behind them. "And multi-level complexes, offices and malls. I invested in other ventures that worked pretty well for me, but building things—that's my true love."

"Basketball was Plan B?"

Paul chuckled, probably at the incredulous sound in Dallas' voice. "Basketball is what I loved, but there were thousands of boys itching to get into the paint. They were just as good as I was. The chances of being chosen were slim."

"So mom wasn't down with that? You being into ball? I don't figure that. She's my biggest cheerleader."

"Anna was raised by a hard man," Paul answered. "Her father hated me on sight. Said I was sly, slick and wicked." Paul crossed his arms over his broad chest. "The only thing good about me back then was my love for Anna. I would do anything for her," he said in a low tone. "Her father chose John because he was a factory worker and church-going man like him."

Dallas gave his father a sidelong glance. His lips twitched in an effort not to form the question on his mind. Sly, slick and wicked.

"Oh, I wasn't a choir boy," Paul replied to the question in Dallas' eyes as he moved to rest against the car right in the space next to Dallas. "But I put my cards on the table, and Anna's father dealt her a hand from the bottom of the deck—either marry John or never speak to her family again." Paul shrugged. "We could've made it on our own, but I couldn't take that kind of a chance with a woman who didn't believe in me. She chose John—a man who would rather work a 9 to 5 than go for his dream of winning a Heisman Trophy."

Dallas' jaw went slack.

Paul slid a glance at Dallas and frowned. "Oh, you didn't know that?" he asked, scanning Dallas' expression. "John was the best running back in all of Marshall, Texas."

Dallas shook his head. "He never mentioned it. And I don't remember seeing any pictures of him either."

"If I had given up my dream just to keep a woman from marrying the man she really loved, I wouldn't talk about it either."

Dallas stiffened and glared at his father for a moment.

"If you want sugarcoating," Paul said in a dry tone, "the bakery's two miles up."

Dallas thought a few minutes and wondered if that was the main rift between him and Pops—jealousy over the fact that Dallas made it and got to keep his women. "I'm surprised you're telling me all of this."

"Well, your mother said to be honest. She feels you need to know before you make a mistake in your own life."

"So, she married my dad because her father wanted her to," Dallas said, realizing just how much it explained about his parents' unhappy marriage. "And look how that turned out," Dallas mumbled.

A vein throbbed at his father's jaw. "Is she ... is she happy?"

"She's married," Dallas replied dryly. "I'm beginning to believe the words 'happy' and 'married' don't live on the same block."

"I wouldn't know about that."

Paul's wistful tone made Dallas give him a hard look. "You never married?"

"The woman I loved was already taken. No one else measured up. Why make another woman's life miserable if you're going to constantly compare her to the real thing?" His smile widened with each passing second. "And your mother ... Anna was the real thing."

The look in Paul's eyes when he said Anna's name spoke to the fact that he was still in love with her. Dallas could not imagine a life without the woman he loved. This was confirmation that his insistence on marriage to Alicia wasn't all that important. Maybe this 'having children thing' was overrated, too. He certainly didn't want to be his father's age and singing a sad love song about how he had let love slip away.

Across the street, the girls had went into their separate houses. The tattered doll had been left on the lawn.

"Are we going to continue having this conversation outside, or are you coming in?"

Dallas lifted up off the car, and his father led the way into the sky cottage, which had a decidedly different architecture than the rest of the modest two-story homes on the tree-lined block. As Dallas followed him through a front patio and to an entryway with only a single wall and three sides of tinted glass, they went up a series of black metal stairs. The living room showcased low-backed furniture and a fireplace that extended the length of one wall, separating it from a stark white kitchen. Every angle of the house had a view of the river. And his father had designed it. Genius!

Dallas took a seat on a camel suede sofa opposite of Paul, who had taken up residence on a matching semi-circular chair. "When did you know you had a child?"

"Anna told me the moment she found out she was pregnant. I proposed a second time. She turned me down."

"Then you forgot all about me. End of story," Dallas said, unable to keep the bitterness out of his voice.

"Not exactly." Paul stood, beckoned to Dallas. "Come with me."

Chapter 30

"What the hell are you up to now?" Alicia demanded.

Tori placed the textbook in her hand onto the nightstand and looked at her aunt, "What are you whining about now?"

Alicia held up a document she printed a few minutes ago. "You created a profile for me on Junglelove.com?"

Tori shrugged. "Just thought you could use some incentive to find a man your own age. Maybe you think there's not enough chocolate out there." She batted her lashes innocently. "So I signed you up for a little vanilla. Ripe vanilla. What's wrong with that?"

"You left that mess up on Dallas' computer so he could see it!!"

"I did no such thing," she lied with a straight face. "I was just trying to give you some options, that's all."

Alicia was more than incensed. Dallas would have thought that she was the one trolling. He would hit the roof.

"Tori, I'm warning you, this foolishness has to end."

"What foolishness?" She slipped to the edge of the bed and walked over to her dresser. "You mean, where you finally wise up and realize that you can't be everything to him?" Tori ran her fingertips along the curve of a diamond necklace that Dallas had bought for her. "Or do you mean the foolishness about why you're still here."

Alicia raised an eyebrow and put a little distance between them, placing her back against the dresser as Tori pressed the necklace to her throat.

"You're just jealous," Tori taunted, turning to face the mirror. "First, I have the balls to become the doctor while you were only a nurse. Then, I manage to get the man that every woman wants. Now you're trying to take it away. All because you're so miserable, and you can't stand to see me happy."

Tori turned one way, then the other, admiring the piece in her reflection before she glowered at Alicia. "I was his friend long before those other bitches got their claws into him." She smiled, but it didn't quite reach her eyes. "And you notice that they're not around anymore." Tori looked over her shoulder at Alicia and gave her a dismissing once-over.

"Why're you staying, Tori?" Alicia asked. "Is it because you can't bear the thought of not having all of Dallas' money? Have you turned into your mother and it's all about the almighty dollar?"

Tori didn't back down. "I'm here because I belong here." She rubbed her stomach. "And I look forward to giving my husband a house full of babies. That's why I'm still here." She gave a wicked smile.

Alicia turned to leave, but thought she'd get in a parting shot. "I'm driving his car, living in his house, sleeping in his bed—all sanctioned by you. Evidently you've forgotten that part." Alicia looked at an imaginary watch on her wrist. "Look at the time. I'd better go check on those investments, balance the books, and get a nap in before our man comes home. He's expecting dinner."

The brush crashed against the door right after Alicia closed it.

❤ ❤ ❤

Dallas followed Paul through the house, past a white marble and silver kitchen, then into a den and study that flowed into a more masculine wood décor—a contrast to all the clear glass and metal throughout. They kept going until they reached a heavy oak door that blended with the wall and shelving. Paul punched in a password on the keypad and the door opened to reveal a vault area the size of a conference room.

Paul stepped in, but Dallas froze at the door. He tried to keep the shock from showing on his face. Pictures of him in every stage of life adorned the walls. Clippings of magazine articles and newspapers were encased in frames that hung from near the ceiling to a few inches before the walls met the floor.

"I guess you have to keep all that cash somewhere," Dallas quipped when he saw rows of drawers, some leading as far up as ten feet over his head.

"I keep my money where it's supposed to be." Paul gestured to the upper drawers. "Those are video recordings and news reels. Official NBA recordings of every game that you've played." He motioned to the bottom ones. "Here are the ones from college, the Olympics and All-Star games."

Dallas was transfixed. He struggled to rein in his emotions. The man who should have been in his life but wasn't, had been silently cheering him on. While the man who was in his life all those years never once applauded his accomplishments.

This man, who was only related to him by blood, had built what could be termed a shrine, a reminder of the son he was never allowed to have.

Paul clasped a hand to Dallas' back and shook him a little, smiling as he said, "I might've gone a little overboard, but hey ..."

Dallas laughed and at once felt something stir deep within his soul. His father was just like him. The man cherished one woman, loved her enough to let her move on with a man who obviously never wanted her, then became successful in whatever he chose to do with his life. No wonder John Avery was so bitter about how his life had turned out. He was angry about the choices he'd made. And he made sure everyone else paid for it.

"Who else has seen this?"

"Only me," Paul said in a solemn tone. "Well, and your mother when she comes to add something to it."

Dallas had the presence of mind not to question that, because it might lead to him knowing something else he wasn't ready to explore.

"She brought these fifteen minutes before you arrived. I haven't decided where I want them to go yet."

Dallas swept a gaze across the rest of his trophies that had been in his parents' den since forever. His most cherished were from playing on the McDonald's All-Star basketball team in high school and the gold medal from his stint with the United States Olympic team. "Why?"

Paul shrugged. "She said something about them needing to be in a safe place right now."

"A safe place?" That could only mean one thing. Reverend Braxton must have put in a call to his dad. And Pops was pretty damn mad right about now if he was threatening to toss out all signs of Dallas. But Dallas wasn't upset by that. He'd always respected Pops. He hadn't been a bad father, just indifferent. Now Dallas knew the man had done the best he could with what he had to work with.

"How did you get those?" Dallas asked, gesturing toward photos of him and Alicia that was a pure visual representation of their love. He focused in on one where her head was against his chest, her eyes closed, and her sensuously curved lips were lifted in a warm smile as Dallas whispered something in her ear. He remembered that day—the day he had taken her to the Jazz Festival and she finally let him do something as forward as place a friendship ring where he believed a wedding ring should be.

"I have my ear to the wire and put a standard feeler out in the Paparazzi pool. I bought them from a man looking to sell them to People Magazine. I made him an offer he couldn't refuse," Paul said, leaning down to scoop up the Olympic medal that was hanging on one of the trophies. "You don't mind if I keep these here? Or did you want to take them?" Something in his tone said he didn't want to part with a single one. And truthfully, even Dallas didn't have this much of his own press and accomplishments in his possession. He would keep the Olympic Medal, but these other new items belonged here.

"I'd like you to have them," Dallas said, keeping his hold on the medal, but gesturing to the rest of the items his mom had brought. "As long as I can come visit them sometime."

"Anytime," Paul said, beaming as though he had just been given the Holy Grail.

"But may I have this?" Dallas asked, gesturing to the picture of him and Alicia.

"Sure. Take anything you like."

Then, Dallas looked right next to it at an image of him and Tori sharing an ice cream cone at the Essence Music Festival the previous summer. Tori looked absolutely beautiful. He had tried to snag a bite, but she moved the cone out of the way. The chocolate ended up on the tip of her nose. In the picture, she was happy—something he hadn't seen from her in a long while. Something she couldn't be if she was holding onto a man with a limited amount of love for her.

"Why do you have so many of me and Alicia?"

"Truthfully?"

Dallas nodded.

"The images of you and Tori seemed staged." He pointed to a row of several shots. "See how much space there is between you?"

Dallas moved closer to examine them.

"It's like that in almost every one of them. But the ones of you and Alicia are more personal," Paul said. "I thought they might be the most damaging for you if they were published because they show something you aren't ready for the world to see."

Paul was right. Everything he felt for Alicia was evident in the fact that in each photo, he kept her within his arms or he lay at her breasts.

Dallas shifted to a small corner where Paul kept photos of Dallas' mother when she was much younger. In one, her arms were wrapped around Paul's middle, and she was looking up at him as though he was all that mattered in the world. His gaze flickered to the photo of Tori once again, and he realized that by trying to spare Tori, by giving her time to end things, he had hurt her most of all.

"Paul," Dallas began. He halted his movements and locked gazes with his father. "You're not angry that I don't call you Dad, right?"

"Wishful thinking, but I'm a realist," he answered on a mild shrug. "What's on your mind?"

"If you knew mom was unhappy, would you have …"

"No."

Dallas cocked his head. "No?"

"She made her choice, Dallas," Paul answered patiently. "She knew she could always come to me. Any time she decided to leave him, she had a home with me."

Dallas frowned, giving that some thought. "Are you sure she knew that?"

"How do you think I got all of these?" Paul gestured to the childhood photos from newborn to high school. "Every time she came, I reminded her of how much I still loved her. Every. Single. Time!"

Each report card and progress report was given as much reverence as all of his sports achievements. That was an awful lot of time shared between two people.

Then, Dallas honed in on a particular photo, which showed him receiving the Oatha Alexander scholarship, which gave him the opportunity to attend any college he wanted. "This scholarship … was it from you?"

"Named for my father," Paul beamed, then pointed to a picture of a balding man with dark brown skin, a wide smile, pearly white teeth and chiseled features that mirrored both son and grandson. "He never went to college. He had ten children to take care of. All of us have done him proud."

Dallas tore his gaze from the document. "Do I have any brothers or sisters?"

"No."

Dallas stared at his father. The man had lived his life unfulfilled—no marriage, no other children. "Do you realize how different your life would've been if you'd had the balls to go after what you wanted?"

"Even if I had, there was no guarantee that things would have turned out the way you're picturing it."

Dallas took several moments to absorb that kernel of truth.

Paul cocked a brow. "At one point, I did think of sending for you to come live with me."

"Why?"

"Your mother said that you and John were at each other's throats. She thought it was going to come to blows and you might end up in jail."

Well, that was about right. When Dallas hit his teens and became more successful at basketball, Pops did everything he could to sabotage Dallas' efforts to play, including tossing out letters from interested schools and not relaying information to Anna or Dallas when schools and scouts called. Pops strived to drum into his head that his focus should only be on church and education.

But it was the way John treated his mother, like she was a servant at times and invisible at others, that angered Dallas so much and caused him and his father to really bump heads. Only in recent years had his relationship with Pops mellowed to a grudging respect for the fact that Pops had provided a roof over his head, food and clothing.

His mother, for some strange reason, was sticking it out, so he thought there was something to be said for keeping to those vows. But at this stage, why didn't they both throw in the towel and find something better to do with their lives?

Dallas scanned the black and white images of his parents, trying to figure out where they were taken. "Mom's from Marshall, Texas. Where were you born?"

Paul grinned. "I'll give you one good guess."

The answer slammed into Dallas. His name was an obvious reminder to John that Anna's firstborn child was not his own but from the seed of a man from Dallas. It dawned on Dallas that even back when the new church was built, when Pops refused to let Dallas put his name on the building, Anna had begged him to name the church's sports building The Paul Alexander Sports Multiplex, saying that he was someone special to her. Then she asked the same for the foundation he started. Evidently, when Mom wanted to make a point, she drove the knife in pretty damn deep.

"So you never tried to see anyone else?"

Paul gave him a low, throaty chuckle. "Now, I didn't say that. Women are plentiful. Good women? Now that's another story."

Dallas looked down at the image of Alicia. "What do you think?"

Paul followed his gaze and said, "My honest opinion?"

Dallas nodded.

He held up the picture of Alicia, stroking a thumb across the image. "It's obvious that your heart is with Alicia." Then he pointed to the image of Tori walking out of the medical school, her brow furrowed with worry. "You're stringing Tori along, when you should end things. I think you like the idea of having both women, no matter that it's hurting both of them."

Dallas grimaced at the reproach he heard in his father's voice, but he was already beginning to respect the man on so many levels. "I thought by now Tori would've kicked up her heels and hit the pavement, but …" he shook his head, "she's hanging on better than Spider Man."

Paul nodded, keeping his focus on the woman he still loved. "Women do that when they feel that they've invested a lot of time in a man. They'll stay in abusive relationships. They'll stay in marriages that fizzle long before the fire even started …" He tore his gaze away from Anna's picture and leaned against the only open space on the wall. "Tori feels you already belong to her, and Alicia's just a nuisance. Evidently she doesn't understand what passion is all about."

"She's a virgin," Dallas said.

"Makes sense, but even before sex, there has to be something there." Paul examined the photographs on his right. "On the outside looking in,

Tori doesn't feel anywhere near what she should for a man she's going to be hitched to for the rest of her life." Paul looked at Dallas. "And if I can see it, then that's something you really need to think about." He put Tori's photo back in place and retrieved another. "With this one," he added, a spark of admiration in his eyes, "this Alicia feels something, but she's afraid. Probably because of the age thing. But from my opinion, what she feels is genuine. And that's something you need to think about, too."

Dallas nodded, extracting the picture from his father's hand.

"I could thank John for raising my only son," Paul said slowly. "But if I was ever close enough, I'd put my fist in his face. He married Anna out of spite, and that's never a reason to do something that important." Paul clasped a hand to Dallas' back and ushered him toward the door. "Enough about the past. Come on, let's put something in your stomach. Don't think I don't hear it growling."

Dallas snorted, and that caused Paul to chuckle.

"Your mother told me that you have one hell of an appetite."

"Mom exaggerates," Dallas said, following his father from the vault and into the dimly lit study.

"Anna says she had to have a cow in the backyard just to keep a few gallons of milk in the house."

"See, she ain't right for telling you that," Dallas grumbled. Then he admitted, "It was the neighbor's cow."

Paul roared with laughter, and Dallas couldn't help but join him.

Chapter 31

Alicia walked back into the kitchen, angered to find that all of her dinner preparations were missing. Dallas had specifically asked her to make him a simple dinner of his favorites. Tori was putting together a meal of her own, seemingly unaware that Dallas was not a fan of shrimp or half the ingredients she had spread out on the counter.

Tori glared at Alicia, practically daring her to say something. The Rap music blasting from the Bose system was a high indicator of Tori's current mood. Alicia could feel the storm brewing. She turned to walk out.

"Have you thought about what I said?" Tori asked in a deceptively sweet voice that held Alicia in place. She lowered the music so she could be heard. "One of the men I'm talking about setting you up on a date with is totally interested in you, and he's your age. Why can't you at least go out with him?"

"Because I don't need to," Alicia replied, giving her a fake smile. "I already have someone in my life."

Tori paused mid-slice, her tense posture looking like she was ready to pounce. "Let's be real, you have my man in your life," she snapped. "I did all the hard work, and you came along and reaped the benefits." She dropped the knife, snatched a paper towel from the holder and dried her hands. "Didn't you tell Dallas that you need a break from all this last week? Well, show him you're serious. See some other people!"

"That was a private conversation—in my bedroom."

"In my house," Tori countered.

"His house. His name is on the deed," Alicia shot back. "Let's talk about the real reason you're so pissed off. Your plan for bringing me here backfired."

"I don't know what you're talking about," Tori said, turning her attention back to her preparation.

"Why're you hanging on to him?" Alicia asked in a sad tone. "Dallas has clearly made a choice. It's not fair, but at some point reality has to rent out some of your brain space since it's obvious you've evicted common sense."

"If he didn't want me, I wouldn't still be in his life," Tori snarled.

Alicia stared at Tori, wondering how her niece could be so clueless.

"I'm not giving up on Dallas," Tori said, going back to the sink. "The old me is stepping in and taking over from now on. He wants me to cook. I'll cook. He wants me to fuck ... then I'll spread it wide and let him go deep." She looked up, as though mulling over a bright idea. "Isn't it normally the other way around? Men trade in for a younger model of the woman they married. Something must be truly mixed up in his head."

Alicia sighed, settling in to humor Tori for another round of bitching and moaning.

Tori snatched up the dish towel and dried off an area of counter space. "You really want to know why I'm sticking it out?"

Alicia didn't bother to answer—she knew how this would go. She could walk from room to room, but Tori was like a stalker. Even with the door closed it was hard to tune her out if she was trying to make a point.

"Do you know what it felt like when those people came to pull me out of class? They told me the tuition check bounced. Bounced! Like we were some low-life ghetto people! Who does that?" she yelled, then took a few seconds to rein in her emotions. "We had lost everything. Ev-er-y-thing! But Daddy didn't tell me because he didn't want me to worry." Tori let go of a bitter laugh and began cutting up more vegetables. "What did he think was going to happen when they didn't get their damn money? That my good looks were going to cover the balance?" Tori's eyes teared up to the point that Alicia feared she would chop off her fingers as she whacked away at the celery.

"All of a sudden we were poor. No house, no cars, nothing! I had to skip a semester because it was too late to get a grant or apply for student loans. Daddy had saved for years so that I wouldn't start my life out in debt," she said in a low tone. "I was so embarrassed."

Alicia yawned softly, but it seemed that Tori took no notice. Instead she put a low fire under the skillet to sauté the onions.

"Then, Dallas," Tori said, her voice breaking with the effort it took not to cry. "I didn't even tell him what had happened. One of my classmates was spreading my money problems around school." She looked up at Alicia. "I had no one. No one to talk to. And somehow, Dallas came in, and he made everything all right." The tears came and for a moment, Alicia's heart went out to her niece.

"You left me!" Tori screamed, pointing the knife at Alicia. "You left me for a whole damn year!"

Finally! The real source of the issue between them.

"What happened to family first?" The pain in Tori's voice was enough to make Alicia's heart constrict. "You didn't call. You didn't write," she sobbed. "While you were off cavorting in Africa and Spain and Tibet and wherever the hell else you went ... You left me ... you selfish bitch!" Alicia moved forward reaching out to touch Tori, but froze when her niece's expression hardened. "And when you finally come back, you take the one thing that matters to me. Because you needed some dick more than you loved me."

Tori turned her attention to meal prep and began hacking a knife into the Andouille sausage. Evidently, she forgot that Dallas had said he was removing pork from his diet, too. "Everything will be fine as long as you keep your word."

"Keep my word?" Alicia asked.

"You'll leave during the wedding ceremony," Tori replied, looking up from her latest victim. "You do remember that you promised to do that."

Alicia wanted to tell her that she never said that, but what would be the point? It was clear that Tori was never going away. So, she would have to do it. Since Dallas didn't want to make the decision, and Tori wouldn't make the decision, she would. This was a wrap!

"You know what, I'll oblige you," Alicia said. "Dallas won't be home for another few hours. I'll pack my things and be gone by the time he gets back."

Tori gave Alicia the first real smile of the evening. "Finally, you see things my way."

❤ ❤ ❤

Dallas walked into the corridor leading to the living room, the sound of DMX's "Y'all Gon' Make Me Lose My Mind Up In Here" hit him the moment he had stepped over the threshold. That was never a good sign. He felt the strange vibes emanating in the house, and kept moving until he reached the kitchen. Dallas was shocked to see Tori at the stove putting the finishing touches on what looked to be shrimp Creole—a dish he couldn't eat since he wasn't into scavengers. He had asked Alicia to prepare a steak, her garlic mashed potatoes, and whatever vegetable she'd like to throw in. Her bread pudding and Jack Daniels sauce was going to be the perfect end to the meal. So why was Tori in the kitchen instead of Alicia? And why was she slashing through a bell pepper as if it had done her wrong?

"Where's Alicia?" he asked.

Tori flinched, her eyes widened in shock, then she frowned. "In her room. She wanted to be alone."

Dallas placed the two packages he carried onto the counter, then whirled around and aimed in the direction of the guest bedroom.

"Damn it, Dallas! Give her some space!" Tori screamed, causing him to freeze in his tracks.

He turned around and walked back to Tori. "What's wrong with you?"

"Nothing," she said in a softer tone. She slid the pieces of tomato into a pot. "I just want us to have a nice, quiet dinner. Alone. That's all." She cornered the counter and was in front of him in a matter of seconds. "I've been thinking; it's New Year's Eve, time for new beginnings. Let's forget about the wedding. Let's hit Vegas and get married," she whispered, gripping the edge of his Polo shirt. "Or we can have a private ceremony right here and just do the damn thing."

It hurt his heart that Tori was still thinking about marriage when he'd promised Alicia that he was going to end this.

"That's not a good idea," he said.

"Why not?"

Dallas didn't feel the need to go into all of it again. The bottom line— he loved Alicia, not Tori. No other explanations were necessary.

"I need to go to Alicia." He pivoted to get out of the kitchen.

"Wait!" she yelled and he froze at the threshold. "Now might not be the best time to talk with her."

Dallas bore down on Tori. "What the hell did you do?"

"I didn't do anything," she protested, but her ears had reddened and she shrank back.

He shook his head. Something was definitely wrong and he hurried toward Alicia's bedroom to repair whatever damage Tori had caused.

Chapter 32

New Year's Eve
7:32 P.M.

Dallas stood in the doorway in shock, watching Alicia gently place her things into the suitcase. She looked at the clock beside her bed and hurried back to the closet.

"You were going to leave without saying anything," he whispered. "Again."

She jumped, and the garment in her hands slipped to the floor. "I would have said something eventually." Alicia bent down to pick up the clothing, then waggled a finger in his direction. "I am not spending another night in this place."

"Come here," he said softly.

"No! No more of that," she snapped, waving him off. "I overstayed my welcome the day I walked through the door, and you know it." She reached for her toiletries and situated them in compartments along the sides of her case. "And I'm telling you, that I'm this close," she snapped her fingers, "to slapping the cow-walking bullshit of that girl."

Dallas had never seen Alicia this angry. And as much as he wanted to talk with her, she needed to let off every bit of steam she had.

"There's a lot you don't know about me." Alicia folded a floral blouse neatly and placed it on the top layer of garments. "And I try, I really try to do right."

"I know," he said in a patient tone.

"Dallas, I love you. And, I thought I could wait until after the holidays for you to do this, but I'm beginning to feel like ..." She grimaced, pausing to come up with the words. When she looked up at him, his heart constricted. "I don't feel safe. I don't feel safe outside of my home with the paparazzi and the public. And, I don't even feel safe in my own home. I never know when Tori is going to go off." She struggled to hold back her tears. "Dallas ... loving you is costing me more than I'm willing to pay."

Dallas cracked his neck right then left, forcing his mouth to stay closed behind that hurtful admission.

"You can't be with me all the time. And I'll tell you one thing." She stopped and looked at him, her eyes flashing with something he couldn't name. "When people push me too far, I might do something that they won't live to regret."

Dallas thought back to when she told him how she had done some damage to a couple of family members who were trying to hurt her. He had no misconceptions that she couldn't back up her threat, especially since she had been only too ready to give Bernice a "Sicilian smile" last year.

"Living in this house, Dallas ... in her space ... it's opened up a place in me that wants to fight, and I don't mean fight fair either. I don't like what I'm becoming. And if I stay here, she's going to say the wrong thing, and I'm going to do the wrong thing, and we'll all end up someplace we don't want to be."

Dallas went to her, curling her into his arms. "I have someplace else you can go."

"I'm going home," she answered simply. "Back to Chicago and I'm kicking Bernice out of my house for the last time. James forgave her for Tori's sake. But I'm not married to her, so I don't have to be that considerate. She has to go, and James can go with her."

Dallas shrugged, nodding as if her talk of leaving him didn't matter. "Okay, I'll go with you, but if you don't mind, we'll need to make one little stop on the way," he said. "Besides, you're in no condition to drive."

Her head whipped to him. "How do you figure that?"

Dallas gestured to the empty bottle of Johnnie Walker Blue Label and the glass sitting right next to it on the nightstand. "I didn't know you drank like that."

One hand slid up on her hip as she glared at him. "I don't. But with what that little heifer's been putting me through? You'd better be glad I haven't polished off the whole damn bottle!"

Dallas extracted his hand from her waist, dove into her bed and lifted the bottle. A tiny bit of liquid pooled on one side. He raised an eyebrow.

"Well, corners count," she shot back, grimacing. "I didn't finish the whole thing." She looked at the painting she had done of him. He smiled at the fact that her gaze lingered where the towel covered his prized package.

"That house on Pernell that you loved so much?" he said, and she turned to look at him. "I put a solid offer on it today." He opened his hand. "I paid a little more so we could live there while the paperwork's getting done."

Alicia looked down at the keys sitting in the center of his palm, then smiled up at him. "When did you get these?"

"Four hours ago." Dallas grinned. "And then I went shopping. A Heavenly Bed is waiting in your master bedroom and a Sleep Number bed is in the guest room. Your choice on where we spend tonight. We'll bring in the New Year the right way."

Alicia practically did a little skip and snatched the keys. "Now you're talking my language!"

He grabbed her suitcase and began to wheel it out of the room. She paused in the hallway, then ran back into the room and reached up to take her painting from the wall.

Dallas returned to the room. "Baby, we can get this next time."

"I don't want anything to happen to it. I can always get new clothes, but I can't get another—"

"Me?" Dallas cut in. "Don't you forget it." He winked and shifted so he could lift the artwork from its anchors.

"I meant painting," she added, giving him a playful punch. "You're so arrogant."

"But you love me, right?"

She looked up at him and whispered, "Yes, I love you."

Dallas leaned down and puckered up. Alicia smiled before she obliged him with a kiss.

He shifted the canvas in his hands. "You might have to do another one of these. This time, I'll take your advice and … drop the towel."

"You are so, so bad."

Dallas grinned, taking that as a compliment, but then he was serious again as he told her, "I'm ending things with Tori for good tonight. I decided I just can't wait until May."

"What made you decide to do it now?" she asked softly.

"My father. My real father. After talking to him, I realize that I want a real life, a traditional relationship. What I've been doing is not right and not good for Tori ... or for you." He set the painting down on the bed and signaled for her to come closer, which she did. "Tori's marrying me out of some misguided sense of ownership. And I was marrying her out of obligation. I shouldn't function like that."

"You're exactly right. That's why I was going to leave. I was done playing her game." Alicia cupped his face in her hands. "You say you're done with her, then be done for real. Or you'll need to be finished with me. You can't keep playing both ends against the middle."

Dallas extended his hand to her, and she clasped it. "I hear you, baby. Let's go break in our new house."

Chapter 33

Dallas walked into the Maverick's locker room and was greeted with a round of curious looks and stares. He trekked across the royal blue carpet, ignoring his teammates until he reached his personal space. Each locker was decked out with a stereo system, a 20-inch flat screen television, a bench and private storage and shelving space.

The team robe hung on a hook in his locker, and he undressed and slipped into it so that he could take a few minutes to meditate before going into warm up.

Dallas had been blessed to have two years with the Lakers, where he racked up a couple of championship rings. But the egos on that team made playing the game a chore. The moment he had a chance to trade out, he signed with the fourth wealthiest team in the franchise, but it was also one that had a lot to prove. His plan was to accumulate as much wealth as quickly as possible, then retire at thirty-two, while his body was still in prime condition, so he could spend the rest of his life doing whatever he wanted, including going back to get his degree and raising a family.

Dallas closed his eyes and took a long, slow breath. Clearing his mind, he envisioned the members of the opposing team. He let a few details from the pre-game prep tapes that Coach Kimbrough showed them earlier in the day run through his memory.

"Yo, man, what's up?"

Dallas opened his eyes to find that Steve, the team's forward, was leaning on the partition that separated their spaces.

"Nothing much," he answered and closed his eyes.

"So um, how was your weekend, big man?" Steve asked with a mild chuckle.

Dallas opened his eyes again to find Roberts standing next to Steve and grinning widely before he cut a look across the locker room at a freckled-faced Collins, who had an eyebrow raised.

Dallas answered, "All right."

"You sure man? Nothing … special?" he asked, and his tone was taunting.

Dallas looked around. Most of the team was tuned in to the conversation in his corner of the locker room. Even pigeon-toed McGushin had stepped out of the wet room and stood at the door. Only the whirring sounds of the hot tub broke the eerie silence.

Dallas peered at the men standing before him. "Man, what's your major malfunction? You know what I like to do before a game."

"So you're really sticking it to that …" Morrison swept a sly glance across the rest of the team, "hot piece of cougar ass?"

Guffaws and peals of laughter echoed, and Dallas felt his temperature spike. He remained silent to get his anger in check. Locker room disputes could carry them into a losing game. Dallas closed his eyes and tried to tune them out.

"Come on, tell us man," Roberts said, waving a glossy magazine page in front of Dallas' eyes. It was a side-by-side image of Tori and Alicia. "What's it like rocking two fine ass women like that?"

"Shit, the Vet looks better than the young chick," Morrison said, laughing.

"And they live in the same house?" Smith shook his pointy head. "Damn, even I couldn't be that bold."

"Peep this, they're in the same family, too!" Thompson chuckled.

"You doing them at the same time, man?" Morrison teased. "Now that's some kinky shit right there."

"Listen up," Dallas growled, standing so he was toe-to-toe with Morrison. "My personal life is not up for discussion with anybody. That's my private business."

Eaves held up the latest edition of Us Weekly. "Not anymore. Lots of good stuff here, man," he said, flipping the pages, then reaching underneath the mag he held and passing a copy of Maxim to Roberts. "That right there must've been an inside job."

Actually, Dallas had thought the same thing when he saw it this morning before practice. The article his teammates were referring to had information that was so personal, so invasive, it could only have come from someone close to them. Alicia would never have done it. His family didn't know his business like that, so it couldn't have been them either. But Tori and Bernice were another matter altogether.

❤ ❤ ❤

Dallas had arrived at the condo on New Year's Day after he moved Alicia in to her new home the night before. He paused at the end of the hallway when he noticed several black garbage bags lining the wall. Though a sinking feeling hit him, he bypassed them on the way to the door.

He shifted his gear into his left arm, inserted his key, but the lock wouldn't turn. He took the key out, tried it again, same results. It didn't take him longer than a moment to figure it out—she had changed the locks.

Dallas banged on the door. "Tori!"

He pounded until she answered, though she didn't bother to open the door. "Dallas, her things are outside. Take them with you."

"Tori, this is childish."

"Childish?" she yelled. "I'm being childish."

"Okay, I get it," he conceded and put his back against the wall. "You're pissed, but I need to get my things."

"You should've thought about that when you strolled your ass out of here last night," she said. "You were only thinking of her and thinking of yourself. You expect me to be fair about things, when you haven't been fair to me."

Dallas lay his forehead against the door, taking a few moments to think his way around this. "Tori, all this time, I thought you'd actually see the truth since you weren't hearing it." He moved a few inches from the door. "So last night, I made the final choice and it's as fair as I can make it—I want to be with Alicia. And since you wouldn't walk away, I had to be the one to do it. This is what I should've done in the beginning."

"Fine. Then go," she snapped.

"My clothes are in there. My gear is in there. My championship rings are in there. I'm not leaving without my shit."

She was silent. Then a few minutes later her footsteps echoed across the hardwood floor as she moved away from the door.

And because he didn't want law enforcement involved, he had to let it ride until she cooled down.

This morning on his way to training he tuned in to the Tom Joyner Morning Show and Tori was on the air, saying that their relationship wasn't over, just on a "rough patch."

Dallas totally agreed with Alicia … what brand of Crazy Kool-Aid were they serving up at the hospital? Because this woman had went in for seconds and thirds!

Dallas turned his back to his nosy teammates and dismissed them in a gesture that said he was done with the conversation. "Gotta get my head in the game."

"Yeah, 'specially since the other one's been playing a whole different game lately," Roberts taunted, elbowing Smith, who raised his hand for a high five.

"I know, right?" Smith laughed.

Dallas tuned out the heckling galloping his way—most of them from teammates who had committed their own publicly-aired mistakes. He showered, toweled off and slipped on his uniform.

Back on his personal bench space, he closed his eyes and focused on stilling his anger. Maybe he should have hired a lawyer and paid Bernice off because this new wave of negative publicity that hit the stands over the last two weeks concerned him. Women were taking shots at him on talk shows like The View and The Talk, and they were ripping into him on his social network page. Several had even asked if he wanted a third or fourth wife to go along with the two women he already had!

For the last three days since Alicia had moved in, she hadn't left the house. She'd had groceries delivered and she'd even stopped watching television since even the reputable news stations had started covering the story. Even as secluded as she tried to remain, she was bound to find out about these new articles. Now, Dallas wondered if their relationship could handle this kind of pressure.

"Hey, kid. Surf's up," Coach Kimbrough said in his signature raspy voice, snapping Dallas out of his reverie.

Dallas lifted his head and looked into a pair of eyes that were the deep grey-blue of a cloudy sky. "Yeah. I know."

"You're catching it right now," Coach Kimbrough said, giving him a reassuring pat on the shoulder. "But you can't let this throw you off your game."

"Right." Dallas walked out to the corridor, making his way to the floor for warm-up. They were playing against the team who'd hit dead last in the standings. The game should net them an easy win.

Two-and-a half-hours later, only three points had separated the teams at the win. The cameras hit Dallas the moment he sank the game-winning shot and his team converged for a victory huddle. Congratulating his tormentors wasn't something Dallas was feeling right now. The fact that a team so out of contention could nearly best them was a sign that Dallas wasn't on point. And that was dangerous if they were going to make it anywhere near the playoffs. The team only had one NBA championship win in the years since it originated. Dallas wanted to change all that.

To please the public, Dallas obliged Smith with a pound, tapping his fist to the man's tattooed one. Then, he followed Collins and Eaves off the floor.

He was approached by Kim Askew, a brunette with a red suit that hugged what she probably thought were curves, but her body had more straight lines than a train track. "Tough game," she said, giving him a pearly white smile. "But it seems like you have the winning formula on and," she winked at the camera, "off the court."

Dallas saw where this leading and quickly came back with, "My comments will be all about the game."

"Come on, now," she teased, looking into the camera at the viewers. "We—"

Dallas felt her staring after him as he headed toward the tunnel.

"He can talk until the cows come home when it's all about the game," she taunted. "But when the pressure's on somewhere else, he retreats to his—"

Dallas turned back and bore down on her. "As many times as I've given you first crack on an exclusive, and this is how you play me?"

She gestured in a slicing motion for the camera to stop rolling as Dallas stormed toward the locker rooms and walked straight into a scowling Coach Kimbrough. "This is not a good time," Dallas grumbled.

"Okay," Coach said with a pointed look at the reporter, then back to Dallas as he fell in step trying to match Dallas' long strides. "Keep it together. Do not show your anger. Do you hear me?"

Dallas nodded.

"Let your teammates handle the after-game interviews for a while.

'No comment' should be your mantra from here on out."

Dallas glowered angrily.

"Do you understand me?"

"Yes, sir," Dallas growled.

Everyone filed into the locker room shooting icy looks at Dallas. The ivory skinned man gestured for Dallas to follow him to his office.

They entered a spacious spot, which utilized the team's colors in its decor. Bookcases filled with binders and playbooks were angled in two corners. An executive desk with a brown leather chair awaited the coach's burly frame. Images that summed up his years of coaching were lined along one wall. All but one showed the team in varying poses of defeat after a particularly hard loss kept them out of the playoffs. Only one frame showed the team cheering in a victory after clinching the only championship they had under their belts.

"What you do behind closed doors is your business," Coach Kimbrough said, "but what you do on the court is mine."

Dallas took a seat across from the older man, settling in for the dressing down he expected, and probably deserved.

"Have your agent and publicist get on top of things."

"I don't even know how Katie or Liz can spin this."

Coach nodded, but the frown didn't leave his round face. "You know the franchise is run by those Evangelical types who don't take to that type of thing—at least not openly."

"Nothing I've done goes against the moral turpitude clause in my contract."

"True, but you know the good ol' boys."

Dallas lifted the snow globe from the coach's desk and twirled it in his hands, contemplating the reference to the white men who ran the franchise. They were the ones to make the rules governing a majority Black roster.

"The minute you cross the line," Coach added, "and someone takes you to task about sleeping with two women who are related, you're going to encounter some problems in other areas."

Coach removed his property from Dallas' hand and put it back in place, peering at him a moment. "So it's true. Two women? An aunt and her niece?"

Dallas slowly nodded. "Yeah. But it's not what they're making it out to be. I had individual relationships with each woman before I even knew they were related. Nothing kinky. And I'm not even with Tori anymore. But people are having a hard time understanding that I'm actually in love with Alicia, the older one." He rubbed his head. "At one time she even felt that I should marry Tori and have a family just to avoid the drama."

Coach leaned in a little. "What do you feel?"

"I feel that I don't want to look back on my life and realize that I let the best thing that ever happened to me slip through my fingers. I want to marry her, but she feels like she's too old to do the marriage thing all over."

"Personally, I understand it." Coach glanced at his wedding band. "My wife is five years older than me."

Dallas smirked.

"It's still older," Coach protested with a grin. "I understand that it's about the experience."

"No, it's not just that," Dallas countered.

"Well, whatever it is, you have to be willing to go the distance with this. It'll shut everyone up."

Dallas remained silent. Going the distance had always been his thing.

"Give it some time, Dallas. Maybe she'll change her mind. You just have to become as important to her as she is to you."

"That's the plan." Dallas stood and extended a hand to his mentor. It felt good to talk to someone and not be judged. "Thanks, Coach."

❤ ❤ ❤

Dallas entered the locker room, which was void of its normal bantering and laughter. In the background, the sounds of the sports commentator picking apart the elements of the game they had just played punctuated their sad performance. He took a seat on his bench and leaned his head against the wall.

"Wonderboy's lost a bit of his shine," Morrison taunted.

"Hey, lay off him," Smith said. "Unlike some people, he's not a glory hog. All of us play a part in this."

Morrison slammed a towel into the hamper. "You act like we lost!"

"It wasn't a solid win," Dallas said, scanning his teammates, who all became silent.

"I'll take any kind of win we can get," Morrison countered.

"And that's the problem," Dallas shot back, getting to his feet. "I've always, always played a team game. Always gave everyone a chance to step up. That's how the Bulls won their championships, even with a different set of players on the roster each time. They weren't just better individual players, they were better team players."

"So don't lay this at his feet," Steve added, maneuvering until he stood next to Dallas. "We all played a part. And if we don't get it in gear, we'll be getting our asses served like some schoolyard bitches."

"I couldn't have said it better myself," Coach Kimbrough said, coming to stand in the center of the room. "You know how ruthless the media can be. You know that." He looked to Eaves. "And Dallas supported you publicly during those alimony and paternity suits. Dallas gave you the best possible advice: man up and take responsibility when the DNA test proved those kids were yours."

His gaze flickered to Collins. "And when you got pulled over for DUI, who was the first to get the media to stop pestering the team for a statement against you? And you," he gestured to Michaels. "When your dumb ass got busted for having a roach in the car, who was the first one to speak to the press on your behalf?"

Michaels grimaced and turned back to his area.

"Now Dallas needs our support," Coach said, sweeping a blue-eyed gaze across the players in the room. "What happens between consenting adults is legal. So show a little respect. He might have been off his game tonight, but then again, so were you. Practice tomorrow is at twelve. Denver is playing one hell of an offensive game these days."

"Sorry, man," Morrison mumbled to Dallas, extending his hand.

"No worries, man." Dallas gave him a shoulder-to-shoulder touch then looked to Coach Kimbrough. "Thanks again, Coach."

"No thanks needed. I came to tell you that your agent's waiting in my office."

Dallas heard the chorus of groans from his teammates as they went back to their respective places. A surprise visit from an agent was never a good thing.

Chapter 34

8:28 P.M.

Dallas showered and dressed in a suit—a requirement for all players if they didn't want to be fined or suspended for violating the NBA's dress code. He entered the office where Katie Walsh, and Coach Kimbrough were having a friendly chat. Today, Katie wore a black power suit draped over her slender frame, and had on a pair of owl-rimmed glasses that were a compliment to her angular face and bright blue eyes.

Katie had presented him with a handmade business card way back when they were in grammar school. An avid basketball and baseball fan, she had said, "I'm going to get a degree in business and learn all about sports management. I'll be your agent when you become an NBA star."

She was the only one besides his mother who even remotely believed he would ever amount to anything in the sport. Even his high school coach had told him that he should focus on his grades if he wanted to get into college. Pops had said the same thing. But it only made Dallas want it all the more. He had practiced day in and day out. Even when he wasn't playing, he spent his time imagining himself shooting, dribbling, and playing in a championship game. He kept his focus on the finish line, and he was offered both academic and basketball scholarships. He took the academic one so he wouldn't be under the restrictions that other sports players found themselves. When his mother became ill, he went on to the NBA.

Katie had showed up at his parent's house during the celebration, laid down an autograph she'd gotten from him in grammar school and said, "I'm ready to take that job I asked for." Though more experienced agents came his way, he chose Katie. "Do your thing, woman," he told her. And she was still doing her thing.

"What's up, Katie?" Dallas asked from the door.

She swiveled her chair in his direction and smiled. "Well, there's good news and then there's something else."

He leaned against the door. "Is it something I need to take in on a full stomach?"

"Dallas, you'll take everything on a full stomach," she teased with an even wider smile. "How about Eddie V's?"

"You want to meet there?"

She shook her head, her auburn curls following with every movement. "My husband dropped me off. I wanted to ride in your new Buick."

"Didn't you get one?" he protested, nodding a goodbye to the coach as he held the door for Katie to pass him.

"Yes, but yours has all the bells and whistles."

Dallas raised an eyebrow. "You're full of shit, you know that, right?"

Katie roared with laughter.

Twenty minutes later, they walked into the restaurant. A few fans approached him for autographs before the host situated them at a private table toward the rear. As he was settling into his seat, Dallas asked, "Were you checking out my ass again?"

"I'm a woman before I'm your agent," she countered. "I can appreciate a pair of cheeks that looks as good as yours."

Dallas gave her a playful tap on her shoulder. "Ooooooh, I'm telling your mother."

Katie smiled at him over the rim of her wineglass. "Hell, even she says you have the best cheeks on the team."

As they feasted on appetizers, he said, "Give it to me straight, Kate."

"I swear you think you're a poet, don't you?"

He playfully popped his collar. "I have been known to spit a verse or two."

"Yes, indeed." She released a drained sigh, a sure sign that she had more on her mind than just his writing skills. "Dallas, your endorsement deals are coming under fire. McDonald's is a little shaky right now."

"What the hell?" he asked around a mouthful of bruschetta. "I haven't committed any felonies."

"Shelley called me to see what is going on with you. He said the higher ups are having an issue."

"And?"

"Women—and that's the audience McDonald's is going for in their new healthy focus commercials—are really up in arms about all of this."

"But I've ended the relationship with Tori," Dallas protested. "And I wasn't sleeping with her anyway!"

"It would have been better for your public image if you had ended it with Alicia."

"That's bullshit!" he snapped. "They're going to terminate because of that?"

"They might try. They're a family-friendly company."

Dallas leaned back in his chair. "What about the others?"

"Since you just signed with Nike a few days ago, and they shelled out forty million dollars, they might not cause as much of a stir. The publicity alone is keeping them in the public eye. Men are their target. Some of them, except those hard asses in the Bible belt, are feeling that whole threesome thing."

"It wasn't a threesome!" he protested with a groan.

Katie flushed bright red. "Yeah, okay."

"Katie!"

"Hold up," she said, pulling something out of her attaché case. "They didn't kick Tiger Woods to the curb, so you'll be fine." She flipped to a page of handwritten notes. "Sprite hasn't said anything, and we're getting close to off-season. The execs can let the current commercials play out. By the time the season starts again, this will all be forgotten."

Dallas leaned back in the seat and waited.

"Spalding's not shaking you down either." She flipped to another page. "Avery autographed basketballs are going for three hundred dollars on eBay. People who collect sports memorabilia are keeping your name at the top of the list."

"Okay, so it sounds like we might lose McDonald's," he said. "You could've told me that over the phone."

Katie looked away and focused on the group of women who had their undivided attention on Dallas. "I wanted to talk to you about something else," she said. "Your lifestyle—" Katie held up a hand when he opened his mouth. "Your former lifestyle," she corrected, "might pose a problem when we try to negotiate new contracts or when it's time to renew old ones. I have a feeling that with everything going on lately, endorsement contracts will get a little tighter on moral clauses. And that would mean that they'll close their wallets and walk away from any kind of relationship that offends the moral majority."

Dallas pushed his plate to the side. He realized exactly what she was saying. The league became more concerned about its image since it had taken a beating following the Pacers-Pistons brawl, infamously named the Malice in the Palace. That game, which started between two players after a blatant foul, spilled into the stands, and eventually led to a few fan and player arrests, as well as nine players being suspended without pay for a total of 146 games and the loss of about eleven million dollars.

"So what I'm saying is keep your dick in your pants when it comes to other women—or be a hell of a lot more discreet than your boys Tiger and Kobe." She made headway on her meal. "If you stay with Alicia, you should marry her to get everyone off your back."

"You don't think I've tried?" he snapped.

Katie frowned and gave him a questioning look.

"To get Alicia to marry me."

"Seriously?"

"She says she's done her time." Dallas growled. "She sees being married as a prison sentence."

"Aw, Dallas!" Katie said, placing her hand on top of his. "Is that what she said?"

"No, but that's what she meant." And that still hurt like hell.

He had shown Alicia, time and again, how much she meant to him. She loved the new house; she was even reluctant to furnish it because she enjoyed the beauty of their sparse surroundings.

"Dallas, you know I've been with you since day one ..." Katie said, halting when the waitress brought dessert.

He nodded, bracing himself and hoping she didn't say something that hit too close to home. The waitress smiled and left the table then Katie continued with, "What is it about this particular woman that's so special?"

Dallas pushed back at her solemn tone and expression. "When I look at her, I don't see age or anything like that. I see class. I see style. I see a woman who has a calm and peace about her that I want for myself. It was easy to get to the love part because we're not wading through a river of game-playing bullshit like I had to do with other women. Even Tori. Alicia doesn't want me for my money. Not at all."

Katie placed her spoon on the edge of her dish and dabbed a napkin at the corners of her lips. "Speaking of Tori, I received a release from her publicist today. They need you to sign it so that she can appear on some reality show about exes, wives and girlfriends of ballers."

Dallas tossed his napkin on the table. "See? This is the Tori that I thought I knew, but I didn't. Tori never loved me, Katie. It was all about the prestige, all about the money."

Katie gave him a sympathetic smile.

He shook his head. "I'm not signing those releases, and I don't care about the contracts. If I lose them, I lose them." He put up a finger, silencing Katie's protest. "Alicia's going to be in my life, so fuck 'em."

Katie shook her head. "You realize that this could significantly lessen the amount of money we're able to rake in. And you're the one who wants to retire early."

He thought about that for a hot minute. "But you know what? Being with Alicia has shown me that there's more to life than cold hard cash."

A few years ago, Dallas would have never believed he would say such a thing. He had thought money was the beginning and end of things. But recently, he had learned that money had paled in comparison to being able to have the things that money couldn't buy.

He looked at Katie. "Are you happy?"

"I married the love of my life." She smiled at him, showing nothing but pearly whites. "Of course I'm happy."

"So, if you had to choose between having your husband or having the money, the cars, the houses, what would you do?"

She didn't even blink. "I can make money anytime, but I don't think I'd ever find anyone as wonderful as Tony."

Dallas lifted his glass. "There you go." His cell rang. "Give me a minute." He stood and walked away from the table. "Mama, what's up?"

"Can you come over?"

He heard the distress in her tone. "Mama, what's wrong?"

"We'll talk about it when you get here." She disconnected the call.

Dallas nearly trotted back to his table. He signaled their waitress, saying, "Check, please!"

Chapter 35

Dallas walked into his parents' house, and an eerie feeling hit him. "What's up, Pops?"

The man ground his teeth, but he didn't speak as he kept his gaze on the blank television screen.

Dallas froze and repeated, "What's up, Pops?"

An angry glare was as much as Pops would give him. Dallas peered at the man, wanted to question the sudden animosity, but continued his journey from the den to the living room where his mother sat on the sofa, her bags packed, her purse slung over her shoulder.

The only thing that came to mind was, *Oh, shit. Things just got real.*

"What happened, mom?"

She slowly raised her head so her red eyes met his. "It's time for me to leave," she explained in a voice that was low and gravelly. "It's time for me to leave this place before he does something stupid and I kill him."

"Did he put his hands on you?" Dallas asked, lowering to his knees.

Her lips pulled into a frown. "He might be dumb, but he's not stupid."

Only then could Dallas relax.

"Whoremongers!" Pops shouted from the door, causing Dallas to get to his feet.

"Man, who're you talking to?" Dallas demanded, squaring his shoulders.

"Both of you," John said with an angry gesture toward them.

"I'm confused." Dallas looked from Pops to Anna. "What's with all the name calling?"

"She told me. She told me everything," he yelled, shaking a fist at them. "How she's been getting money all these years from him to take care of you. That what I've done was never enough. Even you," he spat, with a disdainful look at Dallas, "putting that money in her treatment when she was sick."

"So you wanted her to die?" Dallas asked.

Pops shifted his stance so that he was closer to Dallas. "She wouldn't have died if it was God's will for her to live."

"Then maybe it was God's will that I did everything I could to make sure my mother's still alive. I would've done the same for you, so get off it!"

"And that's what angers him," Anna said softly from her spot on the sofa. "He hasn't done anything to deserve your love, and yet, you still give him respect." She looked to her husband. "Quality comes through, John, no matter how much you try to shape it into something else. It's in the genes." Then she smiled a smile that sent a shiver of alarm through Dallas. "As beautiful and book smart as Carrie is, you can't find an ounce of common sense in her. That must come from your side of the family."

Pops moved forward, his hands balled into fists. Dallas quickly blocked his father's path. "Hey! Don't lose your mind up in here."

Seconds ticked by while his parents did nothing more than glare at each other.

"So what happened?" Dallas asked his mother when Pops gained whatever little hold he had on his senses. "Why are you packed?"

"Tell him, John," she taunted. "You were man enough to say it to me. Now that he's here, be man enough to say it to his face."

Pops looked up at Dallas. "If you continue to do things that disrespect the Avery name, then you're not welcome in this house."

"So why are you packed?" he asked his mother again.

"Any place my son isn't welcome," she said, "is a place where I'm not welcome either."

Dallas shook his head and gestured to his father. "I mean, why isn't he packed? You shouldn't have to leave."

"I want to leave this place and him behind. I need a fresh start," she said, with a haughty lift of her chin.

"Sounds like a plan." Dallas turned to his father. "I still love you as my Pops, and I'm feeling you on this whole name thing. Maybe you'd be a lot less angry if I wasn't an Avery anymore. I'll get with my lawyer and get rid of it as quickly as I can."

"She doesn't have to leave," John grumbled, turning to make his way from the room. "I'll go."

"It's what my mother wants to do. The least I can do is make sure you have a roof over your head. If you're too pissed to take that, then that's on you."

Dallas extended his hand to his mother. "Come on, Mama."

Chapter 36

Dallas stood at the door of the condo he and Alicia had vacated weeks ago, eyeing the man that his former fiancée had thought worthy of her time. Max Eaton, a man who had been Dallas' nemesis since college days, was as arrogant as they came. He had been cut from the Houston Rockets after underperforming for a couple of seasons. Max was the only player on Katie's list of potential clients that Dallas asked her to turn down. Thankfully, his agent was loyal to a fault.

When Alicia and Dallas had walked in fifteen minutes ago, the man's nearly seven-foot-frame was stretched all out on the sofa as if he owned the joint. He grinned at Dallas, giving him a head nod as a greeting. Before Dallas could get a word out, Alicia yanked him toward the back of the house, so he could get his things.

Tori bypassed both of them and began serving dinner, but was halted by Max's angry voice.

"Hey, I don't want none of that fancy shit," Max quipped, his golden skin peppered with sweat. "Make me something else."

"Right away," Tori answered and hopped off to do his bidding.

"And bring me something to drink," he yelled.

Seconds later, she appeared with a bottle of Dos Equis. The man didn't even bother to say 'thank you.' He simply snatched it from her hands and peered at it as though it had offended him somehow.

"This bottle looks dirty. Wipe it off," Max demanded. Tori used the tip of her blouse to do as he commanded.

"When did slavery kick in?" Dallas grumbled, which caused Alicia to give him a swift kick to shut him up. Dallas was only too ready to snatch the cornrows off the man's odd-shaped head. This was still his house!

Dallas shook off Alicia's hands, and stood there, watching as Max continued commanding Tori as if she were mere chattel instead of an educated woman.

Hanging on to his self-control required every ounce of willpower he could muster. After one too many nudges from Alicia, Dallas finally had enough and went toward the guest bedroom. He felt like going postal when he found a few of Max's clothes in his closet next to his jerseys and suits.

This fool—who didn't have two dollars to fold in his wallet, and was in one hell of a bitter divorce battle—had practically moved into a house where Dallas was still footing the bill. "Tori has lost her fucking mind!" he growled and made a mental note to put an end to this as quickly as possible. How the hell had she gotten tangled up with his low class ass in the first place?

Dallas snatched up the majority of his things, then returned to the dining room just in time to see Max stroke a hand across Tori's buttocks. She froze and practically shivered with disgust. Dallas gave Max an icy glare. Only then did the man release his hold on Tori's rear end.

"So how're things over in the Mav's camp?" Max asked, chewing like a cow with a mouthful of cud. "You think y'all gonna hit the playoffs this year?"

Dallas gave him a comedic lift of his left eyebrow. "We've got a better chance than some other teams I could name." Dallas grinned so

Max would know exactly which team he meant. Max's former team had the same championship history as Dallas' team.

"Hey," Max said to Tori, "get me some hot sauce."

"Was that a request?" Dallas snapped. Alicia placed her hand on his arm to calm him down.

"Aw, man," Max said, blowing him off with a flick of his scarred hand. "She knows what I mean. A woman should be taking care of her man's needs. She wasn't with that program at first," then his lips lifted in a clever smile, "but she's learning fast."

"Is that what you want?" Dallas asked Tori. "To be his servant?"

Tori couldn't even look at him. Instead, she quickly glanced at Max, who gave her a hard look before she scampered into the kitchen.

She was afraid of him! When did Tori become someone's mouse?

"Is that your Maserati parked in my space?" Dallas asked.

"My brother," Max said with a shrug. "What's your problem? You don't live here anymore, right? Perfect time for a real man to step in." Max chuckled, cramming in another spoonful. "Can't believe you fell for that 'let's wait for marriage' shit for a whole year. That's definitely not how I roll." He gave another head nod, and it caused Dallas to bristle. "Time's up tonight and I'm tapping that ass."

Alicia glared at Tori, who had just returned and sat a small bottle in front of Max. She avoided her aunt's gaze, along with everyone else's.

Max leaned back in Dallas' designer dining room chair, rocking in it as though it had wheels as he said, "Bring some of that Royal, too, babe."

A stunning silence descended in the room. A vein throbbed at Dallas' temple, and he closed his eyes against the anger building inside. Tori's hand was trembling when she returned to the table with Dallas' celebratory bottle of Chivas Regal Royal Salute. The fifty-year-old blended scotch was in a blue flagon that cost nearly ten grand and was only one of ten bottles that made its way into the United States. Dallas was waiting to break it out when the Mavs won another championship.

Dallas swiped the bottle before Max could break the seal. "My man, I think it's time for you to leave." His tone was so low and deadly, it caused Alicia and Tori to stiffen. "You can reapply for your position as Tori's man when you learn how to treat a woman." Dallas said, keeping a solid hold on the flagon. "You act like you were raised in a cave somewhere."

"Man, you must be smoking something," Max said, smacking his lips around a mouthful of food. "This woman sho' can cook."

"I'm going to say it one last time," Dallas growled. It was all he could do not to sprint toward the man, especially with Alicia's grip on his arm. "You need to make a hasty exit. Now!"

"What's your problem?" Max asked, with a sly grin. "Oh yeah," he snapped his thick fingers. "You think she still wants your ass." He shook his head, chuckled and then shrugged. "It's all good, brother man. I'ma take real good care of her. Trying to make a nigga wait for marriage and shit. That's where you went wrong, stud. You have to break them in early. Bitches gotta know their place."

Tori went crimson. Alicia's mouth fell open. Dallas was around the table snatching Max from his seat in the time it took to draw a single breath.

"Man, get the hell up off me," Max yelped, struggling to get out of Dallas' grasp. Dallas had the man pinned to the floor and in a chokehold within seconds.

"I said get the fuck out of my house!" Dallas boomed.

Max tried to grab at Dallas' shirt.

"Dallas, stop!" Alicia shrieked, trying to reach between the two men and almost tumbling to the ground when they rolled her way. "You're going to kill him!"

Dallas released Max. Tori lowered her gaze to the floor.

"I need to holla at you for a moment," Max said to Tori, while rubbing his neck.

"The only 'holla' you'll be doing tonight is from your own address," Dallas snarled. "Get the fuck out!"

"You didn't tell him what's up?" Max yelled at Tori while scrambling to get up from the floor. "I live up in this joint now."

Dallas flexed, and Max grabbed his leather jacket, then beat a hasty retreat to the door without even looking back. When he slammed the door behind him, Dallas focused on Tori. "Is that what you're about now? Some low-life thug?"

"He isn't a thug," she whispered, covering an arm that was beginning to show signs of bruising.

A new wave of concern washed through him. "I know more about him than you ever will," Dallas said, barely hanging on to his temper. "You wouldn't let me come get my shit, but you let him put his shit next to my clothes? And he's drinking my liquor, too? My best liquor? Tori you have lost your fucking mind if you thought that was going to fly."

"He doesn't normally act like that," she said so softly, they could barely hear her. "It was worse tonight."

"So this is how you're rolling now?" Dallas said to her. "Is this what you really want?"

Tori looked at Alicia for a minute before tears welled in her eyes. "I want things to go back to the way they were. But since you don't want me, then I have to move on. Max is it." Tori folded her arms over her bosom. "So, I'm dropping out of school on Monday. He wants me to be a housewife, to focus on taking care of him. Just like Alicia does for you." She squared her shoulders. "And he wants to have sex before we get married. We all know I learned my lesson on that one."

"How did you even meet him," Dallas demanded.

"At a coffee shop not too far from the hospital," she answered in a low tone.

Something about those words didn't ring true, but Dallas was too angry to pull the real answer out of her.

"Tori, you really need to think about what you're doing," Alicia finally piped in, moving closer to her niece, who finally looked her way. "Max is not the answer, sweetheart."

Sadness flashed in Tori's eyes. "I invited you here so I could apologize to you for the way I treated both of you." She then looked at Dallas. "I wanted you to see that I've gotten over my broken heart. Max and I will work things out. And that's all I'm going to say about it." She turned her back to them; her shoulders lowered as though she felt defeated.

Seconds ticked by before Dallas said, "Alicia, take the car and go on home. I need to talk some sense into Tori."

Alicia stared at Tori, then looked at Dallas, who only took his eyes off Tori for a few seconds.

"Dallas, I don't get a good feeling about this," Alicia said.

"Now is not the time," he said, and his tone caused Alicia to flinch. "Tori's about to make the biggest mistake of her life. And as her friend, as a man who once loved her, I have to clue her in on some things about Max Eaton."

Alicia glared openly at him. "Dallas, I'm going to say this one thing— I'm not going through this back and forth thing again."

"Alicia, go home," he snapped at her, but kept his focus on Tori.

Alicia snatched up her purse from the floor, and was at the front door in a matter of seconds. She turned in time to see Tori look over her shoulder at her, and the small smile that was on her lips and in her eyes let Alicia know that her suspicions had been right. She'd been playing that "little miss in need of a rescue" character to the hilt.

Turning back to Dallas, Alicia said, "I'm going."

His eyes were softer now when he looked at her. "Thank you. I just want to talk to Tori."

"I understand," Alicia said.

"Would you mind taking a couple of my binders with you?" he asked. "They're up in the loft."

The moment he took off, Tori stood straight, shedding her look of helplessness, and she smiled.

"He'll be home a little later, Auntie," Tori said in a low, husky voice that was unusual for her. "Actually, much, much later. Endgame, Auntie. Endgame."

Alicia saw the gutsy determination in her niece's eyes and smiled. "Tori, I choose my battles wisely," Alicia whispered back. "And this is one you might win tonight, but when you think victory is yours, life will snatch it away—especially when you're coming from a dark place. And this," she circled her finger in the air, "is going to come back and bite you in the ass."

"Oh, don't be bitter, Auntie," Tori said sweetly, removing a piece of imaginary lint from Alicia's dress. "I've always known Dallas loved me. Now, I'm about to see exactly how much. I know Dallas better than he knows himself. Why do you think I chose Max in the first place?"

"Little girl, you don't know who you're playing with."

"Sure I do." Tori gave her a winning smile. "No one's ever told me the truth, but you practically raised me at some point—at least that's what I think."

Alicia gave her a pointed look and said, "But there's a lot about me you don't know. And I'm hoping you don't ever have to find out."

Tori's smile wavered a little.

Alicia winked before she swept from the condo. She couldn't shake the feeling that her life was about to change for the worst.

❤ ❤ ❤

5:57 A.M.

Dallas had fallen asleep. How, he had no idea, since the last thing he remembered was sitting on the sofa trying to talk some sense into Tori and intercepting every one of Max's angry calls. She'd fixed him a drink … and well, he didn't remember much after that. Now, here he was, on the sofa, while she lay in his arms. He was startled, but he knew he hadn't slept with her. Still, he felt guilty when he looked over at the clock and saw it was almost six in the morning.

It had been a long and stressful night. Trying to talk sense into Tori when she got it in her mind to do something was like pulling a freight train with two rows of dentures. At least he had extracted a promise that she would immediately end things with Max. Dallas would introduce her to someone he hoped would be as good to her as he had been. She deserved at least that.

The sun was making a dash for the horizon when Dallas extracted himself from under a sleeping Tori. He hurried from the condo to make it home to Alicia. He walked into the home on Pernell Lane and continued to the living room. With the flick of a button, panels expanded from a hidden place in the wall to block the outside world from looking in. At night, those panels were always drawn, and it concerned him that this time they were not.

He continued his journey into the kitchen, which was a blend of silver fixtures and shelving to accent the white Formica cabinets. It was a showcase kitchen and the perfect place to prepare the type of cuisine that Alicia favored.

When he didn't find her there or in the bedroom, he went to the rear of the house to the sunken pool, only to find the cool aqua waters as devoid of her body as the untouched bed had been.

The bathroom, done in white Carrara marble, had a large circular window within a wall of heavy frosted glass. She was not soaking in the tub, and Dallas froze at the threshold as reality stabbed him in the heart.

He didn't have to do a second sweep of the house to confirm what he already suspected. "I'm not going through this back and forth thing again," is what she had said when he forced her to leave Tori's house. Alicia had kept her word.

There was one more frightening thing that spoke to her state of mind. She had left her painting of him on their bedroom wall.

Chapter 37

If he had just minded his business, if he hadn't gotten angry seeing Tori with Max, if he hadn't sent Alicia home alone, Alicia would still be where she belonged—in her rightful place: in his heart, his home, and in his bed.

But he had lost her, and now, nothing mattered.

It had been three days since she'd disappeared and he'd hardly left their bedroom. Either he was sleeping in the bed that he didn't get too many nights to share with her, or he was walking around, trying to remember their moments together, trying to capture her scent. The phone rang, but he didn't answer. It was either his mother, maybe his father, definitely his coach. But he didn't care about the outside world. All he could think about was that he'd lost the love of his life—twice. He'd already been given his second chance at love. He knew he'd never have that chance again.

So when he began to feel weak from dehydration and not even remembering when he'd had his last meal, he didn't care that he no longer had the energy to move around. That was good. All he wanted to do was sleep.

But then, he was awakened, and her arms were around him. He couldn't believe it, she had come back to him.

"Alicia," he called, barely able to open his eyes. "You're here."

"Dallas!"

He must have been delirious. Because though the arms that held him felt like Alicia, it was Tori's voice he heard. And then, his eyes opened fully. And it was Tori.

He groaned. "Go away." He tried to push her, but he didn't have the strength.

"Dallas," she whispered. "You can't do this. You can't give up. She's not worth it."

"Go away," he mumbled. "I don't want to see nobody."

"I'm not going anywhere," she said. "Not until I know you're all right."

"Go away!" he roared.

"No!" she roared right back. "I'm going to stay right here until either you get over her or grow a pair and get your ass back to work, whatever you can manage to do first."

She gripped the edges of his robe and shook him until he was able to look at her. "This melodramatic bullshit right here…that's for punks. And the Dallas Avery I know, ain't no punk."

She released him and as he fell back on the bed, she grabbed a suitcase from the closet, tossed a couple of his sweat suits inside, packed his toothbrush and a few other necessities, then stood looking down at him on the bed.

He rolled onto his back and peeked at her through half-open eyelids. "What the hell are you doing? How did you even get in here?"

"I broke in through your bathroom window. I've been calling you and your mother called me."

Dallas moaned. "Look, just go home. I'm fine."

"You're not fine. But you will be as soon as you get out of here. This is her domain," she said, moving back to his dresser. She pulled a pair of boxers from the top drawer and tossed them to him. Then, inside his closet she pulled a shirt and pants off of hangers. "I don't do my best work in someone else's territory. Get dressed. You're coming home with me."

He growled, but Tori just stood there with her arms folded, and after a few minutes of the stare-standoff, Dallas gave in. Silently he dressed and then, he let Tori lead him outside to her car.

"We have to call someone to fix that bathroom window," she said as she maneuvered her car away from the home. "And we definitely need you to get an alarm. I couldn't believe it when I broke all that glass and an alarm didn't go off."

Dallas said nothing.

He hardly talked for the next two days, though he was slowly coming back to life as Tori met his needs. He listened to his messages, the dozens that had been left by his mom (sounding desperate) and his coach (sounding pissed.) Even his agent had blown up his phone, leaving message after message, reminding him of the fines for each of the games he missed.

He didn't return any calls, and he hardly talked to Tori. But she was there for him, just like she'd been there for him during those desperate times with his mother.

A week after Tori found him, he returned to work, showing up for training, then practice, determined to put all of his energy into the game. He didn't offer any excuses, because he didn't have any to give. Coach nodded, gestured to the court, and it was business as usual.

The sportscasters and media was all abuzz about his mysterious disappearance and then his abrupt return. But the main thing everyone agreed on was that Dallas Avery had changed. He was harder, sullen, quiet, driven and it took its toll on the team. He drove them just as hard as he drove himself—and that was a relentless pace. Though they won games, the cohesiveness they once had faltered a little. After a few days the team adjusted to the "new" Dallas, one who had very few words for anyone and very little time for small talk or bullshit.

He came home and every night, Tori was waiting for him. Dinner on the table. Conversation if he needed it, silence if he didn't. Her warm body was there, curled up to him at night. She was a different woman, more loving, more affectionate, more attentive. It was even to the point she would give him a hand job or head to make sure that his needs were met and her virginity was kept intact.

But though he was falling into a comfortable routine with Tori, he couldn't get Alicia out of his mind. Without telling anyone, he hired a private investigator. But after a few weeks, the investigator found nothing. It was as if Alicia had fallen off the face of the earth and Dallas began to believe that maybe she had finally taken that trip to India and never planned to return.

So, he turned his focus to who he had at home—Tori. Maybe he was where he was supposed to be. Maybe things had worked out the way they were supposed to work out. Maybe he'd been wrong about Alicia and Tori was really the one.

Those were his thoughts as he tried his best to push Alicia out of his mind. He spent as much of his free time as he could with Tori, enjoying the way she was with him now.

There was no talk of their relationship; they were taking it slow, taking it easy and it was weeks later, when one night Dallas was stretched out on the sofa, with his head resting in Tori's lap, as they watched a marathon of movies, that they finally talked about what had happened.

"Everything I thought about love was all wrong," he said.

She answered him right away. "No, it isn't Dallas," Tori said, stroking her fingertips across his lips. "You can't stop believing in love because one woman broke your heart. True love is out there. You just have to wait for it. You have to know when the time is right."

Shaking his head, he said, "There's no such thing as true love. I'll never believe in that bullshit again. They can save that for music and movies, 'cause I'm not buying it."

Tori just let their conversation end there and continued to just be a constant in his life. She proved that she brought something to his table—even if it wasn't anything close to what he had with Alicia. Passion clearly was fleeting, but loyalty and consistency was what he now craved. And loyalty and consistency was what he had in Tori.

This time, he was the one to propose.

Chapter 38

SATURDAY, JUNE 8—3:30 P.M.
DALLAS, TEXAS

Dallas stood next to his father at the front of an archway at the exclusive Towers Club. The place was forty-eight floors above the streets of downtown Dallas, which provided a dramatic backdrop for the type of elegant wedding that Tori had wanted.

Though Reverend Braxton welcomed Dallas back to the church with open arms, Dallas had only set foot inside the place long enough for Tori to ask him to perform their ceremony. The good pastor had tried to talk Tori and Dallas into pre-marital counseling.

"Every couple should have it," the pastor said.

Tori had nodded. "Let's do it, baby."

"No!" Dallas had exclaimed and then softened his voice. "We don't need it."

Tori had only nodded again and agreed and for a moment, Dallas felt bad. Tori had to know. She had to know that he wasn't marrying her because he wanted to. It was because she had been there to pick up the pieces when Alicia had shattered his belief in true love.

"Well, big man, are you ready for this?" Paul Alexander asked, clasping a hand over Dallas' shoulder. He looked dapper in a black tux, lavender shirt and bowtie.

"It's a little late for second thoughts, don't you think?" Dallas answered solemnly.

Paul's smile disappeared. "Never too late for that. If you're having them."

"Second, third, but it doesn't matter," Dallas said, focusing on the flowers that had been placed in the ballroom. "Tori signed the pre-nup. She gets the wedding she wants, the husband she wants. I get a wife and a family. Fair exchange ain't no robbery."

"Provided the exchange is really fair."

Dallas didn't have an answer for that. Tori had changed in a lot of ways, and he believed that she was happy. That was all Dallas needed since he'd given up on the idea that he would ever find happiness again. All of his energy went to making sure Tori would have what she wanted.

That morning, though, he'd had to pray. Before he even got out of bed, he prayed that God would help him to be the husband he should be, the father he would be and a good man overall. He asked God to bless his heart with the kind of patience, compassion and love that would sustain him for the rest of his life.

And then, he had rolled out of bed and got on his knees when he prayed a special prayer of love and protection for Alicia, that wherever she might be, that she was happy.

"I want to thank you, Son," Paul said, pulling Dallas away from his thoughts.

"For what?"

"For acknowledging me publicly. You didn't have to do it."

"Yes, I did," Dallas said, nodding. In interviews since the season ended, Dallas had told the story of finding his real father to the press. It had been received well enough, it didn't seem like anyone was going to dig too deep in his past. All the stories had been about how

much Dallas looked like Paul Alexander. And now today, during the
ceremony, everyone—including Paul—would learn that not only was
Dallas telling everyone that Paul was his father, but today, Dallas Avery
was now Dallas Alexander.

"Well, it's about that time," Paul said.

Dallas nodded as Paul walked away. When his father cast a worried
glance over his shoulder before he took a seat next to Anna, Dallas gave
him a gentle smile.

A scraggily looking reporter had been steadily working the room, but
was getting closer to the front with each pass. He kept an eye on Dallas,
and for some reason, Dallas didn't get a good vibe from the man. Why
had he been given roving privileges when all the rest of the press had to
remain in the rear of the Tower's main ballroom?

Dallas left his spot next to six of his tuxedo-clad teammates. "I think
it's best if you leave," he said to the cagey man.

"I wanted to speak with the bride, but they won't let me near the
anteroom."

Dallas frowned down at him. "Why do you need to see her?"

"Because we have a little business transaction," the photographer
said in a hushed tone.

"What kind of business?"

The photographer first looked left, then right. "I'd rather not say, but
she owes me some money."

"If you want your cash, you'd better start talking."

The man held up a manila envelope. "She owes me for taking these."

Dallas honed in on the words Personal and Confidential stamped on
the front. "How much?"

"Two grand."

Dallas reached into his inside pocket, snatched out a pen and scribbled
on the blank side of a business card he pulled from the opposite inside
pocket. He slipped it to the man and said, "Send the invoice to my
accountant. You'll get your money."

"Cool. Thanks. The name's Bill," he said, reaching into his jacket and
handing a card to Dallas. "She said if there were any new developments,

she wanted me to come right away, and I've been trying to get ahold of her for the last week." He kept his grip on one of the edges of the envelope. "These are sealed and they're for her eyes only."

Bill walked away, stuffing Dallas' card inside his camera bag. Paul walked up to Dallas. "What's wrong?"

"I'm not sure," he answered with his gaze following Bill's journey to where all the other photographers had congregated. "Dude just handed these to me. They're for Tori."

Paul held out his hand, "Why don't you let me hold those for a minute?"

"Naw. I need to know what's going on now." Dallas pivoted and went to the private area right off from the ballroom. His father was right on his heels and closed the door behind them.

Dallas broke the seal and slid out a set of photos that made his heart stop. Picture after picture. Photo after photo. All of Alicia. A pregnant Alicia. He shuffled through each one, then shuffled through them again before he pivoted and dashed toward the door.

"Dallas, wait—" Paul began, but Dallas was already out the door. He went to the arch and scanned the group of photographers, though he couldn't see the man who'd given him the photos. Whipping out his cell, he dialed the number on the photographer's card. "Meet me in front. Now!"

Bill broke through the crowd, threading his way up front saying, "Excuse me. Pardon me. Let me through" along the way. When he finally stood in front of Dallas and Paul, he asked, "What can I do for you?"

"You can tell me where these were taken," Dallas demanded, holding up the stack of pictures.

Bill drew back, his beady eyes darting from Paul to Dallas as he said, "How much are you willing to pay?"

"How much are you enjoying your teeth?" Dallas growled.

"She's in Chicago. Mermaid Towers," he answered right away. "But she won't be there long," he added. "I saw her schlep in some boxes. The packing kind. That's why I wanted to get the pictures in."

Dallas turned the moment he felt a hand on his shoulder. Anna glanced at the photo in his hand and covered her mouth. She looked up at him, taking in his thunderous expression. "Son ..."

"The woman is carrying my child, Mom. And Tori knew!"

Her hand slipped down to his arm. "There's no guarantee that she'll take you back."

"I'm not looking for guarantees. I'm just looking for what's mine. It's as simple as that."

"So what are you going to do about today?" his mother asked. "What about the wedding?"

"What do you think?" he asked. "The wedding's off!"

"Dallas, wait!" they chorused, as Dallas stomped through the ballroom.

There was no way to stop his determined steps and within seconds, he was standing under the arch where he and Tori were to recite their vows in just minutes. Dallas held up a hand to silence everyone. "People, I'm going to say two things. First, thank you for coming out to support what should have been a beautiful day. And second, I apologize, because there won't be a wedding today."

Chatter filled the room and the reporters stepped forward.

"Does it have anything to do with the pictures you're holding?" one bold, crew-cut sporting reporter asked. "Did you catch your fiancée in a compromising position?"

The many cameras in the room started rolling.

"Dallas," Paul whispered his son's name and gripped his arm, "speak to Tori. You have to go to Tori before you say anything else."

He nodded and turned toward his guests, "Please, everyone," he said, raising his voice to speak over the loud din. "Stay, enjoy the food and party 'til you drop." He gestured to the table in the rear overflowing with beautifully wrapped boxes. "Please be sure to take your wedding gifts back with you. Once again, I apologize."

As he turned toward the anteroom, James Mitchell blocked his path. "You low down, dirty motherfucker," he growled, shaking his fist in Dallas' face. "How can you do this to my little girl?"

"Your little girl has a lot to answer for, Mr. Mitchell," Dallas answered. He then shifted his gaze to Bernice, who parted her mouth to take him on. "I suggest you get out of my way before you see what kind of ass I can really be."

James blanched and stepped to the side. Bernice struggled at first but finally clamped down on what she was about to spit out.

Tori sprinted up the aisle, her form-fitting lace dress raised about her ankles as she hiked in four-inch satin-covered heels. Her bridesmaids— Dallas' sister, two classmates, and a cousin—trailed behind her.

"You're telling everyone the wedding's off?" she shrieked.

He grabbed her hand and pulled her into the side room, away from the cameras and curious stares.

"Dallas! What's going on?" But before he could answer, Tori's eyes focused in on the pictures he held.

"Oh, my god!" Her golden skin went practically white in two seconds.

"You've known all this time," he accused.

"She didn't want you to know where she was!" Tori countered. "She doesn't want to come back to you."

Rage shot through him faster than he could put it in check. "You've spoken to her?"

Tori lowered her gaze to the plush carpet, and it was just the thing he needed to confirm his suspicions. He shoved the envelope in her hands. "Next time, pay your hired hands, and your dirt will stay underground."

"Dallas, it wasn't anything like that!" Tori answered, trying to get a hold of his lapel. "She told me that she never wanted to see either one of us again. I only had him taking pictures so I'd know she was all right. After that one time, she didn't talk to me again. She won't take my calls or anything!"

There was a soft knock on the door and before either could say anything, Reverend Braxton stuck his head inside. "This is just a minor obstacle," the reverend said as if he knew what was going on. "Your mother told me, but just know that you're being tested. You can get past this. I believe—"

"Reverend, now is not the time," Dallas snapped, and the pastor frowned as he stepped back outside of the room. Turning back to Tori, he said, "You know what this means?"

"It doesn't mean anything. She doesn't want to be with you. How many times does she have to leave you for you to believe that?"

"I'll never believe that," he said, brushing past her. When he stepped back out into the ballroom, the cameras were rolling.

Tori was right behind him as he pushed his way past his guests, ignoring their questions and statements.

Behind him, Tori cried out, "When she confirms that she doesn't want you, there's no coming back to me!"

He swung around, taking in the angry lines of her face in a single glance. "Tori, that has never been the threat you thought it was. You might want to call Max in again. But I advise you not to get pregnant by him because your child will have to stand in line after his first ten kids."

Her eyes widened in horror.

"Oh, damn. You didn't know about that either?" Dallas taunted, then turned to the musicians, whose eyes were on the same spot as everyone else. "Fellas, now would be a good time to play something with an upbeat."

They struck up a Jodi Whatley classic—"I'm Looking for a New Love"—as Dallas made his way down the aisle and out the door before anyone could stop him.

Chapter 39

Dallas knocked on the door for what seemed an eternity. Alicia cracked it open to see him standing on the other side, still wearing his black tux. Her eyes widened in shock as she tried to angle herself so the door hid her round figure. Dallas pushed past the opening and faced her full on.

Alicia looked absolutely gorgeous, though her eyes were filled with sadness. As much as he wanted to rant and rave, he didn't have the heart. Evidently, she had been hurting as much as he had.

He held out his arms. Moments ticked by, and Alicia didn't make a move. She looked up at him, silently pleading with him not to make her life any more complicated.

Finally, she made a timid move forward and then another. Soon her head was laid against the soft beat of his heart. He scooped her up, carried her with him to the sofa and cradled her in his arms. The time for questions would come much later. Right now, all he wanted to do was hold her.

Dallas rubbed a hand over the small swell of her belly and smiled. The television was tuned to ESPN, where the anchor was reporting on the ill-fated wedding of Dallas Avery.

"That's Dallas Alexander," he said to the screen

Alicia looked up at him. "What happened?" she whispered.

"Four words: I love you, Alicia."

She splayed a hand over his chest as she whispered back, "I love you, Dallas."

And for the time being, he knew that was all that either one of them needed to know.

Dallas awakened a few hours later with Alicia still in his arms. She stirred and snuggled closer to him, and he stroked a hand over her belly. "I looked for you, you know."

"I thought that you would."

"I thought you'd left the country."

"I was going to, until I found out about the babies."

"Wait, hold on. Babies?"

She nodded with a grin. "Twins."

"And so I changed my name; that's why you couldn't find me. I changed it to Alicia Alexander."

Dallas frowned, but then quickly, he smiled. "You chose my father's name."

"Yes, because I wanted the twins to have a part of you, even if we weren't together."

"Twins," he whispered, and then Alicia laughed as he pumped his fist in classic Tiger Woods style. "Yes!" Then he was serious again. "Are you all right?" he asked. "I mean I know you didn't want to be pregnant. You were worried ..."

"I was, but there wasn't an alternative for me. I found out that I was pregnant right when I left, and I couldn't bring myself to ..." She shrugged. "I just couldn't. They would be the only part of you I would have."

Dallas pressed his forehead to hers. "Thank you. Thank you, baby." He kissed her cheek, but then, he pulled back. "So why did you leave? And when you found out that you were pregnant, why didn't you come back?"

Alicia looked away, and when she focused on him again, he was taken aback by the look in her eyes. "I was so angry with you," she said hoarsely. "You stayed there ... and you slept with Tori."

"I fell asleep," he countered. "But I didn't have sex with her."

"Dallas, come on, you've never lied before," she said, her tone suddenly abrasive. "I saw the picture."

Dallas angled so that they were eye to eye. "What the hell are you talking about?"

"She texted a picture of you holding her that night and—"

"And I didn't touch her!" Dallas said between his teeth. "We talked, she was upset, I held her, and we fell asleep. But, I promise you, I didn't have sex with her that night. I have never had sex with that woman!" Then he grimaced, realizing those weren't the best choice of words.

"I think Bill Clinton wore that line out."

"Alicia, you know me enough to know that I wouldn't lie," he said. "If I do some shit, I own up to that! Tori is still a virgin. The most she did was give me hand jobs or head, and that was long after you left." Dallas made Alicia look into his eyes. "I promise you that we didn't do anything that night.."

"But, you were marrying her?"

Dallas looked out of the window at the panoramic view of the Chicago skyline. His hand stroked the smooth, silky skin of her arms. "Yeah, I was. But not because I loved her. She stayed beside me when you left. She was there when I broke down and couldn't think straight. She helped me get back on my feet and I was grateful."

Alicia nodded. "Your investigator couldn't find me, but Tori's found me four months ago."

"I found out today. Right before the wedding."

"Ah," Alicia said, understanding it all now. "Well, there's something you should know. I'd only been gone a month when she came to see me."

"She didn't tell me that."

"Well, she did. She flew here to Chicago, found me and practically begged me to come back. She said you needed me. She admitted that you needed me more than you ever needed her."

Dallas opened his mouth then closed it.

"I told her that what we had was over," she whispered. "I told her that you and I would never be together and that you two were meant to be together."

"Well now, I feel a little bad about running out on her today, but I had to come to you. She had to know that."

"And, I feel bad about telling her to go back to you because the truth is, I never stopped loving you. And once I found out that I was carrying these babies ... Dallas, I'm sorry."

"It's all right, baby." He kissed her temple. "But I feel like putting you over my knee and spanking that ass."

"Negro, I'd like to see you try," she playfully shot back.

"But not with my children in here." He closed his eyes and stroked the taut skin that stretched across her belly.

These were his children. This was his woman.

He thought about the prayers he'd said that morning and everything had been answered.

"Well, there's only one thing left to do," Dallas said.

Alicia frowned until Dallas, still clad in his tuxedo rolled off the sofa and knelt on one knee.

"Alicia, will you marry me? Be my wife, my friend, my lover, the mother of my children?"

A tear spilled down her cheeks.

"Pretty please, with me on top," he said, giving her a playful pout.

"With me on top," she corrected.

"Baby, I'll take you whatever way I can get you."

Dallas kissed the tip of her nose, and she said, "Yes, Dallas, I'll marry you."

The swell of joy he felt at that moment, couldn't be put into words. It wasn't something he could buy or lease, it was the type of love that a man had to earn and maintain. And he would do everything in his power to make sure that she realized she didn't make a mistake by taking this chance with him.

"Can we go to Vegas tonight?" he asked, planting a kiss on her shoulder. "You know, before something else happens ... like changing your mind."

"I'm not going to change my mind," she whispered.

"You promise?"

"I promise," she said, giving him a megawatt smile.

"My dad's private jet is at the airport. We're going to get this thing done." Realizing it sounded more like a command, he quickly added, "Please?"

Alicia's lips spread into a slow smile. "I'll change my clothes."

Dallas stood and did his best—and possibly his worst—imitation of the Godfather of Soul. Because he really did feel good.

Chapter 40

A week later, Dallas and Alicia were back in Texas, traveling down an all too familiar road for him, but not so much for Alicia. She focused on the rural surroundings, checking out the two-story homes up and down Billingsley Lane and along the townhouses stretched out on Murray Avenue.

"Dallas, this isn't the way to our house," she said, shifting her gaze to him.

"I want you to meet my father before we go home."

Her head whipped to him. "Don't you think you should phone first?"

Dallas frowned at the concern in her voice. "He told me I can come by anytime."

She grimaced at that statement. "I'm sure he meant after you gave him notice."

"Sometimes surprises are good," he said, grinning as he made it to the circular drive leading to the sky cottage. "You were surprised to see me, right?"

Alicia remained silent for a few moments, but when she took in the structure, her eyes widened. "This looks like our house! Same material, but with three levels instead of just the one."

"My father's firm built the house we live in. But this one came first."

Alicia gripped his arm, holding him in place as she said, "Dallas, why don't you just call him and tell him we're out here."

"I," he whipped out a set of keys, "have these."

She looked at the set and back to him. "He must trust you an awful lot."

"He does. We're building a great relationship." Dallas jumped out of the car, then trotted around to open the door for her. Moments later, he was entering the code on the keypad of his father's place.

"Dad!" he called out as he led Alicia through the entry and up the stairs. A thump and then a quick scramble caught their attention as feet hit the floor and a sudden yelp floated down the stairs.

Alicia froze at the top of the entry stairs. "That wasn't your father, was it?"

Dallas frowned and shook his head. "He couldn't hit a note that high."

"See, I told you we should've called," she warned, elbowing him in the side.

"He said he never has female company here," Dallas protested. "And he doesn't go to bed this early."

"We'll come back later," Dallas yelled, following Alicia back to the staircase.

"No, that won't be necessary," Paul Alexander said, making it down to the first level, his bare feet slapping against the bamboo floors. He grinned at the woman standing next to Dallas. "You must be Alicia."

"And that must be ... Mama?" Dallas said, bucking his eyes at the familiar figure ambling behind his father.

Anna Avery pulled a plush white robe about her body, which practically swallowed her petite form. "Dallas, let me explain."

"No, you don't have to do that," he said, trying to hide his smile, despite Alicia's warning nudge not to say anything. "He's in a robe; you're in a robe. Last I recall, neither one of y'all was in massage school." His eyebrows lifted as he asked, "So y'all getting back together?"

Anna pinned her gaze on the woman beside Dallas. "Alicia."

The tone made Alicia flinch. Dallas quickly took her hand in his. "Yes, this is my wife. Alicia Alexander."

Anna stopped walking, but Paul nodded his approval and moved forward, extending his hand to Alicia.

"Welcome to the family. I'm Paul."

Alicia took Paul's hand, and he enveloped her in a hug. As he released her, he said, "I've heard so many wonderful things about you."

Anna's gaze narrowed on Alicia, and she cleared her throat, causing everyone to look her way. "You married her?"

"As fast as I could," Dallas replied, not liking his mother's attitude. "I'm taking a page from my father's book. He said next time he would sweep you away and marry you and to hell with everyone else."

Anna's head snapped to Paul. "You said that?"

"I sure did," he answered. "If I had taken you with me that night, we would've been too far away for your father to stop us. Then he just would've had to deal with it." Paul draped a finger across Anna's cheek before he leaned in to kiss her lips. "I loved you then, and I love you now. The minute John wises up and signs the divorce papers, I'm not taking no for an answer."

"Wises up? What do you mean by that?" Dallas asked.

Anna turned to him. "Your fa—" she corrected herself, "John is fighting the divorce. I filed it the day after you took me to the hotel. I called Paul to let him know that I was bringing the last of your things from that house," Anna said. "We talked, and when I told him what happened, he wouldn't let me leave."

"He wouldn't let you leave or you didn't want to leave?" Dallas asked with a chuckle.

She looked at Paul and gave him a sheepish smile. "Both."

Paul put his arm about her shoulders and pulled her to him. He leaned down to kiss her forehead, and Dallas said, "I would say get a room, but I realize we're in your house. So on that note, we'll just catch y'all some other time."

"You don't have to leave," Anna protested with a pointed look at Alicia.

"Yes we do. Especially if y'all don't have on anything under those robes," Dallas joked, to which Paul grinned.

"Alicia," Anna said to the silent woman next her son. "I'd like to have a word with you."

Alicia's chin lifted, a flash of defiance in her eyes that made Dallas stiffen. "I prefer we didn't right now."

Anna's gaze lowered to Alicia's belly. "You're carrying my grandchild?"

"Yes."

Dark brown eyes narrowed to slits. "Isn't that a little dangerous at your age?"

Paul frowned, putting a warning grip on Anna's upper arm.

"And you wonder why I don't want to have a chat," Alicia said. Dallas could tell she was trying desperately to be respectful. "I'm not for anyone making me feel guilty about what I feel for Dallas." Alicia looked to her husband. "I'm ready to go home."

"Alicia, wait." Paul said. He then turned Anna so that she faced him. "All those years, you deprived me of having the two things I wanted most—you and my son. So Dallas, who loves just as hard as I do, is in love with this woman. It doesn't matter if you don't approve or don't understand. Look at all the time we've wasted. You can't condemn our son to the same fate."

A full range of emotions crossed Anna's face before she looked to Dallas, then at Alicia. She gave Paul's hand a gentle squeeze and said, "You're right." Her gaze was much softer when she spoke to Alicia this time. "I apologize." Anna looked at her son before asking Alicia, "Please stay and have lunch with us so that we can begin to get to know one another."

Dallas swept a look at his father, who quickly shook his head, causing Dallas to say, "Ah, no. We were about to—"

"Yes, we'll stay," Alicia cut in, taking in the pleading expression on Anna's face.

Dallas shrugged and only smiled at the look of complete frustration on his father's face.

Chapter 41

Dallas entered the locker room of the sports center, toweling off after his hot shower. Basketball season was all set to start in a couple of months, so he was gearing up by keeping his mind and body in shape. The workout with his assistant and personal trainer had gone well, and he looked forward to getting home for whatever lunchtime surprises Alicia had in store for him. It had been two months, now, and he was the happiest man in the world, and though he still had to field some negativity from time to time, things were going pretty well.

And not only for him. His mother and father were vacationing in Hawaii, while still waiting for John to come to grips that there would be a divorce.

He hadn't seen Tori, though he hadn't sought her out. He knew that she'd moved out of his condo when he'd received the keys in the mail, though she hadn't sent a note or anything.

That concerned him a little. He knew that Tori could be vindictive and he was just waiting, wondering if this was the calm before the storm.

Dallas checked his watch and realized he needed to hurry. He never liked to be away from Alicia a moment longer than necessary. But before he could stand from the bench, Marlon, his new assistant, crashed through the doors, locs slapping his back, and panting as he said, "You have to get to the hospital right away."

Dallas jumped up from the bench and grabbed his gear. "Alicia?"

"She's in labor."

Dallas froze. "The doctor said they could come earlier than nine months, but not this early! She's at 36 weeks!"

"Babies come whenever they feel like it," he said, giving him a toothy grin. "Ask me how I know."

Dallas didn't ask him a thing as he jumped into a pair of sweats and a t-shirt.

"Want me to give you a lift?" Marlon asked.

"That's all right. I drove here."

"Yeah, right." Marlon grabbed the rest of Dallas' things and placed them in his duffel bag. "I've seen the way you drive in an emergency."

"Good point," Dallas countered. "But I'm not trying to fold my legs into your little Lego mobile."

"Aw, that's cold man," Marlon said, frowning. Then he perked up. "I can drive your car."

"And what's the real reason you want to take me to the hospital?"

Marlon chuckled and followed him from the locker room.

Twenty minutes later they arrived at UT Southwestern Medical Center, and Dallas was immediately ushered into the birthing center. "How is she?" he asked the slender brunette RN who greeted him at the doors.

"She's doing all right," she answered, cornering the end of the hall so they could make it to the other wing. "But the babies are giving her a hard time. Her water broke, which is her body's way of saying that she's ready for them to come. But they're asleep and not even trying to budge."

"Stubborn. Just like her," he mumbled, causing the nurse to smile. "So what's the doctor going to do?"

"He's going to give it another thirty minutes, then we'll have to go in and get them."

"A C-section?"

She nodded, her solemn expression matching exactly how Dallas felt. "It might be too dangerous if we wait."

Dallas walked into a hospital room with cream walls, pink and blue accents that was supposed to give the place a cheery feel. What Dallas saw from the threshold didn't make him feel so cheery. A group of people in white coats surrounded Alicia's bed. Some of them looked too young to be doctors.

But then, his wife saw him and she lit up. Dallas though, frowned. "What's with the tribe?"

"I'm trying to figure that out, too," Alicia said smoothly, eyeing each of the nine people around her. "This is their second time here. I'm about to charge admission."

Everyone chuckled, but Dallas leaned in to the doctor, asking, "Don't they have a private room?"

The doctor followed his gaze to the small group of students and said, "This is a teaching hospital, Mr. Alexander."

"Yeah? Well they're not going to learn anything on my wife." Dallas pointed to the open door. "Take the tribe somewhere else."

"Dallas!" Alicia frowned at his tone.

"I don't want everyone looking at you like that."

"If they've seen one," Doctor Webb countered, "they've seen them all."

"Well, they're not going to see hers," he quipped, shooing the rest of the people from the room. "Get to stepping, people."

The doctor shook his head, but Dallas gestured for him to hit the door, too. "And you can go with 'em, 'Chief Looks-a-lot'."

"I'll be right back," Doctor Webb said to Alicia, who was unsuccessfully trying to hide the fact that she was uncomfortable.

The moment the doctor and nurses cleared the door, Dallas took a seat next to the bed. "How you doing, baby?" he asked, leaning in to plant a kiss on her cheek.

"As well as could be expected."

"You in any pain?"

She shrugged. "A little, the breathing exercises are helping, but mostly I'm just tired."

"The doctor told me that they might have to ..."

"I really don't want that, but whatever's best for the babies." She looked up at him, and he could see the worry lurking in those green depths. "Dallas?"

"I'm right here, baby," he whispered, kissing the back of her hand. "I'm not going anywhere."

"Promise me ... that if something happens to me, you'll take good care of them."

"Baby, don't talk like that!" he admonished, putting a tighter hold on her hand, hoping it would reassure her. "Nothing's going to happen to you. I forbid it."

She smiled.

"We're going to raise them together," he added. "Love them, teach them how to dribble and shoot free throws before they can crawl." Dallas gave her sheepish grin. "You know, normal stuff."

"Normal stuff?" Alicia laughed and shook her head, but she was smiling and it set his mind at ease.

The monitors were holding steady and Dallas reached out to switch off the news. "No more of this," he said, "it's depressing."

She nodded, stroking a hand across her belly. "I never thought I would be somebody's mother," she said. "It's frightening if you think about all the weird things going on in the world. It's so unsafe for children these days. And here it is, I'm about to have not one, but two. What was I thinking?"

"You were thinking that you loved me."

She laughed a little before she moaned. And then, she groaned. "Baby," she said. "You better get the doctor in here. I think it's time."

Dallas ran to the door, called out, and moments later, the team was back in the room. After a quick exam, the doctor flipped the sheet back down and said, "This mother's ready to rock and roll!"

"What does that mean?" Dallas asked.

"I don't think we'll have to do that C-Section." Doctor Webb signaled for the crew to speed things up. "Let's get her in the delivery room."

The hospital team went into action. The IVs were hooked onto the clip at the end of the bed, and they rushed down the hall.

The pair of green scrubs they gave Dallas didn't quite fit, but it didn't matter as he tried to stuff himself in as best he could and followed them into the delivery room.

Alicia reached for his hand, and he held onto it, worried when he saw the numbers on the monitor start peaking into the higher digits.

The team moved with fluid synchronicity as they performed a number of maneuvers that seemed to keep them away from the delivery bed for longer than Dallas preferred.

"Well, people," Doctor Webb said, rubbing his latex-covered hands together. "It's show time."

"I bet you say that to all the girls," Alicia joked, causing the good doctor to laugh.

"Depending on what time of night it is." He angled himself onto a stool at the business end of the birth process. "Let's get these little rascals out into the real world."

"If they knew what I know, they'd want to stay inside," Alicia quipped, continuing a series of breathing exercises to keep calm.

"Yes, I think they got that message loud and clear. That's what's taking so long. Sleeping while you contract and dilate! Hmph. Of all the nerve."

Alicia laughed, but Dallas couldn't find humor in any of this. He was worried for no reason he could name. Alicia's pleas for him to promise that he would take good care of the children echoed in his ears. He tried to push the thought away and focus on the doctor's actions.

Doctor Webb had a pudgy hand positioned on Alicia's belly.

"Would now be a good time to ask for those drugs?" Alicia croaked.

Doctor Webb shook his head. "We're a little bit past that. On a scale of one to ten, how bad is it?" Doctor Webb asked. His worried tone matched exactly how Dallas felt.

"It's hitting fifteen, but I'll live."

Alicia tightened her hand on Dallas and he asked the doctor, "You can't give her anything?"

"It won't take effect in time for this."

"But she'll need it after, right?" Dallas protested. "She n—"

At that moment one of the babies' heads crested and Alicia hadn't even gotten to the push part! On a few whimpers of pain, Dallas' son slipped into the doctor's hand, and a heavy wail was his protest at being taken from obscurity and into a light-filled world with a bunch of strangers suddenly touching him, cleaning him, weighing him and fussing over him.

Dallas craned his neck to where the nurse was clearing the fluids from his son's nose. "Is he all right?"

"Did you hear the lungs on this little fella?" she teased, placing a tiny blue cap over his soft silky hair.

Dallas nodded and couldn't help but smile. His son was definitely making his feelings known. Moments later, the nurse placed the baby in his arms, gesturing for him to move away from the bed. Dallas refused to release Alicia's hand. She smiled up at him. "Dallas, are you crying?"

Dallas shook his head, but he could barely see the bundle in his arms because the very tears he denied blurred his vision.

His son, by the woman he loved. He was so overwhelmed with joy. "All of his fingers and toes. And he has your eyes," he said to Alicia as he angled the baby so she could see him.

"Hold up, people," Doctor Webb said, signaling for the nurses to come over. "Baby number two is hanging on the rim. Probably trying for a lay-up instead of a straight shot."

"Man, stick to your day job," Dallas shot back at the man's lame attempt at basketball humor, which caused everyone but the good doctor to laugh.

"What are you going to name him?" the nurse asked.

"We talked about a lot of things, but it's time to put a lock on something. Paul after my father and Michael after yours?" he asked, looking down at Alicia.

"That's a good compromise," she conceded, and he leaned in with a towel to dab the sweat that peppered her forehead.

Baby number two came soon after, but she wasn't as ticked off by the process as her brother had been. She calmly looked up at the nurse and yawned as if totally bored by all the commotion.

"Oh, yes," the blonde said. "This one's going to be quite the character."

Alicia looked up at Dallas and he smiled.

Though her voice was filled with exhaustion, she said, "India Anna Marie Alexander."

"Three names?" he croaked. "Why not just Anna Marie?"

"You know why."

"I'm still going to take you. I always keep my promises, baby." He kissed her forehead. Amid romantic sighs from the females in the room, the nurse extracted their son and placed him in Alicia's arms, then placed India in Dallas' hands.

He crooned a lullaby to his daughter. "Daddy's going to buy you a diamond ring ..."

"Dallas, you are not spoiling them like that," Alicia said wearily.

"Okay, I won't," he said, giving her a sheepish smile and that famous lift of his left eyebrow.

"We are not spoiling them."

"I said okay," he whined. But no one, judging by the smiles in the room, believed him one bit.

Chapter 42

MONDAY, SEPTEMBER 30 - 7:23 P.M.

Six weeks had passed and Alicia had never felt so complete in her life. She'd just laid the babies down for a nap and this would've been the perfect time for her to catch a quickie herself. But all she could do was stand over their bassinets and stare. She'd probably stay right there until they woke up again since her greatest pleasure was being with them.

It was hard to believe that she had created these two human beings. She and Dallas. There was no way that life could get any better.

Then, the doorbell rang and she frowned, checking to make sure that the sound hadn't awakened her babies. When she saw that they didn't even stir, she rushed from the room, taking the baby monitor with her. And she dashed to the door before whoever was outside rang the bell again.

She swung the door open, and then stood there with surprise.

"Hi, Auntie," Tori said softly.

"Hi." That was her automatic response, but inside all kinds of wheels were turning. She and Dallas hadn't heard a word from Tori since he'd left her at the altar, though Alicia suspected that she'd returned to Chicago to her dysfunctional parents. She hadn't reached out to any of them, not even James. That was a crew of crazies that Alicia didn't need in her life and around her babies.

"May I come in?"

Alicia couldn't believe that she'd been so rude. It was just that she was trying to figure this out. What did Tori want?

When Alicia closed the door behind her, the two stood awkwardly in the massive foyer before Alicia led Tori to the living room. But as Tori sat on the love seat and Alicia, on the couch, the awkwardness remained. They sat, stiffly facing each other.

"So," Tori began and then, she stopped, looked around the grand living room filled with photos of the Alexander's. The place was still nicely decorated, but it felt more . . . homey. "This is really nice."

"Thanks."

Then there was more silence until they spoke together.

"Auntie."

"Tori."

They chuckled and both of them sat back.

"You look good, Auntie."

"You do, too. Where are you living now? Did you move back to Chicago.?"

"I did. Doing my residency here. I thought that would be best," she said, and lowered her head.

Alicia inhaled. Tori was still in love with Dallas. Of course—it had only been three months. She needed time ... and distance.

"Glad to hear you didn't abandon school." She paused again, struggling to find words. "So, what're you doing in Dallas?"

Tori's eyes were glassy when she looked up. "I came to see you." She hesitated. "There is so much I want to say, so much I want to apologize for." She sighed. "I wanted to win this one, Auntie. Even though I knew that you were better for Dallas, I wanted him."

Alicia nodded. "You were in love and ..."

"No!"

The strength behind her exclamation surprised Alicia.

Tori continued, "I mean, yes, I did love him, but not the way you do. And he certainly didn't love me the way he loves you." Her chuckle was filled with bitterness. "I've never had that kind of love." The tears that had welled in her eyes streamed down her face. "I've never really had love," she cried. "Not even from you."

Alicia's heart cracked and she jumped up and joined her niece on the love seat. "That's not true, Tori." She pulled her head to her shoulder and held her. "I have always loved you. Loved you like you were my own daughter."

"Then why didn't you keep me? Why didn't you raise me?"

Alicia's lips trembled as she thought back to those heartbreaking days. In the beginning, it had been so beautiful. She had a baby girl, even at the detriment of her marriage. But it didn't matter. She loved Tori beyond anything that she ever thought possible. And the little girl had loved her back the same way.

Until the day James found out he had a daughter. He was angry at Alicia for keeping the secret. And even more pissed at Bernice for never telling him. They'd had a horrible fight, and he'd left. The one time he'd had any balls in that marriage. Bernice had decided that the best way to get him back, was to get their daughter back.

James had been so mad at Alicia, that he had gone along with Bernice's demand to return Tori. And at age five, Tori was ripped from her arms and returned to her parents.

"I didn't raise you," Alicia finally began, "because you deserved your mother and your father."

Tori sniffed and raised her head. Looking into Alicia's eyes, she said, "But you never told me about the court battle."

Alicia reared back a little, surprised that Tori knew about that now. Bernice had threatened her at the time, telling her that if she'd told Tori about how she'd fought to keep her, Alicia would never see Tori again.

That didn't concern Alicia. Nothing that Bernice ever said did. But without James in her corner, she didn't want to take that chance. Besides, she wanted to give Tori the best chance with Bernice and James. All kinds of strikes were against her already having a mother like Bernice.

Alicia didn't see how it would help to complicate the situation even more for the young girl.

"Who told you about that?" Alicia asked.

"Dad. Last week. He said that you did try to keep me. That you even took it to court, but the judge said that you had to give me back."

Alicia nodded.

A small smile curved Tori's lips. "I thought Dad was lying. I thought he was just trying to make me feel better about everything that's happened."

"He was telling the truth. And did he tell you that I didn't give you back?"

Tori frowned and shook her head.

"You were at home with a friend of mine while I was in court and the judge told me that I had two hours to turn you over. I told your parents that I would bring you to their apartment, but I didn't have any intention of doing that. I went home, got you, and went straight to the bus station."

"You were going to take me away?"

Alicia nodded. "And through the years, you don't know how many times I wished that I'd gotten on the bus. Every time I saw you with Bernice, every time I watched her destroying the joy that had filled your heart when you were with me." She shook her head. "But I didn't get on the bus because I didn't think that it was fair to you. You were only five years old; what kind of life would you have had? No real family. No ties. Looking over your shoulder all the time. I would've had to teach you to lie about who you were. I didn't want you to grow up that way. I didn't want you to grow up, figure it out, and then end up hating me for taking you away from your parents."

"That would've never happened. Especially not with the way Bernice is."

"But you wouldn't have known that. You wouldn't have known her and you would've had this picture in your head of a perfect mother, baking brownies all the time and playing games with you all day." She grinned. "And maybe a mother who even let you have ice cream for breakfast."

Tori laughed. "I remember that. I always wanted ice cream for breakfast and you always said no."

"See what I mean? You would've wanted a mother who said yes." Then, Alicia's smile faded. "Seriously though, I wish I could've kept you, but the one thing that you have to know is that I loved you with every bit of my heart. You were the reason why I knew that I could love. With the way I grew up, with the man I married, I was just never sure. But I held onto the love I had for you. Even when you started getting distant at twelve, I loved you."

Tori lowered her gaze. "That's when Bernice told me that she'd given you to me at birth because she was dying. And that after five years, you didn't want me anymore and made them take me back since she hadn't died."

Alicia could only shake her head. She should've been angry, but nothing Bernice did surprised her. "Your mother is a trip." She patted Tori's thigh. "No, baby. That's not what happened. I never wanted to let you go."

"Thank you," Tori whispered.

"For what?"

"For telling me that. For all of that. For loving me and wanting me."

"Oh, sweetie," Alicia said as she knelt down in front of Tori. She held her niece's hands in her own. "I would do it all over again. And maybe this time, I would get on that bus and let you have ice cream for breakfast."

They chuckled lightly together.

Alicia said, "That's why all of this was so hard for me. I didn't want to do this to you."

"And that's why it was so easy for me," Tori said. "Because I wanted to win. I wanted to get back at you for not wanting me. For being just like Bernice and my dad."

"Now hold on," Alicia joked. "That's going too far. I'm nothing like your mother."

Tori smiled. "No, you're not." She paused. "Daddy left her again. He and I are sharing an apartment."

She nodded. "Wow! That's good. I hope James will stay away from Bernice this time. She's his weakness in so many ways."

"I understand weaknesses," Tori said. "Dallas was mine. I knew he was a good man, the right man. But, I wanted him for all the wrong reasons."

Alicia cupped Tori's face in her hands. "It takes a very mature, very strong woman to recognize that."

"I think I knew that all the time," she said, with a wavering smile. "Even when I was putting together this ridiculous scheme of an open relationship that would lead to an open marriage. It just sounds crazy to me now." She sighed. "But, I thank you for not hating me for what I tried to do to you and Dallas when I just should've let him go."

Alicia finally stood. "It wasn't all your fault. All three of us could have made better decisions."

Tori nodded. "And, it all worked out the way it was supposed to, right?"

Alicia didn't respond. Tori knew the answer to that. They stood in an awkward silence for a minute before Alicia said, "Do you want to see the twins?"

Her smile was instant, but Tori shook her head. "You had twins?"

"You didn't know?"

"No. I only used the investigator to find out where you lived, though that wasn't hard to do. I probably could've found you myself."

"Come on, they're sleeping. But come meet your cousins."

Slowly, Tori shook her head. "Would you be upset if I said not this time? It's just that ..."

"I understand," Alicia said, not letting Tori continue.

"It's kind of emotional overload for me today," Tori explained anyway. "And I'm staying downtown at the Hilton, so maybe I'll give you a call tomorrow?"

"That would be great. And I'll tell Dallas ..."

"No!" Tori exclaimed. "I don't want to see him. I'm not ready to see him. I'm sure, he hasn't forgiven me." She paused as if she was waiting for Alicia to tell her that she was wrong. But Alicia said nothing. Tori continued, "I hope that one day he can. I hope one day he'll understand."

"Like I said, this wasn't all about you," Alicia told her. But at the same time, she was relieved that Tori didn't want to see Dallas. There was no need for any new complications. Time and distance. And then, maybe one day ...

"Okay," Tori exhaled as she moved across the living room. "Well, I'm really glad that I came."

"I am, too." Alicia hooked her arm through Tori's as they walked to the door.

"Thank you for being in my life," Tori said before she wrapped her aunt into a hug.

Alicia kissed her cheeks before Tori stepped out of the door. She stood there and watched her niece and even as the car drove away, she remained at the door. The whole idea of them trying to make it work between the three of them had been asinine from the beginning. But Alicia was grateful that things had worked out like they did. She'd finally gotten her happiness. She had children she never thought she could. She knew love she never thought she would. And maybe one day, she and Tori could really heal.

Alicia smiled as she closed the door.

Naleighna Kai is a national bestselling and award-winning author of several controversial novels, contributor to a *New York Times* bestseller, and the E. Lynn Harris Author of Distinction. She has penned *Every Woman Needs a Wife, Loving Me for Me, Was it Good For You Too?, Open Door Marriage, She Touched My Soul, Rich Woman's Fetish*, and other contemporary fiction novels that plumb the depth of unique love triangles and women's issues.

In addition to successfully cracking the code of landing a deal with a major publishing house, she continues to "pay it forward" by organizing the annual Cavalcade of Authors which gives readers intimate access to the most accomplished writing talent today. She also serves as CEO of Macro Marketing & Promotions Group which offers aspiring authors assistance with developmental editing, publishing, marketing, and other services to jump-start their writing careers. She also founded NK Tribe Called Success for her clients and author members who participate in literary events and media advertising as a group. Additionally, she is Editor-in-Chief for Naleighna Kai's Literary Café Magazine.

She was born and raised on the Southeast side of Chicago, the setting for most of her novels and where she is currently working on her next books: *Slaves of Heaven* and *Mercury Sunrise*.

Find her on the web at www.naleighnakai.com
www.facebook.com/naleighnakai
twitter.com/NaleighnaKai
instagram.com/NaleighnaKai
www.thecavalcadeofauthors.com
BookBub and GoodReads under Naleighna Kai